About the Author

C T Sullivan lives in Midhurst with his wife, Deborah, and golden Labradors, Woof and Splosh. A twenty-five-year career as a foreign exchange broker in the city was followed by spells as a lorry driver, landscape gardener, singer-songwriter and stand-up musical comedy entertainer, while learning his craft as an author. He began writing poems and short stories from the age of ten. His love of the written word is equal only to his passion for music, sport and humour.

Fractured Web

C T Sullivan

Fractured Web

Vanguard Press

VANGUARD PAPERBACK

© Copyright 2025
C T Sullivan

The right of C T Sullivan to be identified as author of
this work has been asserted by him in accordance with the
Copyright, Designs and Patents Act 1988.

A CIP catalogue record for this title is available from the British Library.

ISBN 978-1-83794-602-0

This is a work of fiction. Names, characters, businesses, places, events and
incidents are either the products of the author's imagination or used in a
fictitious manner. Any resemblance to actual persons, living or dead, or actual
events is purely coincidental.

*Vanguard Press is an imprint of
Pegasus Elliot Mackenzie Publishers Ltd.*
www.pegasuspublishers.com

First Published in 2025

**Vanguard Press
Sheraton House Castle Park
Cambridge England**

Printed & Bound in Great Britain

Dedication

To my lovely wife, Deborah.

Chapter 1

March 1990

In the Arcadian village of Much Hadham, it didn't take long for the rumours to spill out across the small community. On several occasions, Pauline Jacks had been spotted at lunchtime drinking in the local with John Partridge, a recently retired insurance broker. Once, she'd been seen leaving his house mid-afternoon. John was divorced. Pauline wasn't.

Pauline's youngest daughter, twelve-year-old Wendy, sat watching early-evening television trying to block out the heated row. Her father worked long hours as a warehouse assistant, but there was never enough money for the bills and her mother's social lifestyle.

Wendy's blond-haired father, Stephen, had arrived home at six pm. He stood holding a letter he had just retrieved from the doormat. 'I had no breakfast this morning because there was none to be had. Not the first time either, is it? And here's a final water rates reminder. How do I pay this?' he said, waving the envelope aloft.'

'There's not enough food in the house because you don't give me enough bloody money,' said Pauline, who sat at the small kitchen table drawing on a cigarette, her hand gripping a glass of rioja.

'It would be enough if you didn't spend it down the pub on drink and fags with that John every week.'

Pauline's head sprung up like a box puppet. She looked at her husband, her mouth open.

'You think I didn't know? Maybe you should go and live with him?'

'Well, at least he wouldn't keep me short of money. Unlike you, John has been successful in his life. He…'

The hard slap held rule over the room like a whipcrack. It knocked the cigarette flying from Pauline's mouth, landing on the beige nylon rug at Wendy's feet. Pauline's white blouse had taken most of the cheap red wine spill, the remainder dripping off the table onto the hardwood floor. Wendy's jaw tightened at the display of aggression, but it wasn't through fear. It was excitement mixed with gratification. It was the first time her father had raised a hand to his wife. She thought her selfish mother deserved it – that it was well overdue. Stephen suddenly looked round at his daughter; his own expression was one of shock. He shook his head, then climbed the stairs to their bedroom.

Ten minutes later he appeared, a heavy suitcase dangling from his arm. He took two steps into the sitting room and stopped. Turning away from the television, Wendy noticed his eyes were red, watery. Had he been crying? Ignoring his wife, who was pouring herself another glass of wine, he gave a last look at his daughter turned and headed for the front door.

'Daddy, where are you going?' Wendy called out.

There was no reply as she watched the father that she idolised open the glass-panelled door of the semi and, without a word, walk out into the night.

Wendy never saw him again.

00000

Wendy Jacks, now fifteen, was a studious pupil but not a popular one, mainly because she didn't mix well with the other girls. Boys? She thought they were immature, stupid, although there was one special one. She believed she was beginning to get close to a lad who appeared to be different from the rest. Matthew had blond curly hair, like her father, and spoke in a gentle manner. Their relationship, in her eyes, seemed to be progressing beyond friendship. That was until her only pal, Melissa, moved in on him. Within a few days, Melissa had now usurped her as his girlfriend.

The following week, after a school hockey match, Wendy, still angry, managed to steal another girl's watch and money from the changing room while they were all showering. First back in the classroom, she hid the items in Melissa's desk.

On seeing the distraught girl's tears, Wendy approached her, 'What's up, Laura?'

'Someone has stolen my watch and I had £5 in my bag as well. They're both gone.'

'Are you sure?'

'Yes, of course. I've searched my bag twice.'

Wendy moved closer to Laura and lowered her voice. 'Well, it has to be someone in our class because the changing room is locked while we're in the showers. Tell the teacher.'

When the teacher arrived to take the lesson, Laura repeated Wendy's words.

The teacher addressed the class, 'Laura has had some items stolen from her bag that was hanging in the changing room. As it was only a matter of minutes ago, the culprit is most likely to be in this room. I sincerely hope I am wrong. I want every pupil to open their bags and lift the lid of their desks and leave them open.'

It didn't take long for the teacher to discover the missing watch. It was wrapped in a five-pound note beneath a book in Melissa's desk. She held the items above her head.

'Is this your watch, Laura?'

Melissa's mouth dropped, her face turning red. The mixed class gasped audibly as one.

Ten minutes later a stunned Melissa stood in front of the headmaster, her small fists gripping the sides of her navy pleated skirt. She went to speak.

The headmaster raised an arm – his open palm a stop sign. 'I've heard your excuses already. This kind of behaviour is not tolerated in this school. I am not expelling you this time but another similar incident such as this and you will be out, looking for another school. That is if another school will have you.'

Deeply wronged and helpless, Melissa broke down in tears. Her reputation was irreparably sullied, causing her to spend the remainder of her school life with a stain against her name. THIEF. She lost many of her friends, much to Wendy's pleasure. But she thought Melissa had not suffered enough, as Matthew did not renew his friendship with her. Whatever bond they had between them had been erased as if it never existed. Instead, he chose another girl in their class.

Wendy had not the slightest feelings of guilt about ruining Melissa's reputation. It was payback. But the incident bore deep into her soul. Briefly, her thoughts went back to her absent father. She set her jaw and blinked them away.

It was the beginning of a noxious recurring pattern in her life that would end in disaster.

Chapter 2

Twenty-Six Years Later, June 2016

Wendy Jacks sat in a parallel world, staring forwards, partly distracted by the black, scuff-toed shoes visible below the desk in front of her. The attached legs had not stopped bouncing up and down for the past five minutes. It was as if the boy's heels were operating bass drum pedals.

She questioned her presence in such an environment – surrounded by the very things that bit deepest into her soul. Children.

The teacher's musings were interrupted by faint whispers coming from the back of the class. She looked up, scouring the thirty young heads. '*Why have all these boys' mothers been blessed... allowed to produce all these healthy children?*' she asked herself. She breathed in deeply.

The whispers were now giggles. Her eyes found the target – two boys at the back of the room. Always the same two boys.

'For God's sakes!' The remark came out in a shriek, more strident than she had intended. Mentally, she hadn't even chosen those words. They had just erupted from her. The rest of the fifteen to sixteen-year-old heads snapped up from their writing, surprised by the outburst. 'Do you think that I cannot hear you two?' She paused – her blistering stare forging an instant wedge between the boys. *If you don't want to learn just fuck off,* is what she was thinking. Instead… 'I am here to teach and you are here to learn. That's the deal.'

The whisperers gave each other a brief glance then got back to their work. But one other boy had not. Sat next to the fidgety legs was Danny Antonelli. She noticed that the handsome boy always made sure he sat in the front row. She was also aware that he seemed mesmerised by the way she moved each time she got up from her desk. And he didn't bother to hide his fascination from his teacher. As much as she tried, she found it hard to ignore his interest in her.

When the lesson ended, Wendy stood and stretched. She looked at her watch. Eleven-fifteen a.m. *One more class before lunch, three this afternoon then home for the weekend, thank goodness,* she thought, as she closed the door behind the last pupil. She sat down at her desk, mentally preparing herself for one more onslaught – twelve-year-olds this time. It had been a long tiring week. She had five peaceful minutes to herself.

Restless, she got up and moved to the row of windows. She stood, arms folded, looking out onto bright sunshine. The summer, as usual in England, had been unpredictable but the last half of August and the beginning of September had been hot and dry. Her eyes scanned the row of slim birch trees spaced uniformly along the roadside. Like US Navy officers, they stood proud, rigid white trunks rich with leaves, incandescent in the flattering sunrays.

Sadly, the previously vibrant lawns decking the gardens opposite the school were now a mixture of khaki and jaded gold. She stared at the blades, dead, burnt into submission. The roots, still alive but dormant, were sitting, waiting for that vital injection of life. She blew air through her nose, an ironic smile on her lips.

She took a few steps back as she transferred her focus on to her reflection in the window. She was a bit overweight, but still felt she was attractive in a comfy sort of way. Not bad for her age. She was proud of her womanly figure but her pride and joy was her deep-walnut-brown hair that hung in heavy curls kissing her shoulders.

She brushed it off her face, admired the result and returned to her desk. Out came her diary from her handbag. She scribbled a name and a few words on today's page and flicked forwards over the next few months. She noted they were blank. The diary was slid back into the bag.

Once again, she would be going back to an empty house after work. Her husband, Edward, worked for a company that bought and sold bespoke furniture. It was a job that took him abroad on a regular basis – occasionally to Europe but mainly to Africa and the Far East.

Married at twenty-five, she suffered a still-birth pregnancy three years later. The painful memory and the angry sense of loss still raw, as she played the traumatic life-changing episode over in her mind. Despite the ensuing years of hope, countless crosses on the calendar, the careful planning on the occasions when Edward was back home, she had never managed to get pregnant again.

At thirty-eight, she felt her life was passing her by. She'd worked hard to achieve the position of Head of Science during the five years she had been at the school. Her career up until this moment had been her main driving force. At times, she felt there was nothing else.

She raised her head as the energy-sapping thoughts were distracted by a chattering of voices. Glancing up she saw the line of boys gathering outside the classroom door. She took a deep breath, stood and moved to let them in. As the lively group filed past, a voice resonated inside her. *There has to be more to my life than this.*

Chapter 3

The gap in the curtains allowed a spear of orange light from the streetlamp to score the back wall of the gloomy bedroom. Outside, autumn rain fell in waves hammering the roof tiles of the nineteenth-century detached cottage.

The face, a picture of concentration, was illuminated by the only source of internal light – the laptop screen. Eyes, filled with intent, devoured every component of the video. A slow-burning cigarette and half-finished glass of wine sat close-by, ignored. The animated pictures of the school's under 16's football match filled the display. The film then moved on to the inside of a changing room. It showed sixteen-year-old boys stripping off their muddy football kit and disappearing into the showers.

The eyes moved closer to the screen.

Every so often, a gusting wind lifted the downpour to drum like intolerant fingers against the double leaded-light windows. When the final screen images had ceased, the cigarette was lifted from the metal ashtray, sucked deeply and extinguished in one continual movement.

A distant gurgle of thunder gave drama to the unrelenting raindrops. It barely registered in the viewer's brain as the wine glass, emptied in one slug, was replaced on the pine desk: the laptop closed, the leather swivel-chair pushed back and the dated, cheaply furnished room, vacated.

00000

Hormones struggled for ascendency beneath the vaulted ceiling of the school gymnasium, reverberating with the swell of animated male voices.

'Whoa! Tossers,' said one of the boys from the winning team.

'Luck. And you lot cheated, anyway' replied Antonelli, as the whistle blew to indicate the end of the PE lesson.

Still buoyed after team sprint relay races, the group of sixteen-year-old lads trooped out into the corridor. They were heading for the shower block. The boastful taunts and mocking banter fired back and forth. Yet, no one was aware of two focused eyes that lingered a little too long on one particular sweat-covered figure.

Danny Antonelli was taller than most of his classmates. His soft-lined features would have not looked out of place on a girl of the same age. His hair, rich, liquorice-black cambered over one eye. As he and his pals shuffled into the changing room, the eyes narrowed, recording the final image of the boy's powerful shoulders. The onlooker then turned and continued along the corridor a few paces, disappearing behind a heavy swing door.

Sir Montague Web Grammar School for Boys, known in-house as the Web, sat in five acres of prime real estate. It was situated on the outskirts of Battersea overlooking the unrelenting murk of the river Thames. It was one of less than two-hundred grammar schools in the UK having survived closure or merger with the country's numerous comprehensive schools. Founded in the early eighteenth-century the building reeked of an age time was struggling to cling on to.

Inside the hallowed, red-bricked walls hope and expectation ruled. Silent corridors, on the sound of a shrill bell, were clogged in a matter of seconds. A swarm of grey flannels, striped ties and dark blue blazers dominated the scene. It was as if the bodies within were in a competition to see who could make the most noise. At the far end of the main corridor teachers filtered into the staff room. The morning classes had finished for the daily hour-and-a-quarter lunch break.

The onlooker joined the throng inside the tutors' retreat.

Local authority school funding had not stretched as far as providing teachers' comforts. The staff room was not the most spacious of venues in which to relax. The faded pistachio walls merely added to the feeling of mild suffocation. But it was a haven in which to escape the daily challenge of restrained mayhem.

In the centre of the floor stood two weary, rectangular wooden tables placed end to end. These were enclosed by twenty or so chairs of assorted shapes and sizes. The right-hand wall was lined with two-tier mahogany lockers. They stood opposite an imposing Gothic window set in Tracery Stone.

This magnificent piece of architecture towered over an enamelled steel sink and tea-stained melamine work surface. This housed an electric kettle and a small microwave oven – probably not the internal view the architect had envisaged.

Casual chat around the table on Friday was always at its most lively. It usually skimmed over the week's classroom gossip, the previous night's TV programmes and any plans for the weekend. These subjects soon lost momentum with a small group of teachers. The conversation turned to the new addition that was about to join the school. On Monday, their ranks would be bolstered by the twenty-eight-year-old ex-pro footballer, Sam Whitmore. He was to be the new English master.

Clive Lawrence had been one of the school's two English teachers for the past fifteen years. The popular teacher's sudden death on the operating table had come as a terrible shock to the school staff and pupils. A few weeks later when his devastated wife, who had nagged him to have the hip replacement, committed suicide it left a dark cloud hanging over the school.

That was almost three months ago. Thankfully, the wound was beginning to heal, though it would be a slow process. But as so often happens, one person's misfortune provides an unexpected opportunity for another. Sam Whitmore was the lucky recipient.

'I hear he was on Chelsea's books until he was eighteen, but they let him go,' said James Shilling. James taught geography, cool disposition, in his early fifties and was recently appointed Deputy Head. He was Twiglet thin with close-cropped silver hair, matching beard, and loved his football. In fact, he lived his football. He had a deprecating and, at times, colourful sense of humour, which made him very popular with the majority of the boys he taught.

'Really!' said Wendy Jacks. Wendy was five feet eight and sat tall. 'We're getting a professional football player. Aren't we the lucky ones? Can he actually read and write? Have we checked his CV?'

James shrugged. *'Huh!* How many employers check a CV? Anyway, he went to Wimbledon FC for a while, which wasn't a good move as it turned out. It was just before the club disappeared off the face of the earth.'

'I thought they moved to Milton Keynes?' said Amy, the young Danish physical education teacher and keen football fan.

'Exactly! Milton Keynes,' said James. 'Anyway, I think he ended up playing for Woking for a few years until he got a nasty knee injury – ended the poor bugger's career,'

'I hear he's going to take over running the under-16's football team,' said maths teacher, Simon.

'Supposedly. That'll put old Rothy's nose out of joint,' said James, quietly, as heads turned towards the far end of the table where Mr Roth sat.

Jeremy Roth, history master, had just turned sixty. He had lived in a dilapidated Victorian cottage with his parents until their death. He was now the sole inhabitant. He was a short man with a head that hung permanently forwards as if he were forever checking-out his shoes.

A narrow band of greying ginger hair wrapped itself around the back of a shiny pate. He had been teaching at the school for six years and had been the under 16's football coach for the last four. In that time, they had not managed to win a single trophy and lost far more games than they won.

At every lunch break, he would take his blue Tupperware sandwich box and a copy of the Guardian from his locker, sit in the same seat at the end of the table and dissolve into his paper. Here, he was immune from what he regarded as the banal tittle-tattle, so loved by his colleagues. No one dared sit in his position.

'I'm surprised; the miserable old sod has remained football coach for so long,' said Wendy, not bothering to lower her voice. 'Old Roth wouldn't inspire *me* to run around in all weathers in next to nothing getting physically abused and covered in mud.'

James's left eyebrow lifted. 'Some people are happy to *pay* for that pleasure,' he said. 'But then, the country's MP's and High Court judges have to have some release, I suppose.'

The small group of teachers giggled.

Jeremy Roth turned his protuberant head and raised his eyes above his reading glasses. He considered the jocular bunch for a brief moment then returned to his paper.

The group looked at each other. There would be some very interesting days ahead.

Chapter 4

The baby girl screamed with an intensity that only the most rugged of tympanic membranes could tolerate. *Freya, it seems, is always screaming,* thought Sam. He pushed himself away from the breakfast table with just one thought in mind; to pacify the little tantrum machine perched opposite him.

'Go on, I'll take over, you don't want to be late on the first day of your new job,' urged his wife, moving in.

Lucy Whitmore, brought up my middle-class parents in Weybridge, Surrey, and with a Graduate Diploma in Interior Design, was not the stereotypical footballer's wife.

She met Sam Whitmore on a night out with her friends. Five months on, much to the disappointment of her parents, she fell pregnant. Three months further on the young couple were married. Tragedy struck just two weeks later when she lost the baby.

When Sam realised that a career from kicking an inflated piece of leather around a patch of grass was not going to happen, he decided he wanted to be a teacher. Up until now, he had no regrets.

When Sam was about to leave, Lucy joined him at the front door. She registered her husband's slight unease. 'Good luck, darling. Never easy on your first day – being the new boy at school,' she said, with a crooked smile. 'I'm sure it'll be fine.'

'Thanks Lou,' he said, his cheeks suddenly resembling a pufferfish.

'Wow – grammar school teacher,' he said, as he drove off. He liked the way that sounded. He was told he was going to replace a well-respected, recently deceased former master. He hoped that would not make his acceptance in the role a little awkward.

The journey from Southfields to Battersea should have taken a smidge over twenty minutes. But his struggle through this morning's nose-to-tail traffic, inching its way towards the country's capital, was not expected. 'Shit! I'm gonna be late. And on my first day. Brilliant!'

He was asked, by the headmaster to be in his office at eight a.m. He assumed the request was by way of a quick 'new recruit' pep talk. He left at seven twenty thinking that would be ample time. At the moment, though, his speedometer was hovering between the 5 and 10 mph mark.

As he sat in the slow-moving line of Wandsworth traffic, he glanced out of the driver's window. Rows of colourless shopfronts met his gaze. He knew this area. His parents were raised here. In days gone by, the high street was lined with independent retailers: a newsagent, greengrocer, baker, ironmonger, shops selling fresh fish and meats.

Those shops had all disappeared. Now, one in every three or four displayed nothing but bare, unwashed windows – vacant dusty shells, victims of the sprawling, impersonal Arndale centres, the B&Q's – cut-price superstores. Small shopkeepers all squeezed out by the corporate bullies. The nameless, ghostly premises left him with a feeling of melancholy. His mind returned to his immediate dilemma.

'Come on! For God's sake, come onnn!' he said, through clamped jaw, as the bumper in front of him moved another few yards.

00000

At eight minutes past eight, his perspiration-coated hands manoeuvred his car through the twelve-foot-high wooden side gates of the impressive school building. Unfortunately, every space in the car park was occupied. He parked behind an old green Volvo. It looked as if it had been there for the past twenty years. 'This is going really well,' he mumbled.

Sam leant across to the passenger seat to collect his bag when he noticed two boys in a corner of the parking area. They were perhaps fifteen or sixteen. One was holding out what looked like a packet of cigarettes. They appeared to be having an argument. As soon as he climbed from his car, the feuding boys stopped and looked over at him. Before he had a chance to call over to them, they turned and scampered off. *Whatever the educational level of school,* he thought. *There would always be the ever-present problem with smoking and drugs.*

As he hurried along the windowed corridor, Sam noticed the headmaster's office was slightly ajar. He glanced at his watch. 'Oh Christ!' he whispered. 'Sacked before I start.' He knocked on the heavy oak door. As he did so, the door swung open and a room full of people stood facing him.

Thirty glum expressions. His stomach tightened. Had he got the wrong room? His mouth opened as if to speak. Then his startled eyes focused on the one man he recognised. Peter Greaves. The headmaster.

The head emerged from the middle of the collection of unfamiliar faces. He was a good-looking man with a full head of greying hair, swept back. But at that moment, his face showed no emotion. A nervous attempt at a smile grew across Sam's mouth as he looked into the headmaster's eyes then up at the clock on the wall behind him. The hands were not friendly, pointing in a near straight line across the face. Eleven minutes past eight. Silence.

As the muscles on his face began to freeze, the room suddenly burst into applause. Smiles appeared.

'Welcome to our school,' announced the headmaster, with a wide grin, striding forwards to shake Sam's hand. 'And you won't be the first new recruit that has underestimated our South London traffic. Mind you, another five minutes and you would've walked into an empty room,' he added, raising his substantial eyebrows. He turned and waved an introductory arm across the rest of his staff. 'This is something we do for all our new teachers, so don't let this welcoming party go to your head.'

The room gave a half-hearted giggle.

Sam was overwhelmed by the head's thoughtful gesture. That was until he made a quick scan of the other teachers' faces. He saw that one or two members of staff were not wearing the same congenial smile as that of his new boss.

Chapter 5

Sam began his career at the Web on September 10th. It was a week after the new school year kicked-off. His first two weeks had engendered a mixture of emotions within him. His English classes had gone as well as he could have hoped. He was already beginning to develop a rapport with the majority of his pupils.

The younger boys in year's seven to ten were reasonably well-behaved. This may have been down to them being a little in awe of his footballing background. Years twelve and thirteen, those who'd stayed on into the sixth forms, were focused and adult enough to not cause him any real bother in class. They didn't have to be there. It was their choice.

It was year eleven – the fifteen-to-sixteen-year-olds. These in-betweeners were not kids any more but they weren't young adults either. This demanding bunch were erupting from their adolescent shells into a much wider world – but one in which they were novices. Boundary pushers.

They were the boys whose blue school uniforms were stuffed full of hormones determined to make their assertive mark in the world. These red bloods were Sam's most demanding challenge. But what he had to consider was that this was the most important school year of their lives so far. GCSE year.

There were three separate classes in each of the years and these were defined by the pupil's annual working performance. Class A contained the brightest and/or most studious boys. Classes B and C were supposed to be of a similar standard, but Class C tended to end up with the most disruptive boys. They had the comedians, the Jack-the-lads, the lazy buggers. Having said that, this was a grammar school. Even the 'C' boys had an acceptable degree of academic competence – they had all passed the eleven-plus exam. So, these boys were never going to be quite the challenge that Sam had encountered in his previous school.

All these thoughts were at the forefront of Sam's mind as he sat at the tidy desk in front of year eleven's class C. He was watching two boys giggling with each other. He wasn't sure, but he thought they may have been the couple he saw in the car park on his first day.

One was Tommy Clifford. His black-coffee-coloured hair was shaved close at the sides with a raised mop on top. His dark, defensive eyes held no innocence – opaque windows with room-only for secrets and schemes. Although slightly smaller than his classmates, he was built like a whippet. Josh Taylor was the direct opposite. Tallest in the class, mousey-haired, fair skinned and not long on ambition. Josh was a follower.

'Tommy, if you've finished your composition maybe you could let Josh get on with his. If you haven't, I suggest you stop talking and get on with your work. Same goes for you, Josh,' said Sam, over the heads of the rest of the class.

The two boys, who sat against the rear vanilla-painted wall of the classroom, looked up at the teacher. Josh, after a swift glance at his mate, returned to his work. Tommy did not. He held the teacher's gaze.

'Well?' said the teacher.

'Yes. Very well, thanks, he replied. The class giggled. Tommy looked around the room at his admiring audience, his mouth twisted into a triumphant smirk.

Sam had to think quickly to save face. 'Good, glad to hear it. That means you must have the strength to get on with your work, now. Doesn't it?' The class laughed out loud this time – there were a few cheers. Tommy Clifford's look wilted in an instant. The eyes narrowed as did his mouth. Sam, having achieved a vital measure of superiority dipped his head and went back to marking books. Tight lipped, Tommy returned to his composition.

Later, back in the staff-room Sam was talking to James Shilling. 'Have you ever had any problems with the pupil, Tommy Clifford?'

'Who hasn't had problems with Clifford?' He leant into Sam. 'He's a pain in the arse, that boy. But it's hardly surprising,' he said, eating his way through a tuna sandwich.

'What's his background?' asked Sam.

'Mixed race. Eldest of three kids. Each one by a different father. All buggered off after their births. His Mum has done a bloody good job in the circumstances. She must have encouraged a young Tommy to study, else

31

he wouldn't be in this grammar school. Poor woman probably ran out of energy 'cos the other two are in the local comprehensive – not sure how they're doing.' James put his sandwich down on a paper napkin and had a swig of his tea. Sam waited.

James leant back in his chair. 'When he started here, he was a very quiet but fairly polite little boy. But as he got older – no father figure, you see – he developed a big chip on his shoulder, which seemed to get bigger with every year. I've tried; we've all tried, to break down that anger in him.' He shook his head, picked up his unfinished sandwich, looked at it, put it back in its wrapper and threw it in the bin behind him. 'Shame really. I can't see anything but bad for that kid.'

00000

Peter Greaves shifted in his chair. He had been promoted from deputy head to the coveted job of headmaster shortly after his thirty-seventh birthday. He was proud of his achievement at a relatively young age. So was his wife, Ruth, who embarrassed him with a surprise party for friends and family three weeks after the announcement. But, two years on, he was still coming to terms with the position. The varied and challenging skills of managing a group of adults instead of kids was a steep learning curve.

Jeremy Roth sat opposite him his feet planted on the cream carpet. He was red-faced, his grip on the leather arms of the chair beginning to tighten.

'Just because he was a pro-footballer, a failed pro-footballer, I might add, doesn't give him the right to waltz in here and take over my team. Four years I've been with those boys. Four bloody years I've trained, coached, and organised them. In all weathers. I've turned up every Saturday, week in week out to watch them play. Now, suddenly, after a few days of being here, Mr wonderful Whitmore is to take over the team. My team!'

The head shifted in his seat once again. 'Jeremy, this wasn't an easy decision. I know how hard you have worked with these lads, but you have to admit, *erm,* we've not really had the, er, success that some other schools have enjoyed these past few seasons. I just think...'

'We were bloody eighth in the league last year. That's two places higher than the previous one. And we've been really unlucky with injuries,' Roth countered, raising his voice.

The head was shocked to see his history teacher so animated. He had always been a quiet, reserved individual, or so he thought. He was also aware that there were only twelve teams in the league but thought better of bringing it into what was becoming a delicate situation. 'All your efforts have been much appreciated, but I'm sorry. I... I just think it's time for a change. Coming at the start of a new season. And it makes sense to take advantage of Sam's background.'

'So, it's decided, then?' said Roth. The headmaster opened his mouth, breathed in, exhaled immediately and said nothing. 'Right, if that's your last word.' The teacher got up from his chair. 'And don't expect me to step in if

Mr Sam sodding Whitmore falls ill or gets a better offer elsewhere.' He turned, looked back without making eye contact, mouthed a few words then trooped out of the room.

Peter sat staring at the back of his office door. He picked up his pen, opened a slim folder and put a line through the name of Jeremy Roth. His eyes narrowed as he leant back in his chair. 'Fuck him… loser!'

Chapter 6

Wendy Jacks watched her class drain out of the room like water from a cracked pipe. Her thoughts went back to last weekend. It was not one to remember with pleasure. Friday night had been one of unrest; her sleep had been punctured by half-remembered, confused dreams. She wouldn't often set her alarm at the weekends, preferring to sleep in till late morning. But on that morning, there was work to do. Her husband's absence meant that she now had tasks to perform that she regarded as predominantly men's jobs.

The work inside the house could wait. She had never had a decent rear garden lawn since they moved into the three-bedroom cottage five years ago. It wasn't a very large space but now, after the long spell of dry weather, it was a disaster. The area was nothing more than a dusty patch of cracked mud and a few sprigs of dead grass.

She wanted to be able to sit on the patio after work, wine in hand and look out on to freshly mowed green grass. Wendy imagined a typical English country garden. She had trolled countless pictures of stunning gardens on the internet. It was then she realised that flower beds were simply the sparkle, the colour, the structure.

They were nothing without the calming canvas of a beautiful, lush lawn. One without the other didn't work. To this end, she'd driven to the nearby garden centre and ordered seventy square metres of lawn turf. It came on a wooden pallet, piled up with eighteen-inch-wide, five-foot-long rolls, mud-side outwards.

The deliveryman had deposited the one-ton load from his lorry onto her front drive via an electronic arm. When she attempted to move them around to the back of the house, she'd underestimated how heavy each roll was. Due to the extended fine weather, they had been watered the day before delivery. So, not only did the soaking make them heavier but the wet mud exteriors stuck like glue to each other.

'Oh, this is ridiculous, they weigh a ruddy ton.' she mumbled. After moving just four rolls, the teacher was covered in wet muck. Her arms and wrists were aching so much she had to stop. She shook her head as she looked at the hefty pile in front of her. A decision was made.

'I'm going to need help with these.'

00000

'Another?' said Sheila.

'Yes please, love,' said James. Sheila was the pub landlady at the Tradesman's Arms; late forties, East End raised, sharp as a pin and ran a second-hand car sales business on the side. She was a woman with a ready sense of humour, but you messed with her at your peril. Her husband was from Southern Ireland and a good deal older than her. He would occasionally sit at the bar reading his Daily Mirror. He had little or no conversation with his regulars. They were a puzzling match.

The pub was situated just twenty yards from the school. James Shilling sat on his usual high stool at the end of the bar. The inn served him well. He'd have two or three pints every evening after work before a ten-minute walk back to his terraced house. There, he would open a cheap bottle of wine and roll a very large spliff. But he had no reason to hurry home.

It was a week before his fifteenth wedding anniversary. On his arrival at school, he realised he had left some test papers at home. He had returned in his lunch break to retrieve them only to find his wife upstairs in bed with the builder who was supposed to be fitting a new kitchen for them.

After kicking the builder out, he stood speechless in front of his cheating wife as she dressed hurriedly. Dumbfounded and unable to comprehend what he'd just seen, with tears welling in his eyes, he lumbered downstairs, collected his papers and, in a daze, returned to school.

After three weeks of bitter rows, silent confusion, and a brief attempt at reconciliation his wife packed her belongings and moved in with her burly labourer. The kitchen was never finished.

That was over six months ago. The memory, still raw, played out as he half-watched a young couple sitting in a corner of the pub. They were holding hands across a small round table oblivious of all around them. The girl was looking at her partner as though he was the only man in the world.

'Ere, y'a mate!' The landlady put the jug of beer on the counter, returning him to the moment.

James squeezed his eyes together then opened them wide. 'Cheers, darling.' He took a swig, wiping the froth from his top lip. 'How's my tab looking?'

Sheila punched a few numbers into the till. 'Thirty-two quid, give or take. You're okay for now,' she replied.

'Okay, thanks, Sheil. I'm not leaving the country. Although I'm not sure why, though. I really don't recognise this place anymore. What with health and bloody safety rules and kids knowing their so-called infringement of rights? Honestly, my job is nigh on impossible these days.' He lifted his pint. 'Thank God for alcohol, that's what I say.'

Sheila focused on her regular for a second, lips pressed together in a faint smile. She nodded and went off to serve a waiting customer.

Whenever his bar tab spilled over the fifty pounds mark, she would want it settled. He appreciated the trust she showed in him. It was how a pub should be with their regulars. It was how a pub used to be, he thought – before they became restaurants, filled with kids and young parents who had never known anything else.

He felt sorry for the latest generation of adults. When he was a young man, pubs were the only places available where adults could escape from children for an hour or two – from reality. It was a retreat in which to enjoy relaxed, grown-up conversations with friends and acquaintances. He looked across at a young parent who had just sat his three-year-old at the bar. James closed his eyes, wobbled his head and saw his father's face looking down at him – his heavy eyebrows furrowed in disapproval.

00000

Sam Whitmore was watching the team he inherited from Roth play their first game under him. His first impression was an obvious one. They needed a lot of work to get them up to the standard he hoped to achieve.

The second thing he noticed was that one boy, a forward player, despite being fleet-footed and performer of some flashy skills, appeared to be playing for himself and not the team. He was also arguing with the referee whenever a decision went against him. The boy was Tommy Clifford.

When the final whistle blew, his team was on the wrong end of a 3–0 score line. After the players had showered and changed, Sam kept them in the dressing room. He got them all to sit down. 'Well done boys for trying your best today. Over the coming weeks, we're gonna change a few things and together make this a team of winners. But you've all got to want it. Hands up all those who would prefer to win most weeks rather than lose?'

After a few surprised looks were exchanged amongst the young faces, ten timorous arms were raised. Clifford sat; arms folded. 'That may sound like a stupid question but wanting to win, that desire over all else to succeed, is as important as your skill and fitness levels. Right. Training. I understand it was on Wednesday afternoons. From now on…'

A hand went up. 'Yes, sir, it was supposed to be, but we hardly ever did any training – or work on the team,' said the slightly overweight goalkeeper.

Sam was not surprised to hear this. 'Okay. Training will be on Mondays after school and Wednesday afternoons on games day. Let me know if any of you can't make it on the Mondays. I want the football that we play to be fun and I want you all to enjoy the training sessions, but we will all have to work hard.'

Sam scanned the faces before him. The majority of the boys looked excited and in awe of their new coach and his rousing speech. There was one obvious exception. As the team filed into the waiting bus, Sam pulled Clifford aside. 'Tommy, you don't seem to be very enthusiastic with anything I've just said. If there is a problem, maybe I could sort it. We need everyone pulling the same way here.'

'Just because you was a pro-footballer doesn't mean you know everything about the game,' said Tommy, avoiding eye contact.

'I'm not saying I do, but I probably know a good bit more than you and the rest of the boys, which is why I'm here to help you. You've got a lot to offer this team but you need to change your attitude on the field. You're fast and have a few nice skills but you play with your head down. You need to be aware of your team mates more – pass the ball to players who may be in a better position in front of goal than you.'

Tommy at last looked up into the teacher's face. His jawbones tightened 'I don't need you to tell me how to play football. Rothy thought I was the best player in the team. What do you bleedin' know? You know nothing about me.' He brushed past the teacher and onto the team bus.

Sam stood, not moving, still staring at the space vacated by the boy. He had mixed with some tough guys in the early days of his football career. He had played with a few insular individuals, often kids from deprived one-parent families. Happily, he had seen the majority of them slowly change, relax. It was a delight to see them lower their social barriers and adjust their pre-conceived ideas of authority. Most had become loyal friends. But he'd never seen such a level of hostility and distrust in a young boy's eyes such as those he had just witnessed.

The phrase "you know nothing about me" nestled in his mind. As Sam boarded the bus, two words stuck to his lips.

Clifford. Trouble.

Chapter 7

Amelie Pederson blew her whistle. 'Right, listen everyone. Come on, stop talking.' She had instructed all the boys in her year eleven class to get out every piece of apparatus from the gym cupboard. They were going to do circuit training. It was now in position and she had finally got the boys' attention.

'Okay, when I blow my whistle, you do two minutes on each exercise. Every time I blow again you move on to the next one.' She licked her lips and put the whistle between them. Now half the class were waiting for the blast of the shrill signal to commence their workout. The other half were dreaming; locked onto those moist parted lips and trying to imagine what delights lay beneath that black, tight-fitting Nike T-shirt.

At around fifteen to sixteen years-of-age, a good deal of male emotions were in a near-constant state of carnal curiosity. Their collective machinery untried and all in good working order was primed and ready to rumble. The trouble was at that age, the opportunity to give it a run out with the most obvious and desired of partners, mostly females, was exceedingly rare.

The soft lips pursed. The chest rose. The hungry sets of eyes watched...

The whistle blew.

At five-nine, twenty-six, blonde and fit, she was the playground talk of the school. She had been the Web's PE teacher for the past three years, much to the joy of the five-hundred-and-twenty boys under her tutelage.

When she was nineteen, her family moved from their home in Frederiksberg, Denmark. Her father was transferred from Danske Bank Copenhagen's head office to their London branch. The family went with him. Amelie, having completed her Initial Teacher Training course back home in Denmark, embarked on a three-year undergraduate course at Kingston University, Surrey where she gained a BSc Honours Degree in Sports Science.

She was delighted when her application for the vacancy at the school was successful. Her Scandinavian good looks were also a success with the male staff when introduced to them on her first day at work.

'I am very happy to meet you all. Please call me Amy,' was all she needed to say in her beguiling Nordic timbre. Hearts melted beneath tired jackets; quiescent testosterone gambolled like spring lambs.

Her morning classes finished, she was now sitting in Peter Greaves' office still wearing her daily uniform of black figure-hugging Nike leggings and t-shirt, discussing the ageing gymnasium equipment.

'The workout mats have to be replaced, Peter, they're getting stained and dirty – some are falling apart. And we could do with two more Swiss Balls; the boys are having to wait all the time to use them.'

'Okay.' The headmaster turned a page of the diary sitting on his green-leather-topped desk, studying the contents. 'This month's budget has been virtually taken care of but, *erm,* I think we can get those replacements next month.' he said, writing a reminder in the book.

'I can't believe you're still using a book to plan your business schedule, Peter. That big ugly computer next to you will do that much more clearly for you.'

'Don't trust 'em. My little blue book just sits there in front of me and does what it's told. It lets me decorate its pages with ink, in order to remind me what I've got to remember. Computers; got a mind of their own. Trouble is they talk back – throw wobblies.' He looked up at the PE teacher. 'They let other people know what you're writing and what you're thinking. I only use them when I absolutely have to. Dodgy buggers all of 'em.'

Amy smiled got up from her chair and walked around the desk. She stood behind the headmaster leant forward, put her arms around his shoulders and kissed him on the cheek. 'And that's why I love being with you, you old-fashioned fool.'

'Is that any way to talk to your boss?' he said. Then, checking that his office door was firmly closed he turned his head upwards and kissed Amy full on the lips. He pulled away and looked up into clear Arctic-blue eyes. 'Do you want me to come around again after work tonight?'

'Yes please, boss,' Amy said, her eyes widening.

Their affair had been going on for over six months. Peter's wife, Ruth, was eight years older than him. After their only child, a son, was born nineteen years ago, the couple's sex life had gone from okay through to occasional, settling on non-existent. He hoped it would improve after his son went off to University in Bristol last year. It would leave the two of them alone in the house again. His hope never materialised.

Amy had had two casual affairs since arriving in England. Both guys, after just a few months in, had started to get too possessive over her leisure time – too serious for her relaxed attitude to relationships. She felt she was far too young to commit to anyone at her age, especially when there was so much fun to be had in her new country.

Frederiksberg was a fashionable part of Copenhagen – posh even – the inhabitants being mainly older and more established. There was much more going on in nearby Copenhagen. But London? London was enticing, new and vibrant. The different quarters and cosmopolitan element were a source of excitement to Amy.

She had hit it off with Peter from the moment they'd met at her interview – their lively sense of humour the touch-paper –their combined good looks the lighted match. That he was married, albeit in a passionless alliance, didn't bother her one bit. In fact, the situation was perfect. He was fun, more experienced in bed than her previous young boyfriends and no threat to her freedom. The only threat being her job at the school if her affair with the headmaster was discovered or their relationship went pear-shaped.

'I'll be over soon after work – about six. That okay?' said Peter.

'Six is fine.'

He would tell Ruth he had a business meeting. Friday night was when she went to the book club with her friends. He would have until at least ten o'clock to get back home.

Amy walked towards the door and turned. 'Do you think your wife knows about us?'

Peter looked up from the papers on his desk, it was if he'd been slapped around the face. It was the first time she'd ever asked that question. She knew his sex life was non-existent at home, but this was different – awkward – crossing a line. He took a moment to answer.

'Well, I think she has an idea, yes. I get the impression she may suspect something is going on but either doesn't really care too much or doesn't want to know – as long as it doesn't affect our friendship. It also takes the pressure off her as far as intimacy is concerned if she does know. Not that I think she really feels any pressure that way anymore. Why do you ask?'

'It doesn't worry me. I just can't understand why any woman wouldn't want to make love with a gorgeous man like you. I'll see you at six. You bring the wine; I'll feed us. Don't be late,' she said, as if talking to a naughty boy. She turned and left the office.

The headmaster, unaware that he'd been holding his breath, emptied his lungs.

Chapter 8

'When light bends as it enters a different medium, it is known as what'? asked Wendy Jacks during her twenty-question-and-answer spot quiz for her science class. The hands went up. She chose Danny Antonelli. 'Yes, Danny?'

'Refraction, Miss.'

'Correct. Okay, last one. And the easiest. What is the earth's primary source of energy?' She scanned the faces attached to the stretched arms. Her scan stopped at Josh Taylor. 'Josh?'

'Porridge, Miss.' The class exploded in laughter. Taylor looked surprised.

'Mmm. I only wished you'd meant that as a joke. Now can I have a serious answer? Up went the hands once more. For the first time throughout the quiz, Tommy Clifford's arm went vertical. 'Master Clifford, you've joined us. Is this a Eureka moment? Let's hope you've got a better answer?'

'Porridge is a stupid answer. The answer's obvious. It's cocaine,' he said proudly. There were a few stilted laughs quickly followed by silence.

Wendy looked sternly at the smirking face. 'I keep giving you chance after chance to be a part of this class and all you do is throw it back in my face. Not this time, Tommy Clifford. I'm putting you on report. Head of Year will want a want a word with you.' Tommy, realising he had no support from the rest of the class, simply shrugged his shoulders.

'The Earth's primary source of energy? Anyone? Yes, Darren,' Wendy continued.

'The sun, Miss.'

'Hooray! Correct.' Just then the end-of-lesson bell sounded. 'Right, well done today. And leave the classroom quietly.' The teacher's last phrase was lost to the sixty young ears beneath the sound of scraping chairs, slamming desk lids and animated conversation.

00000

The atmosphere in the staff room had always been relaxed and genial. That was until Sam Whitmore arrived and was given the job of running the under 16's football team. He was a popular figure with most of the other teachers but the hostility emanating across the lunch table from Jeremy Roth was palpable. It hadn't started well when Sam had parked his car behind Roth's old Volvo on his first day in the job, thus preventing him from leaving early that day.

The rancour came in the form of snapshot withering glances, dismissive body language. Roth would moan to anyone who was willing to listen to him. But he had never actually spoken to the young English teacher himself. A couple of the older teachers had even sided with Roth concerning his loss of football manager.

Sam had been told that Roth had been good buddies with Clive Lawrence the previous English teacher. That had not helped. Now, this young novice who had stolen his football team was taking over his sadly departed friend's old post. It was as if Roth was blaming him for Clive's death.

Sam, having just finished his last class of the morning, proceeded along one of the beeline, window-studded corridors. He stopped when he saw Roth at his desk in one of the classrooms. He was on his own. He was concerned about the sharpened vibes he'd been getting from him, which had been confirmed by some of his colleagues. Now was his chance to get it out in the open; build a bridge with the history master. He knocked on the classroom door and entered.

He took a deep breath. 'Can I have a word, Jeremy?'

The teacher, having already seen him approach the door, quickly lowered his head back to his work. 'It's Roth. Mister Roth,' he said, without looking up.

This is going to be harder than I thought, Sam said to himself, as he stood in front of his desk. 'I know you must be upset about losing the coaching duties of the under 16's team…'

'My team, you mean.'

'Yes, of course, your team. But I want you to know that it was offered to me. I didn't ask for the position when I arrived. The head thought it made sense to utilise my background and previous experience.'

Roth continued to remain fixed on his paperwork and said nothing. Sam continued, 'I just want, well, I hope this doesn't get in the way of our relationship in the long term. And I want you to know that I'd be very happy for you to come and watch the team play on Saturdays whenever you wanted.'

Sam waited. His offer was met by silence. His soft, conciliatory approach had not been appreciated. His frustration built. The rudeness of the man now manifested the words he'd wanted to say all along. 'It's just that the school's football reputation tends to rest on the most senior teams. So, I'm determined to take this group of boys to another level if I can.'

Roth went to speak, stuttered then stopped. Sam noticed that the history teacher's face was almost scarlet, a protruding vein visible above the worn collar of his green-checked brushed-cotton shirt. The brown knitted tie suddenly appeared too tight around his neck.

Sam just stood and watched. The teacher's thin lips pulsed as he appeared to be talking to himself. The silence continued. He was astounded that this pathetic little man hadn't the courage to at least argue his corner.

'Well, anyway, I just wanted to, *erm,* you know…' said Sam. Roth's eyes remained fixed on the timeworn surface of his desk. Sam shrugged, shook his head and left the room.

As he closed the classroom door Roth raised his large shiny head and watched the young English teacher walk off down the corridor. 'Another level. Another fucking level.' The words were spat towards the disappearing figure. 'We'll see. We'll see, Mr pretty boy Whitmore, what level I can go to.'

Chapter 9

Friday lunchtime was, to the young football players, the most important time of the week. Emotions ran high. It was when the school teams that were due to play on Saturday were posted on the notice board next to the gymnasium door. The gathering of boys was looking up at the various team sheets, searching for their names. What they discovered engendered four main emotions: confirmation, relief, elation or disappointment.

Tommy Clifford and his pal Josh Taylor sauntered up behind the dozen or so kids checking the line-ups. Josh being taller than his mate spotted his own name immediately over the raft of bobbing heads. Gradually, his mouth dropped open as he realised that the name of his pal was absent from the eleven starters. He wasn't named as one of the three subs either.

He turned to Tommy his expression still one of surprise but now mixed with trepidation. There was no way he was going to be the one to announce to his volatile friend what he'd just witnessed. He didn't speak. The look said it all. Tommy's relaxed, smug face hardened as he shoved the younger boys out of his way to get to the board.

He stood motionless scanning the under 16's team sheet. Once, twice, three times his disbelieving eyes searched the list. He'd been dropped. 'Fucking bastard

Whitmore!' The words came out in a whisper, but his senses were screaming.

He'd never before been dropped from the team. The humiliation was too much. Bitter tears clouded his eyes. He turned, slapped a youngster around the top of his head who innocently had stood in his way, and marched off from the throng of blue blazers.

Josh studied the team sheet once more. There was a new name in the starting line-up that appeared in the position where T. Clifford would usually be. The name was D. Antonelli.

00000

The seventy-five-minute lunch break, as far as the teachers were concerned, always went by too quickly. The staff room was filled with the smell of coffee and the busy sounds of spoons, cups, rustling crisp packets and chocolate wrappers. James Shilling sat with his hands wrapped around a mug of tea. Despite the hot late summer/early autumn temperature outside, the dense internal stonewalls and heavily armoured Gothic window never allowed the room to get anywhere near approaching cosy.

He turned to Sam, who had now become a firm friend. The young teacher always made a point of sitting next to him. 'Had any more trouble with the Curse of Clifford?'

Sam, who had a mouthful of custard tart, put his hand over his lips and managed a garbled. 'Afraid so.' He swallowed the rest and continued, 'I tried to talk to him after my first game in charge of the team but he's impossible to get through to. There's so much hostility in that boy. The thing is, he could be a good player if he wasn't so greedy with the ball. I've dropped him from the team for the time being. I hope that will make him realise he can't…'

James whipped his head around to look at Sam. 'You've done what?'

Sam tried to continue, 'James, he…

'Bugger me, you're brave… or mad. He's never been out of any of the year's teams since he's been at the school.

Sam looked a little taken aback. 'He's ruining the team ethic at the moment. The rest of the boys are scared to not pass the ball to Clifford in case they get a load of verbal from him. It's almost a one-man team. I had no choice.'

'Listen, I get what you're saying. I've watched him over the years, and I know my football. I happen to agree with you but, well, just be aware that he's not gonna let this drop. He's a scheming little bastard is Master Clifford.'

Sam took a deep breath. 'I'm hoping by leaving him out of the side it may just make him realise that there are other decent people in this team… in this world, even! If he wants his position back then he will have to change. And maybe, just maybe, it could be the making of him. I really hope so.'

James dipped his head, raised his eyes above his glasses and stared at Sam. He turned away. Immediately he turned back. He gave him another stare; this time his eyes narrowing to slits.

'What?' said Sam, a puzzled smile growing across his lips.

James released his hands from his mug, threw them in the air, waving them about. *'Hallelujah! Hallelujah!* It's a miracle!'

A few teachers peered across at them. James now wore a know-it-all smirk on his lived-in face. Sam, to all those watching, just appeared to be laughing, enjoying the charismatic geography master's not out-of-character performance. The workings of his face reflected that cheery emotion – his brain told a different story.

00000

When the school day had come to an end, Wendy Jacks sat for the next forty minutes marking an exercise she had set for her last class. When finished, she rose, scooped up the books with an exaggerated sigh and made her way to the staff room. Surprisingly she was alone; all the other teachers on the sound of the bell had either made a quick exit home or were still working in their classrooms.

Opening her locker, she took out her sneakers she wore for driving and her empty Tupperware lunchbox. Off came her low-heeled shoes and on went the comfortable pumps. She put the shoes and lunchbox in her carry bag and departed.

As she entered the deserted corridor, she was surprised to see Danny Antonelli walking towards her. As

54

the student drew close, she stopped. 'Hello, Danny. Surprised to see you still in school; I thought you boys couldn't wait to get out of this place?'

'I was just doing a bit of extra training in the gym, Miss. I'm in the football team now and I want to stay in. Mr Whitmore said I need to get fitter'

'Were you on your own?'

'Yes, Miss.'

'Did Mr Whitmore or Miss Pederson say you could train in the gym without a teacher present?'

'Er, no Miss,' said Danny, looking at his shoes.

It was then that Wendy realised she may just have the perfect opportunity to get the muscular help she needed at home. 'If you had an accident in there with no one around to oversee your training session, what then? If there were no one about to help you if you were badly hurt, the school would be in big trouble. Do you understand?'

Danny's gaze lifted from his feet. It rested briefly on the stern face in front of him then lowered slightly. 'Sorry, Miss.'

As in the classroom, the teacher was aware that this boy was again focusing on the front of her cream chiffon blouse. 'Look, I will pretend this didn't happen this one time.' She hesitated. 'In return, perhaps you could do something for me. And I will pay you for your time and effort.'

The unexpected reply changed the schoolboy's expression in an instant. His eyes widened as they locked onto the teacher's face. It was softer. 'What do you want me to do?'

Once more, she hesitated. *Is this a good idea,* she thought.

'Erm, well. I need you to carry a load of new lawn turfs from my front garden around to the back of the house. They are wet and sticky and just too heavy for me. I don't think it would take a fit young man like you more than an hour to complete the task and I'll pay you £20 for your trouble. Would that be er… could you do that for me?'

Wendy gazed at the boy who was still one month shy of his sixteenth birthday. He was already threatening the six-foot mark; a good three or four inches taller than her. He could have easily passed for a young man of eighteen. She felt herself flush as she waited for his reply.

Twenty pounds was twice what he was paid for cleaning his dad's car. This was a no-brainer. 'Yes, I could do that, Miss.'

She returned the smile that the boy now offered her. 'Splendid! But listen, Danny. I don't think I am supposed to be hiring my pupils to carry out private work for me, so this will have to be our secret. Do you understand?'

There was no way that he was going to pass up the chance to earn that much money. This would be a quick and easy job. 'Of course, Miss. I won't tell anyone. When do you want me to do it?'

'Have you got time tomorrow morning?'

'There is no football game this Saturday so no worries,' he replied.

'My address is 42 Rupert Street. As in the bear. Do you know where that is?'

'Yes, Miss. I know nearly all the roads around here. It's a three-or-four-minute run from my house.

They both lived under a mile from the school and just half a mile from each other. So, it was arranged. Danny would go to the teacher's cottage tomorrow morning at ten o'clock.

On the short drive home, Wendy was aware that her heart was beating faster than normal.

00000

At fifteen minutes past six, Peter Greaves parked his silver Audi A3 outside the early twentieth-century Victorian style building. The long arrow-straight road was located behind Earlsfield Station in the borough of Wandsworth.

The up-and-coming area consisted mainly of two-storey terraced dwellings. Some were divided into lower and upper two-bedroom flats. Amy had bought one on the first floor with the help of her father and a mortgage she could handle. It was ideal for work, being a mere fifteen-minute drive to Battersea.

As he approached the black gloss-painted door, his level of excited anticipation was through the roof. He was nineteen when he met his wife-to-be but by then he'd already been to bed with several girls. He had fallen in love with Ruth after only a matter of months and was overjoyed when she had accepted his proposal of marriage.

But that was twenty years ago. This feeling was different; electrically charged. This liaison was naughty, wicked even and had arrived after nine years of enforced

57

abstinence. Ironically, he had never cheated on any one of his casual girlfriends. And even after the complete withdrawal of sex in his marriage, he'd remained faithful to Ruth. Until now.

The unexpected arrival of the younger, desperately attractive PE teacher was one thing. That she actually wanted *him* – a man two months off his fortieth birthday, and a touch wide around the girth was life changing. For the first time in years, he was desired and needed physically; it was wonderful. He was young again.

A bottle of Sauvignon Blanc in one hand, he opened the door with the key Amy had given him some months ago. As he turned in the narrow passageway and started to climb the stairs, a voice above him said, 'Good evening. You're late!' Peter looked up; his heart jumped. Amy was perched on the top step. Her blonde hair, still wet from the shower, draped itself across the smooth pale skin of her shoulders. She sat naked with her legs slightly apart. One hand between them the other proffering her firm breasts to her visitor. He noticed that the hand between her legs was not still.

'I couldn't wait any longer, you naughty boy, so I've started without you.' Peter's eyes widened, his jaw loose as he became more aroused with each step he took towards his paradise. When he was four treads away from his prize he leant forward, laid the wine on the carpet next to her, dipped his head down between those smooth shapely legs and replaced her busy hand.

Most of his work had been done as just thirty seconds later Amy, now laying back on the hall carpet whilst holding her boss's head firmly in position, moaned and squealed her way to orgasm.

Moments later, she raised herself up onto her elbows as she watched Peter stand up. 'Head Master, in more ways than one! Man of many talents,' she breathed. The lithe P.E. teacher then stood, grabbed the bottle, grabbed his hand, led him into her bedroom. Pushing him backwards onto the bed her face lit up. 'Your turn.'

Her attention immediately switched to the wine. As she started to unscrew the cap, Peter leant over, grabbed the bottle, and replaced it alongside the two glasses sitting on the bedside table. In one movement, he pulled the naked Amy onto the bed and straddled the beautiful body of his Danish lover. 'The wine will have to wait,' he said. 'I can't!'

Chapter 10

Friday night had been one of conflicting dreams for Wendy. Her husband had played a major role in most of them. They consisted, for the most part, of jealous arguments loaded with blame and resentment. But then, there were overlying visions of Danny Antonelli's face, but one that she hardly recognised. He was at least ten years older – more assertive, more mature.

Saturdays were when she would usually sleep in till mid-morning. Not today. She rose at eight a.m. and dressed in jeans and an old t-shirt. After a quick breakfast, she began the big clean up. If Danny ever told anyone that he had been to her house, she didn't want it known she lived in a pigsty. There was two days washing-up in the sink and her clothes were scattered all over the house. During the week, she was less inclined to keep her home shipshape, especially when most of her evenings were filled with school duties. The weekend was the time for housework.

When she finished her chores, she was sweating. The late September temperature was still in the early seventies, the atmosphere humid. She opened the rear glass patio doors, enjoying the slight breeze that brushed her face.

The next thing she opened was a bottle of white wine from the fridge. It was not normal for her to start drinking this early but this morning she suddenly felt a need. She poured herself a large glass and sat down on her sofa. As she took a welcome drink, the doorbell rang. She jumped. 'God. Why am I so nervous? He's just a boy.'

When she opened the door, Danny was standing there in ragged denim cut-off shorts that finished halfway up his thigh and a tight-fitting t-shirt. She hadn't realised how toned he was as she took in the view of his suntanned muscles.

'Hello Miss. Here I am, ready for work,' he said with a smile.

She was surprised how confident and relaxed he was, compared to the boy she'd been talking to at school yesterday afternoon. 'Hi, Danny, thanks for coming. Right, the turfs, as you can see, are there,' she said, pointing to the mud heap in front of the garage. 'I'll just go around the back and open the side gate for you.'

Danny wandered over to the pallet and went to pick up a turf from the top of the pile. It was heavier than he had anticipated and was stuck to the others, putting more strain on his fingers and forearms than he expected. He quickly decided to transport one at a time. As he moved to the side of the property, he heard the scraping of the bolt as it slid across the lock. The wooden-slatted door opened. He was led through to the back garden.

'You can stack them up here on the patio, please Danny.' She then noticed a smear of mud on his white t-shirt. 'Oh, you're going to get your top filthy by the time you've finished. Would you like an old shirt to wear?'

Danny looked down at the smudge. 'No that's okay. If it's all right with you, I'll take it off to work.'

Wendy nodded. *'Erm,* yes. If you're comfortable with that.' Danny pulled the figure-hugging shirt over his head, ruffling his thick mane of olive-black hair. He shook it back into place and hung the garment over the back of a weather-beaten garden chair. It was immediately obvious to her that he was happy to show off his fit body to a relative stranger. And at that moment, so was she.

She took a breath. 'Can I leave you to get on with it? I need to get out of these clothes and have a quick shower. Will you be okay?'

Danny looked into her eyes, a slight smile on his face. 'Yes, Miss. I'll be fine.'

By the time she arrived in her bedroom, she was aware that the teacher pupil relationship had suddenly altered. She was not on school premises anymore where strict rules between staff and students were followed and readily accepted. And he, out of his school uniform, had escaped from the institution that exemplified those rigid guidelines. *We are both in uncharted territory,* she thought.

Standing in the shower Wendy turned her face upwards letting the powerful water-jets wash the shampoo suds from her hair and down her body. When her head and face were soap-free, her hands slid slowly downwards over her breasts, stopping on her thighs. The earlier sight of Danny's ripped body dominated her thoughts.

She had not felt like this for years. It was intoxicating. Exciting. It scared her. Her mind went back five years. She was beginning to get a bit too close to a sixteen-year-old boy at her previous school. Before it got too serious, she had a decision to make. She knew she was weak, so the only way she had the strength to end it was to leave and find another job.

Now she was in the same position. But this time, the need for self-control was losing an unfair fight against the unquenchable need for satisfaction. At that moment, desire was overruling good sense.

After Wendy had dried herself, she slipped on her white towelling bathrobe, then moved to the window overlooking the rear garden. She stood and watched Danny carry the turfs in and place them in a neat pyramid on the concrete. But her focus was on one thing; his glistening shoulders.

00000

Danny had been having erotic thoughts and dreams about his science teacher for months. His sexual fantasies had, more often than not, centred on Miss Jack's weighty breasts. Their hypnotic movement as she turned and moved about the classroom made it near impossible to concentrate on his work. It probably accounted for his average marks in most tests she set the class.

She was quite attractive for her age, he thought, but there was something else apart from her physical appearance. Something other than the obvious, that had ensnared his attention. Beneath the strict teacher's guise, he saw something different. A need. Despite her seniority in age and lofty position, he sensed a vulnerability in her. He found it irresistible.

Although nearly sixteen, he'd had a certain amount of experience with the opposite sex. But these were with girls of the same age. Sex mainly consisted of fumbles in and around various items of underwear. Officially, he was still a virgin. But he could tell when females were attracted to him.

The first hint of that animal attraction was yesterday. It was back at school, when his teacher had asked him to do some work for her. She seemed nervous, almost unsure of herself. He was certain he hadn't misread her body language. His first reaction was surprise, but today when he turned up at her house, his instincts were confirmed.

The imperious teacher had disappeared. In her place was a slightly flustered, expectant teenager. He had registered his teacher's reaction as he took off his top. It was then that he thought he could be in with a chance of something more than twenty pounds and a mud-covered t-shirt. If he was wrong, he would at least get the money and take home the fantasy of what might have been with his busty teacher.

00000

Wendy walked slowly down the stairs and through the sitting room to the open patio doors. She was still dressed in her towelling robe. She saw that the pile of turfs had grown a lot quicker than she had anticipated. Danny's job was almost done. As he deposited another mud roll on top of the neat pile he had created, she walked out into the garden. The boy was covered in sweat, streaks of dirt smeared his arms and chest.

'Oh dear! You look very hot. I'm sorry I should have offered you a drink before I showered. I'm sure you could do with one.'

'Water will be fine, please Miss.'

With just a pair of shorts and trainers covering his lithe body, Wendy's imagination didn't need much assistance in picturing him naked. 'You've done really well in getting all these here in such a short time. Is there much more to do?' she said.

'Only three or four left, I think,' said Danny, proudly. While he spoke, his eyes were fixed on the considerable amount of the teacher's soft cleavage that the loosely tied dressing gown was now revealing.

A shiver went through Wendy's body as she saw the effect she was having on her pupil. She didn't bother to rearrange her gown as she turned and headed for the kitchen to get the drink. She pulled a tumbler from the overhead cupboard and stood watching the water from the tap fill the glass. As she turned off the supply, she froze.

'My God! What am I doing?' she whispered, to her distorted reflection in the glass. 'He's still fifteen for God's sake. My career and my freedom are at stake here.' The teacher shook her head. 'You must be out of your mind, Wendy.'

But even as her brain was admonishing her for setting up this potentially life-wrecking situation, an animalistic urge was trying to ignore her words. The glass went down on the draining board. She tried once more to reign in her wanton desires.

'I can't do this. This is wrong,' she said, her clenched fist tapping against her mouth. This time she listened to herself. She drew in a massive breath. Her flustered mind had decided to control her depraved thoughts and emotions. She would go upstairs and get dressed.

Then, there was a tap on her shoulder. She jumped once again. She turned and stood face to face with the mud and sweat covered youth. They were less than three feet apart. 'I've finished the turfs,' he said, his emerald-green eyes drilling deep inside her. He was wearing a smile that Wendy read as hunger more than pride.

Whatever restraint she had decided to exert over her desires, evaporated like frosted breath. She stood... flushed... heart racing. Without speaking, she brushed her long chestnut curls off her shoulders. Then, she gripped the collar of her dressing gown. With trembling hands, she opened the robe to reveal her nakedness to the boy.

Danny's mouth dropped; his eyes agog as they explored every inch of her voluptuous body. He stepped forwards and lifted Wendy's heavy breasts with his muddy hands; those secretive yet conspicuous breasts that had been dominating his dreams for months. Danny dipped his head and ran his tongue over her already erect nipples. Wendy gasped as she held the boy's head to her chest, watching him feed on her growing teats.

Suddenly she pushed the boy away. Neither spoke. Danny looked startled. What had he done wrong? The teacher pulled her gown together, tying it around her waist.

She then breathed deeply, took his hand and led him up to her bedroom. Off came the gown once more, as she lay on her bed. Her hungry eyes studied every inch of him as he tore off his shorts and pants in one move. There were no preliminaries in either mind. Danny climbed between his teacher's open legs and thrust himself inside her.

Chapter 11

Sam's weekend had been a good one. His under-sixteen football team had scraped a 1-0 win on Saturday morning. The scorer – Danny Antonelli.

Monday morning, like most of the country's workforce, was not a day to which Sam looked forward. But this one was buoyed with positive thoughts. During the school lunch break, he had bathed in the compliments over his team's win from the majority of the teachers in the staff room.

His first afternoon lesson was with year eleven's Class C of which four boys had played in Saturday's victorious side. On the way to the classroom, he realised he needed a pee and had to turn back.

As he stood facing the porcelain in the male teacher's urinal, he reflected on his team's performance. It wasn't wonderful but he was pleased with the way the boys had listened to his basic pre-match tactics. They had responded to his words of encouragement. It was the first win for the under 16's this season, and the first time Tommy Clifford was not in the side. For that reason, he decided not to mention anything about football to this class.

As he hurried back towards his classroom, he realised he was running two minutes late. When he neared the top of the stairs, the noise hit his ears. He opened the classroom door to a group of animated boys who had formed a ring around something he couldn't see. Sam knew immediately what was in the middle. A fight.

On seeing the teacher, the circle of lads scurried back to their seats. Clifford and Antonelli were still rolling around on the floor between two desks. Sam bent down and picked both kids up by the scruff of their necks. 'Enough, you two,' he bellowed at the dishevelled pair. He turned to the class. 'Page 35 of your textbooks. There's a précis to do. Get on with your work,' he said, as he marched the two boys out into the corridor. 'Right, what's all this about?

Danny spoke first. 'Just because I was in the team instead of him and I scored, he called me an arse licker. Said I must've been giving you a blowjob to get in the side. I'm not taking that from any...'

'Yes, all right,' said Sam. He turned to Clifford. 'Is that right, Tommy?'

'I don't give a fuck about the football team anyway.'

'Well, you must do because you wouldn't have been so nasty to Danny, would you?' Tommy went to speak but Sam carried on, 'Your place in the side has nothing to do with him anyway. It's for the reasons I told you. You've got to learn to play a team game. When you do, you're back in the side. Simple as that.'

Tommy looked up at the teacher. 'Anyway, I didn't start the fight. It was 'im. He's a...'

Sam cut in. 'I don't want to hear any more from either of you. And I definitely don't want to hear that language again from either of you; or you'll be in serious trouble. Is that clear?'

'Yes, sir,' said Danny. Tommy gave a brief reluctant nod.

'You're both lucky that the class next door is empty and no other teacher saw or heard this fight, otherwise I would have had to report it to the Headmaster. But I'm giving you two another chance. This is the last I want to hear of it. Now get back into the class and do what you're both here for, which is to learn.'

The boys, surprised to be let off so lightly did as they were told.

00000

James Shilling stood in front of his year-nine class. Their last two lessons had been about earthquakes and volcanoes. James was renowned for starting his lessons with the occasional geographical joke and today was no different.

'Right, you 'orrible lot! I want you to write a two-page essay on the causes of major volcanic eruptions and earthquakes. Before you start, I will leave you with this one thought.'

The boys, who loved his relaxed, sardonic approach to teaching all knew what was coming – a terrible pun, a silly one-liner. But they loved him for it. None of the other teachers had that gift of communication, where the boys felt they were all on the same side as the person in charge.

'So,' James continued. 'There are two tectonic plates having a conversation. One says to the other, "There's just too much friction between us!" The other replies, "Well, it's not my fault".' Most laughed, some groaned but James knew that the joke would soon do the rounds in the playground.

'Okay. Two pages. Off you go.'

Five minutes had passed. The geography teacher now sat at his desk staring aimlessly at the assortment of head tops of the fourteen-year-old lads. He should have been proud to see his young students all busy writing, but he was elsewhere. Since his personal life had experienced its very own major eruption, he had lost focus. Daydreaming was a growing pastime.

His unfaithful wife was the catalyst for his lack of direction, manifesting itself in a slanted outlook on the world around him. For the first time in his memory, he found himself questioning every aspect of his existence.

He had never been a deep thinker before, sailing through life with a light touch; always seeing the funny or ironic side of events. Most things simply brushed past him. That had ended the afternoon he walked into his bedroom to be confronted with a scene no loving partner should ever witness.

He still had his sense of humour, but it had become more cynical. Shilling's smooth-running ship had hit stormy seas so rapidly there was no time to adjust; no opportunity to change course or prepare for survival. The vessel was in need of repair.

James needed a purpose.

00000

Sam had been at the school for just under three weeks. On entering the staff room at the beginning of the lunch break, one of the teachers approached him. 'Hi, Sam, you've just missed the Head. He asked if you could see him in his office before you settle down for your lunch.'

'Oh! Okay thanks,' Sam said, frowning.

He was standing outside the imposing door marked, Headmaster, imprinted in gold letters on age-worn oak. The floorboard just in front of the door, also oak, squeaked when anyone stood on it. Sam wondered if the headmaster had manufactured it as a warning of someone approaching.

His hands were slightly moist. He had no reason to be nervous. Well, apart from his memory of the last time he was summoned to see a headmaster. He was thirteen years old and had been caught bunking off school with a friend one afternoon. The plan was to hook up with two girls they'd met the day before at a neighbouring school.

The stern lecture from the headmaster was frightening but hadn't been a real problem. It was the fact that he had phoned his parents to inform them of the incident. It was his dad that gave him the hard time. No pocket money and no football for two weeks. It was the 'no football' that hurt the most. But it worked. He never gave his dad another reason to repeat the painful imposition.

For a moment he was that young boy standing outside the headmaster's office awaiting his sentence. 'How old am I?' he said to himself. The answer appeared in his brain

72

in a flash. *You never grow up. You just grow old.* He knocked on the door.

'Come in,' said Peter. *'Ah,* Sam, take a seat.' The head sat back in his chair. 'So, what do you think of the Web after your first month here?'

Sam, picking up on his boss's body language, eased back in his chair as well. 'I love it here. To work in such a highly regarded school was my dream. And yes, I feel I've settled in quite well.'

'You're here because I want you to know that I've had reports back from members of staff.' Sam stiffened slightly. 'You've been warmly accepted, and they say you've fitted in splendidly. Also, just as importantly, I understand you are quite popular with the boys,' Peter said, with an impressive nod of his head.

'Thank you, Headmaster, that is really nice to know.'

'And you're doing sterling work with the under-16 football team, I see.'

'Yes, I'm happy with the way the boys are responding. It's early days, but I've got some decent players, and I'm aiming to try and win something with this lot in the near future.'

'Excellent. Right, that's all I wanted to say. I know how important your lunch break is so I'll let you get back to the staff room to enjoy it. Keep up the good work. Oh, and don't hesitate to let me know if there's any questions or problems that arise whilst you're here.'

Sam got up. Tommy Clifford and Jeremy Roth got up with him as they paddled briefly across his mind. But just as quickly, he dismissed them. 'Yes, I will. Thanks very much. Bi, then.'

Peter smiled and nodded.

As he left the office, he felt as if he could have floated back to the staff room. He was liked by his colleagues and his boss. On top of that, he was earning twenty-five per cent more than in his previous job, which meant more money for Lucy to spend on the house and their daughter Freya. His move was everything he'd hoped for and more.

The fact that the head was taking notice of his work with the under-16s was another plus. He was proud of his initial achievement with those boys. In the three games he'd been in charge of this football team, they had won two and drawn one. He had kept Danny in the main striker position. He wasn't the most skilful of players, but he was big, strong and fearless. And he scored goals. At that age and in that standard of football, size did matter.

Sam had included Tommy Clifford in the squad at every training session and had tried to encourage him to come on board with his way of thinking. So far, the boy's response was disappointing. Every time he received the ball in the training games, he disappeared into Tommy's world of selfish play and showboating. The rest of the players around him may just as well have not been there. There was no way he was going to get back into the team with that attitude. He thought it was regrettable – a sad waste of his talent.

Chapter 12

After Danny's first visit to his science teacher's house, he returned the following two days. He helped Wendy prepare the garden soil before starting to lay the turfs, creating the new perfect lawn she had always wanted. They both knew that her invitation for further help in the garden was a convenient ruse for what they really wanted. On each occasion, before he went home, she would lead him up into her bedroom. The sex was always urgent taking little time to completion. It seemed to satisfy both parties for the moment.

It was on the Monday, after school when he came to finish off the job in the garden that the relationship began to change. She had never asked him about any details of his life before. She had never wanted to know. It was garden, bedroom, goodbye. Now she wanted more. She needed more.

When Danny walked in from the garden, Wendy was standing by the kitchen door. He looked at her then in the direction of the stairs.

The teacher didn't move. 'Have you ever drunk alcohol?' she asked.

He turned. His voice deepened. 'Yes, I've had some lager with my friends. And even managed to get served in a pub twice.'

'That doesn't surprise me. You look a lot older than you are.' She turned and grabbed the bottle she had placed on the kitchen shelf in anticipation. 'I thought we'd celebrate you finishing the garden off with a glass of red wine.'

'Erm! I've never had wine before... but yeh, why not.'

Her idea being to have a glass or two before going up to the bedroom. She hoped it might just relax the young gun, slow him down and make the experience last a little longer. She was looking for more satisfaction from their dalliances.

Ten minutes later Wendy lay in bed watching Danny get dressed. The glasses were empty but the contents had not worked this time. She would try again.

It was after that session that the pretence of her pupil being simply Danny the handyman was dropped. Phone numbers were swapped and the teacher's sexual needs were now to be arranged between them. Whenever she told him that Edward, her husband, was away on business, which seemed to be most of the time, he could visit.

The intimate texts from Wendy were now being sent to her young pupil on a daily basis. Whenever possible Danny would reply with a prompt and equally personal message. The teacher, always thrilled to receive them, felt like a silly teenager once again. What had started as a need for male attention and intimacy was turning into infatuation.

00000

Sam, after arriving home from work was sitting at the small table in his kitchen staring into a cup of tea. When Lucy finished unloading the dishwasher and sat facing her husband at the table, Sam told her about his meeting with the headmaster. When he'd finished, Sam pulled his wife onto his lap.

'Yep, he told me that my colleagues were pleased with me and that I appear to be popular with the boys.'

Lucy gripped her husband's head and kissed him on the lips. 'That's great. Oh, I'm sooo proud of you. Well done, you.'

'There are a couple of minor issues that slightly muddy the water but otherwise I can't be happier there.'

'What do you mean minor issues?'

'The teacher who used to run the football team has had his nose put out of joint and really doesn't like me at all. He's a bitter man, Lucy. I've been told he was good buddies with Clive Lawrence the previous English master.'

Lucy's head tilted to the side.

'You know. The guy I took over from – who died on the operating table and his wife killed herself a few weeks after. Another reason not to like me, I suppose.'

'He's just jealous, Sam. A young man taking over his domain. It's understandable. He's probably still upset that his friend has died. I shouldn't worry too much about it. He'll probably calm down over time. If he doesn't, well, it's his loss. You've tried your best. Anyway, what's the other issue?

'I've had to drop a boy from the team. His attitude is all wrong on the field… *and* in class. He's got quite a hostile personality. I worry for his future 'cos he doesn't seem to want any help or ever take in advice.'

'Then, he needs someone like you. Someone who doesn't pander to him but still wants to help him. Tough love, they call it. You'll talk him round. That's what you're good at.'

'*Mmm!* We'll see,' said Sam, as he took a swig of tea.

00000

'Why is it you never drink in here with any of your fellow teachers?' asked Sheila, pouring James another beer.

'Listen. I did say to a teacher once, that I was pally with, "Do you fancy one up the Tradesman's?" He's never spoken to me since,' James said, with an innocent frown.

Sheila howled with laughter. 'I'm not surprised. So, come on. What's the news on the block Mr Shilling?'

'Ha, ha. It all goes on in schools, Sheil. The common mistake that everyone makes is that they all think it's a place where children go to learn things. It's not, of course.' James took a swig of beer.

The governor of the Tradesman's Arms gave him a look, waiting for the punchline.

He placed his pint back on the bar. 'It's a hotbed of frustration, mental and sexual. It's an environment in which insecure adults with restricted life skills and abilities, apart from the knowledge of their required school curriculum subject, get to rule the roost over a bunch of ingenuous kids.'

He took another swig. 'Have you ever watched a schoolteacher on one of those TV quiz shows? The majority are bloody useless. If the question isn't linked to their particular job requirements, their wider scope of knowledge is, at most, unimpressive. Everyone thinks teachers must be clever. There's a misnomer that being a teacher requires them to be intelligent with an understanding of the world and its facts and figures.'

Sheila for once was speechless. She was all ears and she was loving it.

James, instead of his pint glass, now had the bit firmly between his teeth. He continued, 'Think on this. What is the life of an average teacher? As children, they go to school, where their achievements are often unremarkable, to say the least. They then go to college or uni, which is simply an extension of school but without the discipline. That is definitely not real life.

'Then they go back to bloody school for the rest of their lives. The outside world is, well, another world to them – a mystery. And these people, me included, are trusted with educating... delivering, the next generation into society. Bugger me, Sheil. What a joke,' he said, picking up his pint.

Chapter 13

Three Weeks Later

An autumn sun shone from a flawless powder-blue sky on this Friday morning, as the boys filtered through the two Gothic arches that lead into the oak-panelled corridors of the school. An hour later, the radiance of the building's exterior was not reflected in the classroom where year 11C were sitting.

The History lessons conducted by Jeremy Roth were the polar opposite to those of James Shilling. Apparently, very little humour existed within the man. There was no employment of innovative ways or tutoring tricks designed to grab the attention of his classes. It was textbook learning all the way. His monotone whining delivery was never going to keep this age group on the edge of their polypropylene chairs baying for more.

It is estimated that two-thirds of male teenage students regard school history lessons as one of the most boring subjects. The irony being that the older we get, as we begin to approach our own history, the more we seem to want to know about it. Sadly, no one had seemed to have bothered to impart these facts to Roth. His delivery, like the man, was grey.

When the lesson ended, the boys began to file out of the classroom. Roth stood from his desk and walked forwards to Tommy Clifford. He was putting his books in his black, nylon backpack. 'May I have a quick word with you, Master Clifford?'

Tommy looked surprised, then defensive. He wondered what he'd done wrong this time. He rolled his eyes and sat back down. Roth waited till the last boy had left the room then put a hand on Tommy's shoulder. He noticed that the boy didn't feel comfortable with his physical approach, but he left the hand there.

'I'm sorry to hear that you have been dropped from the football team. I always regarded you as my best player. First name on the team sheet. You must be very upset with Mr Whitmore?'

Tommy's mistrustful nature stopped him from giving an immediate reply. What was old Rothy's reason for talking to him? It was as though he was his best friend? Was it a trick to get him into more trouble?

'I want you to know that I don't agree with his decision. If there's anything I can do to help put right this very unfair situation you find yourself in, I will. How many games is it you've missed?'

Realising the teacher was probably on his side, he let fly. 'Three. I've not even been a substitute since he took over. He just doesn't like me. He thinks he knows everything about football. Well, he didn't make it as a professional footballer did he, so he can't be that good, can he?'

'There may just be a way that we can get you back into the team.' He lowered his voice. 'But it means removing a certain person, doesn't it?' Roth watched the boy's face closely. The youngster's wary eyes suddenly flickered into life. His mouth opened as if to speak.

Tommy's reaction was exactly what the history teacher was hoping for. It was now or never. 'Would you be prepared to do anything to remove that person from this school, so I can run the team again with you as my main striker?' His words came out in little more than a whisper. As Roth spoke, he scoured their surroundings like a shop employee about to steal money from the till.

Tommy looked up at the teacher. The old man, his head bowed even further forwards than usual, hovered, waiting for an answer. The teacher had a look on his face Tommy had not seen before. His eyes bulged. There were small particles of spittle around the corners of his mouth. It reminded him of a hungry animal waiting to devour its prey.

Yes, I would,' said Tommy.

00000

One hour later, Sam stood with his back to year eleven's class C. He was wiping off the punctuation exercise from the board. As he turned to face his students, his eyes scanned the back row. He was a little surprised how well-behaved Clifford and Taylor had been throughout the lesson. Part of him was pleased, the other part wary. When he sat back down at his desk, the bell rang for the end of the lesson. The inexorable chair scraping, desk banging, and chit-chat lasted just under a minute until the classroom was vacated of thirty-one boys.

Gathering his books together, he rose from his chair. He bent down to retrieve his shoulder bag, glad for a moments calm.

'Excuse me, sir.' The voice behind surprised him.

Sam turned to see the unexpected sight of Tommy Clifford. The teacher's eyes narrowed to a squint. 'Thomas Clifford. What can I do for you?'

'I just wanted to say sorry for not listening to you about my place in the football team.' Sam's eyes now bounced opened wide as he studied the boy's face. 'And that my attitude will change.' He moved a step closer to the teacher and held out his hand.

Sam hesitated. Tentatively he extended his arm and shook the limp hand of the boy. 'Okay. If you mean what you say, then that's great news for you and the team.' He waited for a reply but Tommy just nodded, swivelled, and headed for the classroom door where Josh Taylor was waiting around and disappeared.

Sam stood tall in the empty room, shook his head, blinked hard and said, 'Wow!'

Chapter 14

James Shilling rose from his desk, rolled his head around in two wide arcs and stretched upwards. The lower sixth class – year twelve – were spread out below his eyeline, silent, concentrating on nothing but their work. In his eyes, they were the best group of students to teach. They were there because they had passed enough GCSE examinations to qualify for further education.

More importantly, they wanted to be there. They had signed up for the next two years, culminating in sitting for A-level examinations. Hopefully, a crack at a university education. These early achievers knew they had to study on a different level going forward. In addition, the gap from year eleven to twelve meant more than just one year's normal growth. It was a leap up in maturity.

Whereas the upper sixth – year thirteen, although not rowdy, tended to be focused on the greater freedom and adult pleasures that university was going to afford them. They could sniff it. They could be a little cocky at times.

Some of the seventeen-year-olds in today's class had bumped into him in the local pub a few times. The occasions were early evening when the boys were out of uniform. James knew they were under-age but just acknowledged them with a nod and a smile. The boys knew they were not going to be reported to the headmaster.

That type of relaxed, trusting relationship he had with them made them feel like rookie adults, not merely schoolboys.

As the lesson came to an end, James addressed his class, 'Good work today gentlemen.' He paused. 'Just remember... without geography, we'd be nowhere.' The audience, always ready for his customary one-liner smiled, laughed and groaned in equal measure.

With an armful of books, he left the classroom, turned left into the blue-blazered corridor, and headed for the teachers' staffroom. As he passed by the door marked, Headmaster the attractive figure of the PE teacher came out of his office with a contented smile on her face. That was the third time this week he'd seen her enter or exit that room. He was lucky if he had reason to enter or was summoned into the bosses' domain three or four times in a term. And he was the deputy headmaster.

Inside the teacher's hideaway, James plonked himself down with his coffee next to his new buddy. 'Young Sam! How's life in the madhouse?'

'Hello, James. That's a very apt description, because earlier...

James interrupted, 'D'you know.' He leant in towards Sam and lowered his voice. 'I've seen the *too lovely to be true* Miss Pederson going in and out of the Head's office more often than the bloody tide on Brighton Beach. Of course, it could just be a coincidence that every time I walk past she happens to, er...' He shook his head. 'No, with my recent history I don't believe in those sort of coincidences.'

Sam was aware of James's shocking episode concerning his wife and their builder. One of the other teachers had filled him in with the ugly details. He had to choose his words carefully. 'Do you think... you know, that they're...' Sam paused, waiting for James to say the word.

'What? Playing hide the sausage. Sharpening the pencil? Having it off? I think there's every chance. Before Peter became head honcho of this parish, he was just another teacher. He mixed and gossiped with the rest of us. I know he let slip more than once to me and others that his marriage was, how can I say... somewhat sterile. I think he expected his comments to be regarded as flippant asides, but I reckon there was a lot of truth in what he said.' He looked into the distance. 'But Amy... not a good move. Not on your own doorstep.'

Sam's mouth had been open throughout James's speech. 'No, I suppose not.'

He turned back to Sam, a crooked smile on his face. 'Mind you, I would struggle to turn down Amy fit-as-a-flea Pederson if she expressed a desire to offer her Danish delights to me. But then I'm a single man'

Sam laughed. 'Well, you're not gonna believe what just happened in my last class. Clifford came back into the classroom when the other kids had left and apologised for his bad behaviour.'

James's face was a picture.

'He promised to change his attitude and do everything to get back into the football team. What do you think of that?' said Sam.

'Maybe miracles do happen at the Web,' said James. Then his eyes narrowed. 'Have a care, Samuel.'

Chapter 15

Sam's lesson, mid-afternoon, was with the pupils in year nine A. He stood watching his class, heads down scribbling away at their individual desks.

He had set them the task of writing a two-hundred-word short story on My Favourite Experience. He gave them all a piece of paper and told them they could write anything they wanted, true or fiction, not to sign it, to fold the paper in four and put it in a box at the back of the class.

It was a bit of fun that also got the boys used to writing short stories. Then, Sam would read out the stories to the class with, at times, hilarious results. The last time he did this was for his class at his previous employment in Wandsworth. The secondary modern school had a few boys there whose behaviour was not what you would describe as exemplary.

He was surprised that one or two of them could manage to eat with a knife and fork, let alone write a short story. But they all did. Trouble was a good third of them could not be read out due to the dubious content. He was hoping the grammar school boys would not be so daring or graphic with their stories.

Sam's thoughts were interrupted when there was a knock on the window of the classroom door. He turned to see the headmaster beckon him over.

He walked to the door and opened it. 'Hello, Headmaster?'

'Could you see me in my office after this lesson please Sam? I've arranged for another teacher to take your next class.'

Sam's heart almost stopped beating. What does that mean? Was it Lucy or the baby?

'Is everything okay?'

'Hopefully. But I'll see you in the office. I'd rather talk there.' He then nodded and left.

When the lesson ended Sam gathered up his books, stuffed them in his bag and fleetfooted it to the head's office. His mind was throwing around all sorts of negative scenarios as to the reason for Peter summoning him in such a way. He rapped twice on the imposing door.

When Sam entered the room, the head was sitting behind his desk. 'Ah, Sam. Please sit down,'

Sam sat on the chair opposite. He waited. The head looked awkward. It sent a chill up his spine.

'Sam, I've had the school welfare officer in here this morning. I had to inform her of a complaint concerning inappropriate touching of a pupil in this school. As I'm sure you know, that comes under the sexual offences act.'

Sam realising that it wasn't about his family finally breathed out. Then his semi-relieved brain immediately moved on to what the head had just said.

'What has this got to do with me, Peter?' he said, dipping his eyebrows.

'The complaint is against you, Sam.'

The young teacher's mouth dropped open. The cosy office all at once felt cold as his skin puckered across his entire body.

'Me? You can't be serious… I mean, it is a very serious accusation but no, I've never done anything like that before or now and never will. That's just not me.'

Sam registered that the man in front of him was studying his every move with a fixed intensity. 'Where has this complaint come from; who is the boy?' he added.

'Look, I don't believe this accusation for one moment, but I have to go through the proper procedure of confronting you with the facts that I've been given. And, of course, how you respond to them.'

He looked at Sam, now balanced on the edge of his seat waiting for an answer.

'Who…'

'Tommy Clifford,' said Peter.

Sam, on hearing the boy's name slowly raised his head up to the ceiling, closed his eyes and started nodding.

'You don't look surprised,' said Peter.

'I'm surprised that he would stoop this low but no, I'm not surprised now you've told me who it is. You know I've dropped him from the football team because of his attitude on and off the field?'

'Well, I wasn't aware of that until this morning,' said Peter.

'And that he has taken it very badly. Tommy Clifford has a regrettable, malevolent, and at times, quite aggressive attitude towards anyone that doesn't fit in with

Tommy Clifford. So, I'm enemy number one at the moment.'

'Well, the boy has claimed that this is the very subject that forms the basis of his complaint. He said that you asked him to remain in the classroom after the lesson had finished. You then told him that there were ways that he could get back in the team. And then you began touching him around the genital area.'

Sam's face tightened. His mouth tinder dry.

'When the rest of the class left the room, as I picked up my books, I suddenly heard a voice behind me. Clifford must have come back into the room. I asked him what I could do for him. That's when he said, to my utter amazement, he was sorry for his behaviour and that he would improve and try to get back in the team. His story, Peter, is a pack of lies. Your Deputy Head, James warned me that he could be vindictive and dropping him from the team would bring out the worst in him. But this…'

'I have no reason, Sam, not to believe your story. I think you are an honest and devoted teacher.' He paused, crossed his arms. He lowered his eyes. 'The trouble is, the boy has a witness who says you were standing very close together and was holding his hand. And he said he couldn't see what the other hand was doing.'

Sam began to nod with a false smile on his lips. 'Josh Taylor… he was standing outside the door.'

The sick smile grew stronger. He realised he'd been set up by the conniving Clifford.

'He's Clifford's best buddy. They're thick as thieves. We were not standing close together until Clifford finished his little speech. That's when he walked forwards and held out his hand to shake mine. I was surprised and sceptical by this complete change in him. But I gave him the benefit of the doubt and shook his hand. He then left the room.'

Peter had held the position of Headmaster for just two years. This was the first time he had cause to deal with a complaint such as this. It was a delicate situation. He recalled some years ago when he was just a teacher, that there had been a similar issue at the school. The Board of Governors had reacted very badly he recalled. They had put the previous headmaster under enormous pressure to suspend the accused.

Nothing came of it as the boy withdrew his statement, but he didn't want to give them any excuse to do the same to him. This was all spinning around in his head as he listened to his clearly distraught teacher.

'I need you to write down your version of events and submit it to me. But I'm going to have to report this incident to the Local Authority Designated Officer (LADO) who will in turn investigate this very unfortunate episode themselves,' said Peter.

'But surely this hasn't got to go any further, Peter. Can't it be kept in-house? It's just his word against mine. Plus, you surely have to consider the boy's unsavoury reputation against my untarnished one. Things like this have a habit of ruining people. Even if the so-called perpetrator is found innocent. Mud sticks. There will always be the question on some peoples' lips of did he, or didn't he?'

The headmaster suddenly put his official head on.

'I'm sorry, but I have to put this through the proper channels. I will inform you when the LADO has replied and guided me as to the next course of action. In my opinion, I don't think you're a danger to our boys so please continue to take classes for the time being. Apart from Clifford's class, of course.'

Peter stood up, walked to the door, opened it. He nodded to Sam who shook his head and left the office, his mind in a bubble of fear and confusion.

00000

Minutes after the bell had sounded to end his last lesson, Sam reached the staffroom, sat down and waited. He just hoped that James had not left school early that afternoon. When James appeared, he stood and met him at the door.

'James, I need to speak to you. Right away.'

James looked at the pale colour of Sam's face and reacted immediately.

'There's an empty classroom opposite where the boys hang their coats. We'll go there,' said James.

James sat tight jawed as he listened to Sam's account of what had just happened.

'Fucking hell, Sam! I told you that little bastard was poison. But I never thought he would do something like this. He had to have a mighty strong reason. So, what does he expect to get out of it all?' He laid his hands on his cheeks for a moment. 'He's been put up to this. He's been bloody put up to this, Sam. And I bet I know by who.'

'Who?' Sam asked.

'I saw them alone. He was talking to Clifford earlier this morning when I was walking past his classroom. It's gotta be,' said James, looking focused.'

'For God's sake, James. Who?' Sam said, in a loud whisper.

James looked straight into Sam's eyes. 'Roth. It's fucking Roth. It has to be. He's lost control of the football team and Clifford has lost his place in the side. This way, if you get the sack or you are asked to move on, they both get what they want.'

Sam stared at James, then at the desk he was leaning on. He slowly nodded.

'You're right. It has to be. Roth has hated me from the moment I started work here.'

'What you probably don't know is that Roth's big buddy here was Clive Lawrence, the previous English master. He went in for a hip replacement and died on the operating table. His wife, who nagged him to have the op was devastated and blamed herself. Two weeks after his funeral, she threw herself off the top floor of Kingston NCP car park. Not a pretty sight,' said James.

'Oh my God! I never knew the details.'

'What with you replacing his friend and then taking away his coaching job, that nasty little man has got two reasons to hate you.'

'Christ! They're that desperate as to ruin someone's life?' Sam's voice rose higher. 'They can have the bloody team. It's not worth all this shit.'

James crunched his teeth together. 'No, Sam. That's exactly what they want. You fight these two lowlifes and

I'll help you. Come on, let's have a coffee and work on a plan.' James walked to the door, turned back to Sam, winked, then headed back to the staffroom.

Sam took a huge breath in, almost choked the air back out and followed the geography master.

Chapter 16

Wendy's affair with Danny had been going on for over three weeks. She was still not receiving the attention and loving touch that she craved. She sat at her kitchen table in her tired, off-white dressing gown and poured herself another glass of red wine – the third one.

She had been in the unusual situation of having only two classes to teach after the lunch break. It enabled her to leave school at three o'clock on this Friday. The long weekend was hers. As soon as she arrived home, she showered and threw on her towelling robe. Her watch read three-forty-five. Danny was due anytime now.

The last two times he had been late. She didn't like his tardiness and wondered whether he was losing interest in her. He'd also cancelled the arranged meeting on Wednesday with a lame excuse; that he'd had to get some food shopping for his mum.

The week had been a long, frustrating and draining affair. She had waited in on Monday for a plumber who was supposed to turn up at nine thirty to fix a leaking tap. He never turned up. This resulted in her missing the whole of her morning's lessons. That didn't go down well with the headmaster.

Then there were endless staff room briefings, after-work meetings and gradings that went on forever. On two nights, she hadn't arrived home until after eight pm. Today was the first time she'd manage to leave school early.

She was about to pick up her glass when the doorbell rang. Her disposition changed immediately. The hairs on her arms bristled.

Danny stood at the door wearing a leather jerkin over his school blazer and a reversed baseball cap. The late October temperature had fallen dramatically. 'I thought you weren't coming,' she said, closing the door after her pupil stepped inside the narrow hallway.

Danny's humourless smile was his only reply.

'Well, you're here now. You go on up and I'll bring the wine,' she said, walking back into the kitchen to open up another bottle.

Danny climbed the stairs as if he were wearing lead boots. The novelty of having sex with his teacher was beginning to wear thin. The constant texting was fun at first – his own clandestine piece of adult intrigue. Initially, it had made him feel more superior than his school chums. Lately, it had become suffocating. He was beginning to feel trapped. And twice he had to lie to his mother when she accused him of drinking when she thought she could smell alcohol on his breath.

Having a glass of wine seemed a good idea to start with. It made him relax a little and feel grown up in his teacher's company. But now, he felt under pressure to have a drink with every visit. And when he arrived a moment ago, he could tell by her eyes and slightly slurred speech that she'd had a good few drinks before he turned up.

It wasn't a good look, he thought. The power-dressed teacher, to whom he was first attracted, commanded respect. She was totally in charge of her class of thirty boys. Formidable. She now appeared far less impressive, pathetic almost, dressed in her loose-fitting dressing gown and slippers.

On reaching the bedroom Danny, who never wore a watch checked his mobile for the time. It read ten minutes past four. The phone then whistled. A text from his pal. *Meeting up at five-thirty.*

I'll get this over with and be back home by five at latest, he thought to himself. *It will give me time to have a shower, wash off the smell of her sickly perfume, and meet my friends for an hour before my dinner at six thirty.*

He didn't reply to the message, replaced his phone in the zip pocket of his lightweight jacket, took it off and dropped it to the floor. The radiators in the room were on full blast. The atmosphere stifling. Danny sank down on the side of the bed. He began looking around the room. It was the first time he had actually bothered to take in his surroundings.

The brass lamp next to the double bed was crowned with a dense, tasselled scarlet shade, which struggled to light the room. On one side of the closed bottle-green curtains stood a single mahogany wardrobe. On the other a small dressing table. He looked at his shadowy reflection in the angled mirror and frowned.

He saw no photographs of her husband or any family members on the cupboards or bedside tables. There were just two pictures in the room. They both hung on the wall opposite the double bed. One was a close up of a rosary and beads draped randomly across an ebony tabletop. The other was of the Virgin Mary wearing a deep blue scapula against a black background. She was holding the baby Jesus.

His own family were staunch Catholics but his mother's picture of the Virgin Mary that hung in their passageway was painted in bright colours. These two prints were dark and dispiriting in the dimly lit room. It certainly didn't raise his unsettled mood.

Just then, Wendy appeared holding an opened bottle of wine and two glasses. She set them down and started to pour. He didn't particularly want a drink this time but said nothing as she handed him a glass.

'Cheers my darling,' she said. As she held her glass out to him, she stared into the boy's eyes for a good few seconds. 'I love you,' she said.

She may as well have said *I'm really a man.* The shock would have been just the same. It was the first time she'd said that; the first time she had said anything remotely like that. It took a few seconds for him to compute those three unexpected, alien words. They alarmed him. Despite his feelings, Danny went along with the now all too familiar performance. He smiled, extended his arm, and clinked their glasses.

'Cheers,' was his only reply.

There had never been a word of conversation during their lovemaking before. This time, shortly after they started, Wendy suddenly grabbed either side of Danny's head. Her mood changed.

'Slow down for God's sake! Take it slowly,' she cried out, through gritted teeth, staring into his face and shaking his head.

Danny, shocked by her aggressive outburst, instead of adhering to her forceful demands pulled away and rolled off the naked teacher.

'What are you doing,' screamed Wendy, as she tried to pull the boy back onto his position.

Danny pushed her hands away resisting her efforts. 'Why did you do that? You've spoilt everything,' he said.

Wendy took a deep breath, her bloodshot eyes blinking rapidly. 'Danny, I'm sorry I just…'

'So now I'm not doing it right. So now I'm not good enough for you. Well, maybe you're not good enough for me!'

Wendy raised herself up on one arm. Her demeanour caught fire once again. 'How fucking dare you! Who do you think you are? You couldn't wait to come round here showing off your body, hoping to get me into bed. Do you think I need immature little boys like you to waste my time with?' The volume of wine was now showing its other face.

The alcohol had also hit a bum note in the boy's unsettled mind.

'You got me to come to your house because you wanted me to fuck you. The grass was just an excuse. You seduced me, not the other way round. And that's how they will all see it. If I'm the underage immature little boy that you just waste your time with, what does that make you?'

'What do you mean that's how they will all see it? So, you're now threatening to tell everybody about us?' she paused as the thought sunk in. Her mouth dropped. 'Danny you can't do that. It would ruin me.' Tears appeared in the corner of her eyes.

Danny sat up and swung his legs over the side of the bed. He was now facing away from his angry teacher. He turned his head in a deliberate fashion 'Well, look at you. You're a mess... half-pissed and... you're old and overweight... I don't know what I'm doing here anymore.' He turned away again. Suddenly he felt dirty and embarrassed with himself.

His insults gouged a deep wound into everything she was and had achieved. Everything that had gone wrong in her life. She had lost control of the situation. Her addled brain was burning inside her head, working at a hundred miles-an-hour. It was searching for a solution to the disastrous threat, she was now faced with. She felt betrayed.

She needed another drink. As she reached for the bottle on the bedside table an uncontrollable swell of anger erupted within her brain. Her frustrations exploded as she gripped the neck of the bottle and swung it backwards in a high arc with frightening strength.

The bottle of Barefoot Shiraz had done a job; but it wasn't the intended one. The beet-red Californian wine was opened with one aim in mind – to relax and enhance the late afternoon sex session.

It was a mistake.

As far as alcohol was concerned, the fifteen-year-old boy was a novice. The effect of the wine kicked in shortly after the bout of interrupted intercourse. There was no contentment. Dissatisfaction had engendered guilt, self-loathing. Anger.

But through her own bitterness and rage, Wendy had found a solution.

The naked teenager now lay on his side across the tangle of bedclothes. Perspiration glistened across his broad shoulders and muscular thighs. The only beet red colour now to be seen in the sultry shade of the bedroom was pouring from the gaping wound above his left temporal lobe – an expanding patch seeping into the duck-egg blue of the bed sheet. His eyes were wide, confused. They were already blind to the empty, blood-spattered wine bottle when it fell from the holder's grasp with a cushioned thud onto the bedside rug.

'You stupid… beautiful boy. What have you made me do?' The words, unsteady, fell from the maroon-stained lips that trembled next to the body of the youngster. Wendy leant forwards and gripped the boy's wrist searching for a pulse. None was felt. What *was* felt was a searing mixture of pain. Regret. Relief.

Without warning the teacher's body reacted violently, gasping in a chest-full of air as her moment of panic, a flash of spite, struck home. Her scrambled senses were suddenly aware of the sickly-sweet smell of blood and fresh hormonal sweat that draped itself over the small room. Wendy's brain was now searching for escape routes;

trying to assimilate the reality of her disastrous action. The end product – a dead schoolboy.

He was just two weeks away from his sixteenth birthday. She had planned a special meal for them both. Now there was nothing. The wine-affected speech was unsteady. 'Everything was just... so good... so perf... Look what you've done. You silly, stupid... beautiful boy.' Then the tears came – rolling off her cheeks down onto the soft olive skin of the youth's rapidly cooling torso.

Wendy sat naked. She wiped her tears with a blood-spattered forearm, leaving streaks across her pale face and forehead. She then climbed unsteadily to a standing position and pulled on the dressing gown that hung from a single brass hook on the back of the door.

All of a sudden, she lurched sideways, threw aside the curtains, opened a window and threw up over a small area of grass in the garden below. Hanging on to the latch with one hand, her heavy head lifted slowly. The watery eyes tried to focus. The rear view of the cottage opened out onto ploughed fields and a distant Anglican church; its sharp, grey steeple drilling into the teacher's conscience.

The window closed. The brain in turmoil began talking to itself: *I had to do it. The consequences; my God... too horrendous. So... I had no choice, did I? ... worked too damned hard to throw it all away... Fuck. Oh, Jesus, Jesus! What have I...?* Huge sobs triggered a low, drawn-out animal-like moan. It was followed by a brief moment of paralysed silence. The brain took the lead once again.

This wasn't normal behaviour. This was not the actions of a sane person, for God's sake. It was definitely not the actions of a highly respected teacher. Christ! His teacher.

00000

Wendy Jacks, Head of Science, respected tutor at the prestigious Sir Montague Web Grammar School sat at the end of the bed, holding her knees tight to her chest in a red-wine-misted nightmare. She couldn't look at the boy. As long as she kept her eyes away from the young corpse then surely, it didn't exist.

Three hours and four coffees later, when the effects of the alcohol were wearing off she knew she had to sort this horrendous problem. She thought of calling the police – confessing all. She thought of killing herself – leaving the mess to someone else.

Eventually, she made her mind up… She was going to get rid of the body.

No one knew of the affair. If she was careful. Who would suspect her, a commendable middle-aged teacher? A pillar of society.

She decided to put the body in the shed at the bottom of her garden for the time being. The rear gate next to the wooden structure led immediately to where her parking space was. It was an unlit narrow track that ran along the back of the cottages. It separated them from the open fields that extended half a mile to the distant church. She could then move him the short distance from the shed to the boot of her car. The next part would be where to dispose of the body. This would take careful planning.

She looked at her watch. Seven-forty-five p.m. She noticed her hand, still specked with Danny's blood. It was shaking. She decided she would wash off the spatters after the whole clean-up was completed. She would then shower and wait till midnight when the lights of the cottages either side of hers had all long been extinguished. She prayed it would then be safe to transfer her young lover's body to the small shed.

But now, she had the immediate job of clearing up. His clothes were in an untidy pile on the floor. She picked the bundle up and placed them on the bed next to the body. Her first attempt to dress him ended in failure. She struggled to manoeuvre the boy's body sufficiently to put his limp arms through the sleeves of his shirt. Each time she lifted him up she lost her grip on his sweat-soaked body and he slumped back down. After the third attempt, she sat on the edge of the bed, looked at Danny and wept.

'I can't do this. I can't...' After a few seconds, she got an unexpected rush of adrenalin from deep within her tortured soul. She wiped her face and stood up. 'Come on. I've got to be strong.'

She decided to roll the body onto the duvet cover, distribute his clothes over him and tie the bundle tight with string. Not the best solution, but she couldn't stand to touch his cold, clammy flesh and look into the waxen face anymore. She just hoped her adrenal glands could supply her bloodstream with the energy she needed to carry out her bizarre list of tasks.

Quarter to midnight.

Wendy's frequent trips outside in her garden confirmed what she had prayed for. The last light of her neighbours' houses either side was extinguished at eleven p.m. She had already bumped his body down the stairs. She had then stripped the bed put the bloodied bedsheet and pillow slips in the washing machine and turned the red-stained mattress over.

Now she had to find the strength to carry out the next part of the plan. She turned her sitting room light off, opened the patio doors, and picked up Danny's encased legs. The initial effect of the cold night air was welcome on her perspiration-covered body. She began dragging him across the newly laid lawn towards the garden shed. A sliver of moon, partially covered by wispy clouds was the only light she had to work with.

Halfway across, the lawn was suddenly lit up next to where she stood. It was a light from next door's house, putting her in a spotlight. Wendy immediately dropped his legs. They landed on the lush grass with a dull thump. She froze. She crouched. She waited.

The light stayed on. Slowly she turned towards the source. It was coming from an upstairs bathroom that had a large, frosted window. She felt dizzy as her lungs emptied. She sunk to her knees, hunched over the body. 'Please, please go back to bed,' she whispered.

She heard the faint noise of a toilet flushing. The light was turned off. She got to her feet picked up the lighter end of the human parcel once again and managed to reach the opened door of the shed. There, she dragged the body in amongst the lawn mower and garden tools, closed the door and returned to the house.

Fortunately, she had the weekend free from work to find a suitable deserted spot to dispose of the fifteen-year-old schoolboy. Not only did she not have a clue where that deserted spot was, but she had a much bigger worry.

Would she have the stomach to carry out this next phase of her mission.

Chapter 17

Earlier That Evening

The Tradesman's Arms was a typical old English boozer. Faded beer-stained carpet, oak-panelled walls exhibiting grainy sepia pictures. They showed the inn as it was before motorcars and electric streetlamps, computers and Coronation Street. Tangles of dried flowers weaved over sturdy oak beams hung precariously over the drinkers' heads. A timeworn walnut bar with a highly polished top was punctured by a military rank of erect beer pumps. Directly above, hanging from the buff-coloured ceiling, a row of chunky-handled glasses and tarnished pewter tankards that no one ever seemed to use.

Behind the bar were endless shelves of curiously shaped bottles containing different shades of liquid to entice the adventurous customer. All this in a sultry-lit environment aimed towards calm and perspective at the end of a working day.

James's second home.

Even for a Monday, early evening, the pub was heaving with customers. What made this tavern so successful was the eclectic mix of punters standing at the bar and sitting at the small round tables. Two groups of young, muck-streaked builders stood joking with each other. They were within touching distance of four middle-aged highfliers in smart suits and shiny shoes.

Pensioners with flat caps and walking sticks sat around copper-topped tables amid groups of young women. The hubbub of light-hearted and at times boisterous conversation enlivened the nineteenth-century building.

'Heavy week?' said Sheila, passing over a freshly poured, froth-topped pint of bitter to James. Despite the crowd, he had managed to grab his favourite stool at the far corner of the bar.

'Is it that obvious?' replied the teacher.

'Nothing that a quick facelift wouldn't sort out. Okay, so what's weighing down those shoulders? Tell Auntie Sheila.'

'If I told you I'd have to kill you.'

'Come on, I could do with a bit of gossip. I've not had the most stimulating week myself.'

James looked intently at the smartly dressed landlady. He was bursting to tell someone the story that was bubbling up inside him. He was also aware that Sheila knew Tommy's mother. She was a regular and would come into the pub with her boyfriend on a weekly basis. And occasionally, on her own. He had recognised her from parents meeting evenings and had seen her chatting away with Sheila at the bar.

She seemed to know everything about her regulars, did Sheila. Maybe she knew something he didn't? Oh, sod it! He thought. He summoned the landlady closer and leant forwards.

'I've told you before about how sexual frustration coats the walls of this country's educational academies.

'Well, I could have told you tonight about a potential blockbusting liaison within our school's corridors. One that would have your toes tingling. But today something far more serious has jumped out of the perilous pit that I work in.'

Sheila checked that her staff were doing their job. There were no waiting customers. She turned back to James, her hands placed wide on the bar top. 'Go on.'

James's mouth barely moved as, in a whisper, he related the false accusation story to the enthralled landlady, initially using no names.

'It's total bollocks, Sheil. He's been set up.'

'That is disgusting. It could ruin that teacher's life for ever,' was her reply.

'Exactly! Listen, I wouldn't tell you this normally, but I think you know the mother of the boy it involves. And maybe, I don't know, I'm grabbing at straws here, you might have heard something about the family?'

Sheila's eyes widened. She leant forwards.

'It's Tommy Clifford.

'Donna Clifford's boy?' She shook her head. 'As if that woman hasn't got enough on her plate. Blimey! Do I know something about that family? Where do you want me to start?'

'Anything that concerns the young Tommy would be a good place.'

She lowered her voice. 'That bloke she comes in with, her live-in boyfriend for the past three or four years, is a complete arsehole. He's never had a proper job since I've known him and I know he knocks her about. And I think he does the same to her kids. Especially Tommy. He resents him going to a grammar school for some reason – as if Tommy thinks he's too good for the local comprehensive.'

'That could answer a lot of questions about Tommy's worsening behaviour at school. Have the police ever been involved concerning his abuse of the family?'

'I've tried to get her to report the bugger but she's too scared of him.'

James sat back on his stool. 'That's been very useful information, thanks, Sheil. I'm determined not to let those two get away with this. I will do everything in my power to show up this scumbag of a teacher for what he is.' He took a swig of beer. 'Keep all this to yourself, Sheil,' he added, knowing that she probably wouldn't.

Wow!' said Sheila, as she went off to serve a waiting customer.

While James's mouth was taking another large glug of his beer his mind was working out ways to trap Roth, delve into Clifford's disturbed brain and, perhaps, do something to improve his dysfunctional home life.

Chapter 18

The smell hung off the walls, ground into the cheap plastic chairs and rows of scarred tables. Always the same smell, Jo thought – stale cigarette smoke and cheap perfume. The fixtures and fittings weren't the guilty ones.

Detective Sergeant Jo Major walked into the prison visitors' room. Her athletic figure and short blonde hair, cut into her neck, drew some admiring glances from the prison officers as she sat down. She was dressed in jeans and a puffer jacket. Her eyes were focused on the door. She was waiting for him to appear – the man she helped put behind the steel door of his cramped single-person prison cell just over fifteen months ago. Jo had missed barely a dozen of her weekly visits out of the sixty-two he'd been there. The man was Nick Summers. They had grown close over his term of incarceration.

Nearly eighteen months had passed since the nightmare had descended on the Summers' home. After a devastating series of events, resulting in two accidental deaths, Nick, in fear of a prison sentence, was persuaded to bury the bodies that had exacted immeasurable harm on him and his wife, which eventually led to his wife's suicide.

Shortly after his terrible loss, the two buried bodies were discovered. Despite Jo's confused feelings about the handsome landscape gardener, her astute detective work, added to the eventual voluntary confession from a guilt-ridden Nick, got him a sentence of five years in prison reduced to three.

Jo expected him to serve only eighteen months of that at most. That meant he had, all being well, about three months to go before his release. She was longing for the day they could take their tentative relationship to another level. Originally at Wormley Prison on the Isle of Sheppey, he had been transferred after a year to its neighbour Standford Hill, a category D open prison. There he was to serve the remainder of his sentence.

As always, when Nick appeared in the waiting room the detective's skin tingled. As they sat together neither could have guessed that Nick would provide a useful lead in solving Jo's first big case in her new role.

00000

On a pearl-grey Monday morning, Jo Major was parked behind her desk at Wandsworth Police Station. It was nine-thirty a.m. She had been promoted from DC to DS due to the 'sterling work' she had carried out on the Summers' case over a year ago. Her boss at the Ashford Nick, Detective Superintendent Jack Jolley, had been posted here five weeks ago. When Jack had offered her the promotion to Detective Sergeant and wanted her to relocate with him, she had jumped at the chance.

He and her late father had been colleagues and good friends. When his pal died, Jack made a promise to himself to watch out for Jo. She was grateful for his father-like care and encouragement. Their bond strengthened when her mother died last year.

The move had gone well. With the sale of her mother's house, she was able to buy a two-bed flat in Wandsworth Common. As sad as her mother's passing was, the timing was fortuitous as property in the outer London area was more expensive than Ashford, Kent. She was excited to work in the Capital despite having to move house. The only downside was the four-hour return journey to visit Nick.

She'd not had anything particular, job-wise, to galvanise her since her move. On this Monday morning, her brain cells were rapidly kicked into gear. She was reading the report that had been sitting in the tray on her desk when she arrived. It was from the Initial Investigating Officer, marked MISPER.

A boy had been reported missing on Friday night. The IIO had visited the distraught parents on Saturday midday when the boy had still not shown up at home. Jo studied the information gathered. A supposed happy and healthy boy, weeks off his sixteenth birthday had disappeared. The tall, strongly built youth had not been seen since he left school on that Friday afternoon. Normally she would wait for the IIO to finish a more comprehensive report but the officer had called in sick this morning.

A lad of that age and stature would be regarded as low risk initially. But now, two days after his disappearance, Jo knew she had to move this up to medium risk.

She instructed Detective Constable Kyra Chand to phone local hospitals and YMCA centres. If he'd had an argument at home, he could be holed up in one of them.

Jo wasted no time to push the investigation forwards and the obvious place to start would be… she scoured the report again.

She wrote it on her pad as she read out the name, 'Sir Montague Web Grammar School.'

Wandsworth police station was actually situated in the Clapham Junction area – a five-minute drive to the school in Battersea. It would be the first time she had been involved in this type of incident. Her encompassing thought as she drove towards the school was how worried and helpless the parents must be feeling. She would have to visit them afterwards. It made her shiver in the warm car. She realised she was nervous.

00000

Detective Sergeant Jo Major sat in the comfortable surroundings of Peter Greaves' office. The headmaster, opposite the police officer, was fiddling with a pen. The clock on the wall behind him read eleven fifteen. Jo had phoned ahead of her visit informing him that one of his pupils had gone missing. She didn't say which one in case the information could have compromised the investigation. If there had been anything amiss at the school she didn't want stories concocted before she arrived.

The headmaster had informed all his staff of the police phone call at mid-morning break. They had all hurried to check their registers for absentees. They narrowed it down to seven possibilities.

'We've been informed by his parents that Danny... sorry.' Jo looked at her notes. 'Antonelli, has gone missing. He has not been seen since he left here on Friday afternoon.'

'Danny? Oh dear!' The head sat bolt upright. He couldn't believe what was happening at his school. The Clifford situation – now this.

Jo noticed him shift in his seat.

'I realise you won't be able to answer all of the questions I'm going to ask you. But if you could write those ones down you can't answer now and try to find the answers, please? It is imperative that I receive these as soon as possible. Meanwhile, I would like to interview some other members of staff.'

'Of course. I understand that time is precious in these situations.' Peter opened an exercise book. 'Okay. Fire away.'

'Right, I need to know who was the last person to see him on that Friday when school finished? I want the names of his close friend or friends? What type of boy was he?'

'Well, I might be able to answer that one. He was a very polite, happy boy. He had just got into his year's football team. He was scoring goals as far as I know. I've never heard any complaints about his behaviour from any of my staff. He was a tall lad and looked quite mature for his age. Academically, I believe he was neither excellent nor poor. He certainly hadn't been brought to my attention for any misdemeanours – or indeed, any outstanding achievements.'

'I would have thought that scoring goals on his debut for the football team was a pretty good achievement,' said Jo, trying to loosen the straight-backed proceedings.

'Oh, quite! But, *er,* his teachers will be able to assess those aspects more accurately than I. That's it really.'

After all her questions were answered or noted down, the Head was then asked to summon two of Danny's teachers into his office.

'Is the teacher who manages Danny in the football team a man?'

'Er, yes,' the head replied, slowly.

'Good. I'd like to talk to him. And I would like to see another one of his teachers. Preferably an experienced woman.'

Immediately the request from the police officer to see Sam sent a panic signal rattling through his brain. Sam had just been accused of sexual harassment of a child. Should he tell the police officer that? He hesitated.

Jo noted his slightly reticent look. 'I want one of each gender. I think a female might see a different side of the boy to that of a man. And I'd like you to be present during these interviews.

'Yes, of course,' he said, nodding.

Peter decided against telling her about the accusation. The police didn't need to know at this stage. He thought for a second. Who would be the most experienced female teacher at Blackies. One immediately sprung to mind.

Wendy Jacks.

00000

The headmaster sent his secretary to inform the two teachers that the detective wanted to interview them both. Up first was the young English teacher.

Sam sat in front of the police officer hoping his face was not revealing how nervous he felt inside. He had no way of knowing whether she was aware of the sexual assault accusation against him. The head had no time to tell him before he was called to be interviewed. He was stunned when informed by Jo that it was Danny Antonelli, his striker, the boy he knew as a confident strapping lad, who had gone missing.

'How would you describe Danny,' Jo asked.

'Well, when I recently picked him to play up front in the football team, he couldn't have been more pleased. And he's already scoring goals, I couldn't ask for more from him. In class, he was just a normal pupil. By that I mean I never had an issue with him.'

He suddenly recalled the fight he'd had with Tommy Clifford. Did he want to bring Clifford's name into this inquiry? If it came up at a later date, it might look as though he had something to hide.

'Actually, he had a bit of a tussle recently just before I arrived in my classroom. It was with the boy he had replaced in the team. But it was nothing serious.'

Jo looked up from writing her notes, her eyes wide open. What's this boy's name?'

118

Sam glanced at the Head, who was sitting in his eyeline. He saw his boss frown.

'*Erm,* Tommy Clifford,' he said, as if he'd just remembered his name.

Jo wrote the name down. After a few more questions, she looked up at Sam.

'Thank you, Mr Whitmore. That's all for now,' she said.

Sam breathed a sigh of relief. The interview was over. The other Clifford incident wasn't mentioned.

Wendy Jacks was next.

Chapter 19

When the headmaster had walked into the staff room earlier with a concerned look on his face, Wendy Jacks knew what the announcement would be. It was the moment she had been dreading all weekend. Her legs felt as if they were going to give way as he told the stunned gathering the disturbing news. The gasps heard around the room made her feel sick to the stomach. She had to ignore the voice that told her to run from the premises.

Part of her secret was now exposed in its nakedness. It would be on the minds and lips of every person at her place of work – the institution where she was highly valued by the staff and respected by the pupils. Inevitably, she would now be drawn into uncomfortable conversations with other teachers. Conversations where she would have to feign shock and fear for the boy. The boy she murdered in her bedroom.

But part of her believed she could do it; that she could brazen out this nightmare.

When, as a young woman, her child was born without a breath of life, no one understood. No one at that traumatic time helped her through the following years of emptiness and pain. Her husband changed from a warm and supporting partner to a stranger from that awful day onwards. She believed he blamed her for the loss. Then there were years of seeing her friends and colleagues produce healthy children at the drop of a hat; how she had to watch proud, boasting mothers carrying their babies around like bloody trophies. She hated those mothers.

Yes. She could do this, she decided. She just had to be strong; had to be one step ahead.

What she wasn't expecting was to be called in for an interview by the police officer in the headmaster's office. The muscles running up the back of her neck were like violin strings. That strength had swiftly turned to uncertainty. She must not let panic get hold of her.

'Why me, out of all his other teachers,' she mouthed, as alone she made her way along the corridor. 'Someone knows something. Maybe Danny had already told one of his friends about us?' One thing was for sure. She didn't know what to expect.

00000

'You are Head of Science I'm told. Wendy Jacks?'

Wendy nodded. 'Yes.'

'You may or not know by now that the boy who has gone missing is fifteen-year-old Danny Antonelli,' she watched the teacher's reaction.

'No, I didn't know which *er*... who it was until you said. I'm... it's *erm*... a big shock.'

Her words struggled for any cohesion. Wendy did not recognise her own faltering voice. Her attempt at holding it together was failing and by the look of the police officer's expression, she had noticed it.

'As his teacher, I presume you are fully acquainted with the boy in question?'

The phrase *fully acquainted* surprised her. Was she testing her?

She put her hands in her lap then on the arms of the chair. *'Er,* yes I know who he is, like all the other boys in my class. But nothing more than that.' Wendy was instantly aware that she was sounding unnecessarily defensive.

'It's just that I wanted to see if you had noticed anything different recently about the boy's behaviour? His relationship with you... or... any of his friends?' said Jo.

Wendy felt herself blushing. 'No, I wasn't aware of any change or strange behaviour in Danny.'

She realised her discomfort was obvious to the police officer.

'Are you okay? Do you want a drink of water?' asked Jo.

'No, I'm just upset about this. I know how these things usually end.'

Jo frowned. 'Well, let's not go down that route just yet, shall we? These things often have a happy ending.'

The teacher forced a smile.

After a few more routine questions the detective was satisfied she had finished with the teachers for now.

'Okay, thanks for your time,' said Jo.

As Wendy left the office, her brain was in a vortex. She almost bumped into Tommy Clifford who was waiting outside the door. He was next to be interviewed. Tommy hated the police. A few of his black friends had been caught shoplifting more than once but they would always tell him how the police were forever picking on the black and mixed-race community.

'Could you ask the boy Clifford to come in, please headmaster.'

Peter suddenly realised that Tommy Clifford would think the police were here to ask him about the accusation of assault. He didn't want this revealed yet, if at all. He walked outside the office and took the boy a few paces further down the corridor.

Bending forward, he whispered, 'Listen. This has nothing to do with your complaint about Mr Whitmore. That is being handled. This is about Danny Antonelli who has gone missing. Everybody's worried for him. That's the only reason you're here. Okay?'

'Okay,' said Tommy, looking puzzled.

He entered the office and was told to sit down. Jo studied the boy slouching back in the chair, his legs wide apart, as if it was his office.

'Thomas Clifford. May I call you Tommy?' Jo said, with a smile.

Tommy nodded slowly. 'Yeh.'

'You are not in any trouble. I want to make that clear to you before we start. But I just need to ask you a few questions.'

Tommy nodded once more.

'Danny Antonelli, the boy in your class has not been seen since Friday end of school. I wondered, Tommy, if you had seen him leave school and if he was with anybody?'

'No, we're not mates and he goes home in the other direction to me.'

'And you have not seen him since?'

Tommy shook his head, the edges of his mouth turned downwards.

'I'm told you had a fight with Danny recently. What was that about?'

Tommy shot a look at the headmaster who looked concerned. He quickly changed his expression and nodded in support to the boy.

'He started it,' said Tommy.

'All right, I believe you. But that's not important. I just want to know the reason you fought with him?'

'Football. He's playing in my place, and I'm a better player than him. He's sucked up to the teacher.'

'And that's the only reason?'

'Yeh.'

'Is he a member of a gang?'

'I dunno. I wouldn't think so. I don't know if he's got any close mates here at school either.'

Jo smiled at the boy again. 'Okay, that's all I need. Thank you, Tommy.

As soon as the boy left, the headmaster spoke, 'I instructed my secretary to find out who Danny's friends are. There appears to be no particular boys that answer to that description. Maybe there's a crowd he hangs around with. I will make more inquiries myself and let you know if I come up with any names.'

'Thank you for that. Meanwhile, could you instruct your teaching staff to ask all their classes if anyone saw Danny after school on Friday?'

'Of course,' said Peter. 'And I'll put up notices around the school to that effect.'

The detective nodded her approval. She then stood, passed the headmaster her business card, shook his hand and departed.

On the drive back to work she felt ill-at-ease. She was running the interviews back and forth in her head. Both the headmaster and the two teachers seemed overly nervous. It was obviously a shock to be told that a boy at their school has just disappeared into thin air. And all schools have a promise of safekeeping that they would be painfully aware of.

Perhaps their demeanour was born out of feeling responsible somehow. Who would want their school associated with such a distressing matter? Their daily workplace associated with such a negative story would soon be open season to the media if the boy was not found? But it seemed to Jo, there was more going on behind the information they were prepared to offer. Were they hiding something? If so, what?

She was determined to find out.

Chapter 20

By mid-afternoon, all the school had been informed of Danny's disappearance. The teachers had carried out the headmaster's instructions. All pertinent questions had been put to the pupils and posters had been written, printed and displayed around the school premises. No one, it seemed, had seen Danny leave school on that Friday.

James Shilling was in the headmaster's office.

'So not only have we got an accusation by a pupil of sexual impropriety hanging over our bloody heads, now another one has gone missing. What is going on? First of all, I want you to know that I fully support Sam in this ridiculous allegation. It is blindingly obvious that the Clifford boy has been encouraged, persuaded whatever, to accuse Sam of this incident and I know who by,' said James.

The headmaster's head rocked backwards, as if avoiding a swinging punch.

'What! You mean by a teacher?'

'Sam's been set up, Peter. Look. Clifford has been dropped from the football team for the first time since he's been at the school. And he's made his feelings known more than once to anyone who will listen to his selfish wrath. He's had it in for Sam ever since.'

James took a breath. He was not completely comfortable with blaming a fellow teacher. Bugger it, he thought, he has to be told. Sam needs all the help he can get.

'Jeremy Roth has, much to his obvious outrage, been relieved of his duties concerning the team. Who stands to gain from Sam Whitmore's disgrace and following expulsion from the Web? There's only two that fit the bill,' said James.

The headmaster let the deputy head's words sink in. His chest expanded. Out came a huge puff of air.

'That's a hell of an accusation James… mind you, Roth was in here the day after I appointed Sam team coach. And he was livid. I have to admit I've never liked the man.'

'He's still livid. He won't even speak to Sam. You don't like him. I don't trust him. He's shifty. We've got to put a stop to this before…'

'Hold on. Listen. I've already informed the LADO of the incident…'

'What. Why? You didn't have to do that. We're allowed to handle problems of this nature in-house, at least initially,' said James.

'I thought it best to follow the official channels. In fact, I received a reply phone call this lunchtime suggesting that I suspend Sam until further investigations have been carried out.'

James shook his head. 'Peter, what have you done? Now it looks as though you're siding with the boy. You have to ignore their suggestion. This is Sam's reputation we are talking about here. More to the point, if the police find out you've suspended a teacher for a possible sexual offence against a pupil, then Sam's suddenly going to become prime suspect for the missing boy Danny Antonelli.'

Stupidly, the head hadn't realised the ramifications of his proposed action. James was right. It could put Sam in the spotlight for both incidents.

'I don't know if I can go against the LADO on this. I'll have to think about it.'

'Peter, you've had my support on every issue ever since you made me Deputy Headmaster. But if your decision on this ruins Sam's credibility, his career, then that support disappears. I want you to think long and hard about what you are going to do.'

On his last word, James got up and exited the office leaving Peter elbows on desk, head in hands rubbing his face.

00000

Apart from the police there would be another organisation actively interested and involved in Danny's disappearance. The early Antonelli's hailed from the village of Plati, in the Calabria region of Italy. Plati was the stronghold of the Ndrangheta, a mafia organisation that ruled throughout the region. Danny's grandfather, Umberto a lesser member of the organisation, decided to move with his wife to London in the early nineteen fifties.

He had relatives who had moved there a few years before to an area of Clerkenwell that became known as

Little Italy. The promise of a better lifestyle in the UK was attractive to this ambitious young man. Via their family's mafia connections, which were beginning to expand throughout the country, Umberto was invited into the lucrative but fiercely competitive mobile ice-cream selling business. Years later Umberto and his only son, Enzo opened their first Italian bistro.

Enzo eventually married. It was another twenty-three years before they had their one and only son. His name was Daniel. Enzo, a successful restauranteur, now lived in an increasingly affluent part of Battersea.

It was a mere seven-minute walk to Sir Montague Web school for the young Danny.

00000

Jo had now reached the most discomforting part of her investigation. The delicate business of getting information from the worried parents. Her DC, Kyra Chand was with her. When they knocked on the door of their house she introduced herself and Kyra to Enzo and Karen Antonelli. At sixty and fifty-five respectively, they were a lot older than Jo had expected.

As they were shown into the sitting room, Jo noted the beautiful furnishings and attention to detail. They sat opposite each other on two cream Francoferri Italian sofas. They were placed either side of an ebony glass-topped coffee table. Everything in the room, down to each artefact and adornment, was perfectly thought out and immaculate. Jo had learned many years ago to study how people treated their homes during an investigation. It would often give an insight into the owners' lifestyles and personalities.

'Has Danny ever stayed out all night before?' asked Jo.

'A few times he has had a sleepover at a friend's house. Once he forgot to ring us until late in the evening to let us know where he was. But, that's all,' said Karen, taking a quick glance at her husband.

'Has there been any trouble recently with Danny? Any family arguments or change in his routine?'

'No, said Karen.' Again, she looked at her husband who nodded in agreement.

'How about his behaviour, any changes there or in his time-keeping recently?'

She hesitated. 'Actually, I thought I could smell alcohol on his breath a few times over the past few weeks. And they were the times he didn't come home straight after school,' said Karen, this time avoiding her husband's eyes.

'What time would you say you smelled the alcohol on Danny's breath,' asked Jo.

'Around five or six p.m. I suppose,' said Karen.

Enzo frowned. 'You never told me this,' he said to Karen.

'You're never home to notice these things. Working all hours in the restaurant.'

'You could've let me know about him drinking, Karen. I think that's important, don't you?' said Enzo, as if the couple were the only ones in the room.

His wife looked at Jo then burst into tears.

It was the first sign of any discord between them.

Jo reacted quickly, 'That is good information, Karen. Thank you. I want to assure you both that we are doing everything now to locate Danny,' she informed his parents, who by now were both perched on the edge of their sofa.

'You told my colleague on Friday that you keep ringing his mobile phone but with no answer. That still the case?' said Jo.

'It just rings and rings then goes to answer phone,' said Karen.

'Very often, in these cases the missing person returns home or is found the following day. Taking into account Danny's age and size, the investigation began as low risk. I want you to know we are now moving the investigation up to medium risk. So, we will need his laptop or tablet, if he's got one here and his mobile number. With the help of his phone provider, we will try to locate the whereabouts of his phone.'

This next question made Jo breathe deep. 'With your permission, accompanied by either of you, if preferred, I'd like Kyra here to make a brief search of the house and garage.'

Enzo looked rattled. 'Do you think we haven't searched the house ourselves. So, you don't trust us?'

'Yes, of course we trust you, Mr Antonelli. But it's part of our routine in these cases. We ask to do this with everyone. It's just ticking boxes to please our bosses.'

The recent case went through her mind where a single mother had hidden her daughter in an upstairs cupboard.

She claimed she had gone missing. Instead, it was a despicable attempt at an insurance fraud. She wasn't going to cite that case to the Antonelli's for obvious reasons.

After her DC had searched the premises accompanied by Enzo, Jo asked Karen for a recent photograph of Danny. After more words of encouragement, the detectives departed.

As soon as they had gone Enzo phoned his cousin Luca. He had texted him on the Saturday morning when Danny had not arrived home, but this was more serious now. He needed all the help he could get.

Although he was close to Luca, he was not an active part of the Ndrangheta organisation that now had a strong foothold in London. Luca, on hearing his cousin's distressing news, then made sure that Danny's disappearance filtered through the London Antonelli's and associates throughout the UK within a matter of hours. Luca's was a side of the 'family' that had the reputation of getting what they wanted and not always by the usual accepted means.

Chapter 21

Monday early-evening. Jo sat opposite the man she hoped would be the catalyst to kickstart a new life for them both after his release from prison. She never found it easy to start the conversation when she visited Nick. Asking him how he's been or how his week had gone was a no-no because his routine would basically always be the same. But eventually, it become a joke between them. And so it went.

'How's your week been then, Nick?' she asked.

Nick smiled.

'Oh, I don't know where to begin. Actually, I feel sorry for the Queen because I never realised that Her Majesty's Pleasure could be so dull and boring. If I was the Queen and I had that much power and influence, my pleasure would be off the scale. And, probably every night,' said Nick, straight-faced.

They both looked at each other and laughed out loud. The rest of the inmates and the on-duty prison officers turned to look at the pair. No one else was laughing.

'So, how's *your* week been?' asked Nick.

'We've got a fifteen-year-old lad gone missing from a school in Battersea. I've held interviews at the school and a couple of teachers seemed very tense. The headmaster appeared to be a bit on edge as well. But then it's not an unusual reaction when a copper turns up on your doorstep asking questions,' said Jo.

'Funny you should mention Battersea because I've got pally with a con in here who was brought up and lived most of his life in that area. I think he moved from there about a year or so ago, but he's still got friends from round that way. He's not a bad bloke. Well, I suppose all of us in here have been bad blokes in some way, but you know what I mean,' Nick said, with a grin.

'What's he in for?' asked Jo.

'Grievous, I think. He got picked on in a pub by two fellas. He laid one of them out cold and smashed a bottle over the head of the other one. That's his story anyway. He's not very big but blimey, he's as tough as a horse's saddle and solid with it.' I have to admit I wouldn't mess with him.'

'Oh, I must remember then to invite him around for tea when he gets out,' Jo replied. They both began to laugh again but thought better of it this time.

'You never know, him or his mates who still live there might know of any dodgy blokes that are interested in kids. If his friends are anything like him then they're probably going to have their ear to the ground. What's the name of the school?' asked Nick.

'Oh, I've got an amateur sleuth on my hands now, have I?'

'I wasn't named Nick for nothing. But you can call me Sherlock.'

'I could think of many names to call you but that certainly isn't one of them. It's Sir Montagu Web

Grammar School. It has been three days since he went missing so we're getting more concerned for his safety. I think the story is going out on the box tonight. On the major channel's news,' said Jo.

'Okay. Leave it with me. I'll see what I can find out,' said Nick, just as the end of session buzzer went. Jo leant forwards, kissed Nick on the cheek and departed.

She loved Nick's humour. But admired his positivity far more. Being locked up for all that he had to go through, then having his wife commit suicide, would destroy most guys. I'm surprised he hasn't tried to top himself in there, Jo thought.

Nick had talked it over with Jo a few times since he'd been in prison. Although he knew he had made a mistake, he wasn't sorry that he had stood up to a burglar in his home in the dead of the night. He certainly didn't feel sorry for the detective. He didn't kill him, but he could easily have done the deed.

'Would you do it all the same again,' Jo had asked.

'Try to protect my home and wife? Yes, I would.'

Jo thought that that was the main reason he was coping with being in prison so admirably. He knew he'd done wrong in the eyes of the law but was confident of his actions against the two criminals.

Chapter 22

James sat in his car scouring the school car park. It was six-fifteen p.m. The October nights were drawing in. The gloomy square of concrete had just one light. It sat on top of a thin, towering metal pole situated at the far corner. His engine was off. Two blackbirds in a nearby tree were having an aggressive singing competition between them. His subconscious may have heard them. But his mind was focused.

It switched on to full alert when the figure of the headmaster appeared carrying his briefcase, climbed into his car and left the school premises. James followed. The head turned left out of the gates. James knew the area where his boss lived. *He wasn't going home that's for sure*, he thought.

Staying two to three cars apart, they drove on through the South London traffic. When they reached Earlsfield Station, the head turned left off the main road into a long, beeline street of semi-detached houses. He parked halfway down on the right-hand-side. James pulled in opposite some fifteen yards behind. He turned off his ignition and lights.

The glow from the lamppost close to the Head's car enabled James to make out that he was on his mobile phone. A minute later a door opened in a house nearby and outstepped Amy Pederson.

'I knew it,' said James, nodding.

The gamble had paid off. He had hoped that Monday may be one of the nights that they met up. He was lucky. His mobile was already on camera, he zoomed in and hit the button.

The PE teacher walked round the car and climbed in. The couple kissed. The camera clicked. They drove off.

James then followed them to a backstreet restaurant in Wimbledon. His camera was busy again as they entered the small bistro hand in hand.

He'd seen enough.

00000

Monday, Wendy's first day back at school, had been fraught with worry. After facing the detective's questions, she was dreading another teacher trying to strike up a conversation about Danny Antonelli. Fortunately, she had managed to avoid any close contact with her colleagues. She spent her lunchtime in her own empty classroom.

The evening found her downstairs in front of her computer. A cup of coffee and a cheese sandwich sat untouched by her right elbow. She had hardly eaten a thing since that macabre Friday afternoon. Food was usually high on her list of simple pleasures. Comfort eating had, for now, ceased to exist. She needed a good deal more than food to mollify her tortured soul.

Her sitting room was best described as cottage cosy. There was enough room for a sofa, one armchair and a mahogany writing bureau. The blue and red chintz curtains matched the sofa upholstery. A small, flat-screen television sat in a corner next to an unmade open fireplace. She sat in joggers and baggy sweatshirt, hunched over the keyboard searching online for remote locations to bury the body of her young lover.

It was a half-hearted attempt. She was still having serious doubts as to whether she was capable enough in mind and body to carry out the aberrant process. It would need a great deal of strength and stealth to manoeuvre the heavy corpse in and out of the boot of her car. Then to dig a grave big enough and deep enough to bury a six-foot body in an unknown area, quickly and quietly? It was surely beyond her capabilities.

Her brain kept playing back a video of her interview at school with the police officer. She was so nervous answering her questions and the detective had noticed it. The thought came up once more. Why was I, out of all the other teachers, chosen to be quizzed by her? Why would she suspect me, his teacher? There would be no reason. Unless Danny had opened his mouth?

Behind her, in the corner of the room the TV was on. Her attention was grabbed when the recognisable opening theme music to the six o'clock news filled the room. She spun round on her stool. The second story was of the disappearance of a young schoolboy. The piece showed a reporter standing in front of the grammar school and then a picture of Danny Antonelli. There was an appeal for witnesses.

As Wendy watched the report, she prayed that they had found no clues that would point her way. The more she watched the more she withdrew into her chair trying to distance herself from the images on the screen. Seeing the incident broadcast on national television hit her like a punch in the gut. If she had managed to eat that sandwich it surely would have made a swift return appearance. The enormity of her actions came into focus once more as she broke down in tears.

'I can't do this,' she whimpered. 'I don't even think I'll be able to manage getting him into my car. And what about my nosey neighbour? He could easily see me struggling with a heavy body from his upstairs window. Oh God. What am I going to do?'

00000

First thing Tuesday morning, before the commencement of daily lessons, James was in the headmaster's office. He took a seat facing Peter across his desk. He said nothing as he considered the body language of his boss. One thing was for sure. If he was compelled to orchestrate what he had in mind, their relationship, both in and out of work, would be irretrievably damaged. The balance of power altered.

'So, have you thought about what you're going to do with Sam? Will you suspend him?' said James.

'I'm afraid I think I must. I was about to call him in this morning to tell him,' said the head.

'I'm asking you one more time to reconsider that decision, Peter. At least give me the opportunity to talk to the boy, Clifford.'

'That's the thing. You can't talk to him, James. If the boy mentions it, it could appear that you were intimidating him. Trying to change his mind.'

'I'd like to do more than that to the little…'

'Look. My mind is made up James. It's the reputation of the school I'm worried about. Especially with the Danny Antonelli situation bringing us unwanted attention.'

'The reputation of the school will survive all this mess. Sam's reputation won't, said James, shaking his head.

'I'm sorry…'

'Right. I didn't want to do this. I really didn't. But you've left me with no option.'

The head looked puzzled as he watched James get his mobile phone from his pocket. He saw him press a few buttons and then push it across the desk towards him. As he scrolled across the photos of him and Amy his face drained of colour.

'You followed me?' whispered the head, while still looking at James's phone.

'Desperate times, Peter. Listen. Although I regard it as a bloody stupid thing to do in your position, I don't really care if you're fucking someone at this school. What

I don't want is you fucking two people at this school. Suspending Sam could do exactly that.

The head pushed the phone back across the desk. His pasty face had now turned red.

'So, you're blackmailing me? You would tell the governors?'

'Peter, I've been dumped on from a great height in my life not too long ago. And I can tell you the hurt sinks so deep down inside of you that it's impossible to ever dig it out. And it changes you. Those you trusted before suddenly have a potential question mark over their head. You allow the negatives in life to creep in, staining all the positives. If I can save someone else from that torture – a good man like Sam Whitmore – I would do anything. Yes, even blackmail.'

The Head sank back into his chair. In the time it took to scan a few photos, his mischievous dalliance with the beautiful Amy had gone from an invigorating secret to a tawdry affair. He ought to have felt violated – enraged that his personal life had been spied upon. He didn't. He was embarrassed. Sitting in front of a colleague, his deputy headmaster, he felt cheap.

'How did you know?' the head asked.

'Ever since I caught my wife having an affair, I began to look at people from a different perspective. I am not even aware that I'm doing it sometimes. But my brain locks on to subtle signs. A smile that seems more than just a smile, a glance that lingers too long. Things like that. Body language reveals a lot of secrets, Peter. Add all that to seeing our PE teacher visiting your office a little too often…'

The headmaster's chin sunk down onto his tie. He raised his eyes. 'Do you think anyone else knows?'

James remembered that he had mentioned the possibility of an affair to Sam but he had no proof then. His boss didn't need to know that.

'I very much doubt it. You must think I am lower than a grass snake to carry out such a spiteful deed. But I've done this for one reason only. It was all I had to bargain with.'

The head closed his eyes. Then, blinked them open. He stared at James. 'This job and my standing in the role mean everything to me.' There was a moment's silence. Peter's chest rose.

'You've got your wish. Sam stays.'

Chapter 23

Much to Wendy's surprise, the headmaster insisted on seeing her early Tuesday morning. When she left her house, the skies were stuffed with black clouds. During the short drive to work, unrelenting rain hammered down onto the thin bonnet of her car. The tinny sound made her shrink down into the driver's seat, adding to her feeling of vulnerability. The nearest space in the school car park was twenty yards from the building. As she exited her car she stepped straight into a deep puddle that leaked into her shoes.

'Shit!' she said, as she ran through the downpour to the rear school door and entered.

The headmaster's door seemed larger than normal. She knocked and waited. An unexpected shiver rippled through her bones as the door was opened from the inside. As she walked into his office, the head immediately closed the door behind her. She noticed that he had not bothered to turn the lights on. It felt unusually cold in there. The single window was the only source of illumination in the dim room. Her attention was drawn to a shady corner. She was startled to see the female police officer. She stood, arms folded, staring at her.

What was she doing there? she thought.

Suddenly, the headmaster began yelling at Wendy, his face purple, the veins on his temples ready to burst. He stepped towards her, both hands grabbing her by the shoulders, almost knocking her over.

'Why? For God's sake, why?' he screamed, into the face of the teacher. 'What have you done to the reputation of this revered grammar school.

Alarmed, she looked across at the officer for support. She just stood there watching the headmaster ranting at her. The policewoman was now wearing a spiteful smile across her face. It was as though she was enjoying the spectacle.

'The boy has told us everything. You're a disgrace to your profession,' he said.

She turned towards the DS again who stepped slowly from the shadows. A sheet drenched in blood was wrapped around the police officer's shoulders. She shook her head and slowly pointed downwards. Wendy gasped as she saw Danny lying naked on the floor in front of the detective. His head a bloody mess. But he was moving… the boy was still alive.

Wendy gasped and screamed, 'No!'

The high-pitched shriek woke her with a shudder from the grisly nightmare. She lay on the bed on which Danny was murdered, soaked in sweat, staring at the ceiling. Once more, her night's sleep had been a maelstrom of haunting images – her brain dropping in and out of grim dramas. Scenes filled with distorted faces and a constant barrage of accusing voices.

She wanted to call in sick this morning, but it would surely arouse suspicion. Wouldn't it? She knew she had to get up and go to work. The teacher hauled herself out of bed and headed for the shower.

When she had finished dressing, she went down to the kitchen. Half-filling the kettle she hit the switch on top, while her other hand reached up and pulled open a cupboard door. She looked at the boxes of cereal then immediately close the door again. Her stomach couldn't face breakfast this morning. She made a strong coffee in her largest mug and sat at the table.

Before she had time to settle, the doorbell rang. Wendy froze. It was seven forty-five am. Ten minutes before she left to drive the short distance to work.

'Who the hell…' she whispered, as she walked hesitatingly towards the door. She paused behind it hoping whoever it was would go away. The bell rang once more.

She opened it to barely shoulder width and was confronted with her next-door neighbour. A corpulent man in his late sixties. She had noticed him from time to time, in his garden and in the local shop, but merely afforded him a half smile. She had a rule not to encourage friendships with those in her street. Neighbours can be nosey. Neighbours can be intrusive.

'Sorry to bother you so early but I thought I'd try to catch you before you went to work,' he said. He wore an orange Champion sweatshirt, green baggy jogging bottoms and yellow tattered slippers. He looked like he had got dressed in the dark in a jumble sale. Two-day-old stubble completed the vision of scruffiness.

Wendy smiled weakly and raised her eyebrows. She waited.

'It's just that I was working down the bottom of my garden.' Wendy's smile instantly evaporated. 'And I heard the sound of a phone ringing. It was coming from your shed.'

Oh, my God, Wendy thought. *I had forgotten about his phone. It must be wrapped up with him in the duvet cover. It has to be in his jacket pocket.* All these thoughts scuttled through her mind in a matter of seconds. But now, she had to think quickly once more.

'Oh… thank goodness. *Erm,* yes. I thought I'd lost my phone. I have searched everywhere for it. It must have fallen out of my pocket when I was in the shed last.' She could hear her voice wavering.

'I guessed as much. Although I thought you might be keeping a secret lover locked in there,' he said, with a creepy smile and a chuckle.

Her heart went into lockdown. She thought it had stopped until she realised she had ceased breathing. She sucked in air and exhaled it.

'*Ha!* I should be so lucky,' she said, eventually. Another weak smile, an attempt to cover the pandemonium running wild inside her. 'I'll go and fetch it now. Thanks very much.'

The neighbour smiled but didn't move. He just stood there on the coconut doormat in his yellow slippers. It was if he was hoping that their first one-to-one connection would go on a little longer. Perhaps he wanted a friendly chat. Maybe an invitation to come inside.

It looked very cold outside but… *absolutely no fucking chance,* she thought. She gave him a polite nod and closed the door in his face. That short exchange was the most she had ever spoken with him. This was certainly not the time to carry the conversation on any longer even if she had wanted to.

'His blasted phone! That was stupid of me. Stupid,' she said, the other side of the closed door. She knew through watching numerous TV crime dramas that the police could find the location of a mobile phone. She wasn't sure how accurate they could be. If they could pinpoint her house, she was done for. She just hoped that they hadn't already started the process.

She had to get to that phone to turn it off. But it would mean unwrapping the body, which was now four days old, to retrieve it. She felt faint at the thought.

The science teacher looked out through the glass patio doors onto her garden. It had been raining most of the night. The new lawn was soaked, dappled with small puddles. The imminent arrival of November was evident. The nighttime temperature had fallen to barely above freezing. The interior of the shed would be cold. She hoped the wrapped body would still be preserved to a bearable extent.

There was no time to change out of her work clothes. She hurried to the small boot room off the kitchen. There, she threw on a sleeveless gilet over her blouse and knee-length skirt, stepped into her garden clogs and returned to the patio doors. The neighbour was not in his garden.

Good. Wendy made her way down to the shed dreading what she was going to find.

She twisted the small metal door latch and pulled open the pine door. On entering, the odour was immediate. She could just about tolerate it. Her hand ran down the inside of the wood slatted wall searching for the light switch. She flicked it down, stepped inside and closed the door behind her.

Wendy looked down at the human package. It appeared fuller, swollen. She still couldn't believe how utterly reckless she had been. More than once, since Friday, she had questioned her sanity. How could she be capable of murder? But deep down she knew. The anger that had been locked up, hidden for so many years, had manifested itself in spectacular fashion. It had erupted into one devastating attack. Striking out at her demons. The innocent victim? A dead child.

But this was a nightmare that would *never* die.

She took a plastic covered cushion she used for gardening from a hook on the wall. Then, laid it on the dry mudded floorboards next to the body. Kneeling down she began untying top and bottom pieces of string that bound the duvet – the substitute shroud. The one at his feet came undone easily. But the knot at the head end was tied too tightly. She spent minutes trying to loosen it. She soon began to get annoyed with herself, losing patience. As she tore desperately at the knotted string, she ripped part of her nail from her index finger.

'Fuck, fuck,' she shrieked, as she flicked her throbbing finger around in the air. She had no time to feel sorry for herself she was going to be late for work. She had to press on. As soon as she started to unwrap the boy's corpse the pungent smell of rotting flesh assaulted her nostrils. It was much stronger than she had imagined. Her lungs instantly rejected the clogging stench that were now under attack. Her body's involuntary impulse was to jerk violently away from the smell.

As she tried to stand, she tripped and swayed backwards. Wendy shuffled her feet to regain her balance. Alas, her body was too heavy to correct itself as she clattered into the side of the lawn mower with a loud crash. On the way down her head struck, the metal handlebar making her cry out. Whilst trying to break her fall she sliced the fleshy side of her hand on a protruding nut. The same hand that contained the ripped nail.

Laying on her back on the grubby floor, she put the cut hand to her mouth absorbing the flow of blood. Her eyes screwed tight with the pain. It was a punishment. It had to be. The tears flowed once again, now accompanied by violent sobs. She stared hopelessly up at the inside ridge of the gabled roof. If her neighbour had been in his garden, he would have wondered what the hell was going on in her shed. She could not have attracted more attention to herself, she thought, than if she had set fireworks off in her garden.

'For God's sakes. What next,' she cried. An ironic smile spread across her face at the farcical position she found herself in. It was an ugly smile.

Wendy crawled to her knees and approached the body once more. The teacher dared not look at what was under

149

the cover. She rolled the heavy parcel over to expose the open flap of the duvet. It was no longer the stiff board she had pulled into the shed. Rigor mortis had dissipated, the body was now floppy and more difficult to manoeuvre. She then turned her bruised head away from what she was about to do.

Leaning gingerly on her twice-injured left hand, she used the good one to rummage inside the cover for his jacket. More than once her bare fingers brushed against the cold decaying flesh of the young schoolboy. The fetid reek was so pungent she could taste it. Bile rose in her stomach as she searched the length of his body trying not to inhale too deeply.

She located his jacket and quickly searched the pockets. 'Got it!' she said, as she pulled out the phone from the fetid bundle. There was still a small amount of life indicated on the front window. Wendy knew there would be a large number of missed calls present. Desperate calls from family and friends. She couldn't bear to read or listen to them. The device was turned off, replaced and the bundle retied.

She climbed unsteadily to her feet, left the shed and wavered, like a drunk, back to her house. A feeling of desolation hung over her as she collapsed into an armchair. She looked at her bloodied hand. It was a mess. But it was so cold, she could hardly feel the pain anymore.

Immediately, she got up again, realising her clothes would be in a state. She took off her skirt and gilet. As she suspected they were covered in greasy dirt and dry leaves from the shed floor. Her head was in a muddle as she glared at the ivory armchair now streaked with dark smears. It was purchased less than one year ago – her prize possession. She screamed out loud. The first part of the scream was aimed at the stranger who used to be the sensible, mature head of science – the remainder at her father and husband who had both deserted her.

Gathering her senses, Wendy hurried up to her bedroom. She washed and bandaged her hand then picked out another skirt and blouse to wear to work. Her immediate thought now was, had she turned off the mobile phone in time?

The next task? To smarten herself up and get to work. Every day from now on, she would have to pretend she was upset about the disappearance of one of the boys in her class.

The schoolboy who now lay rotting in her garden shed.

Chapter 24

The headmaster sat heavy in his office chair. The discovery of his affair was a huge shock. He thought they had been discreet enough during their working day not to have given any indication of their close relationship. He was horribly wrong and surprised how naïve he had been. He had allowed his juvenile excitement of his tryst with a beautiful young girl to cloud his judgement. He was headmaster, for God's sake.

When his nerves had settled enough for him to think clearly, he picked up his mobile to text Amy Pederson. He had to tell her their affair had been discovered. But he didn't want to say by whom. It would surely cause a toxic atmosphere within the staffroom if she ever let her anger towards James spill out. He knew that Amy was a free spirit and could speak her mind without thinking of the consequences at times. It was a trait he admired in her. But not one for this time.

More to the point, he did not want to upset James. He still had those photographs.

Please come to my office as soon as possible. URGENT. Peter. The text was sent.

Fifteen minutes later the track suited PE teacher entered the headmaster's room.

'What is it, Peter?' she said, with a furrowed brow.

'We've been found out. You and me.'

'What do you mean found out? How is that possible?'

'Someone suspected we were having an affair, followed us and took photographs. But it was done for a reason.'

'Photos? Photos of what?'

'You, getting into my car. Us kissing. Us holding hands going into a restaurant.'

'Is that all?' Amy said, shrugging her shoulders.

'Is that all? It's enough, Amy. People are not going to think that was all we did. They are not stupid. I'm the head… blooming master of a reputable grammar school. I've got governors who expect unquestionable behaviour from me. We already have enough problems on our doorstep now.'

'Who did this? Who followed us and took the photos?'

'It doesn't matter who. The person has threatened to tell my employers. And if they tell the media my chances of getting another job in education again will be zero.' He pointed at Amy. 'So will yours. And Ruth doesn't deserve the shame, it would bring on our family. Her finding out that I'm having an affair is one thing. Having it plastered all over the newspapers is… well, it's not going to happen. Not if I can help it.'

'What does this person want in return for not telling on us?'

It's about Sam Whitmore. There's been an allegation against him from a pupil of a sexual nature. I don't think for a moment he is guilty but I felt under pressure to suspend him,'

'That would not look good for Sam. No smoke without any fire,' Amy said.

'Exactly. If I don't suspend him the photos and the story of us never sees the light of day. So, I've not suspended him. But I had to tell you. No one else knows about the Sam situation. And it's not him who took the photos, by the way. I am asking you to keep this to yourself. I'm hoping this can be sorted out between the parties involved.'

'Is that the end of us, then?' Amy asked.

The head breathed in, went to speak, looked into Amy's eyes and breathed out again.

00000

Sam had still not told Lucy of Clifford's accusation. She'd been having problems with Freya who had not been well. Teething problems, the doctor had said. Maybe that was the cause of her constant crying, thought Sam. On top of that his mother-in-law, who seemed to have a catalogue of perennial physical and mental problems, had spent much of Friday and the weekend describing them all in detail to Lucy. Half of it had come his way. It was not a good time to weigh her down with more distressing news.

At mid-morning break, James waited for Sam outside the staff room. When he hadn't arrived after five minutes, he thought he may have not gone to work that morning, pre-empting the head's final decision. Then he caught sight of him in the corridor, amongst the bobbing heads and blue blazers, walking towards him.

'Thank God, I've caught you.' He pulled him to a windowed recess. 'You're not going to be suspended. I was in Peter's office this morning, and it's all okay for now.'

'How... that was you, wasn't it?' How did you manage that?'

'A little bit of the old Shilling persuasion. It at least gives us time to try and break down the murky alliance between Roth and Clifford. That's my next job,' said James, rubbing his hands together as if he was rolling pastry.

Chapter 25

Wendy's day at school only added more stress to a fragile spirit that was ready to snap. After the morning's horrors, she arrived at work twenty-five-minutes late. She was never late. She missed taking the register for her year eleven class – a vital omission to the start of the school day. But she could still make assembly.

As she walked through the iron-gated entrance, she passed beneath the imposing school badge – a gold falcon atop a red and white shield. Beneath it was written the school motto in italics. *Rather Death than False of Faith.*

She did not look up at the apocalyptic message. As she entered the corridor, she would normally turn left to the staff room. There was no time to drop in there this morning to change out of her driving pumps into heeled shoes. Instead, she turned right heading for the Grand Hall. Still carrying her bag, she hurried up the wide sweeping staircase, decked with ornate framed paintings and photographs of formidable-looking past headmasters.

Wendy, red faced, entered the baroque style assembly hall five minutes after proceedings had started. A line of perspiration sat on her top lip. She sidled between the back row of canvas chairs across the rear of the stage, where all the teachers sat. In her hurry, she inadvertently kicked the metal leg of the vacant one she was about to sit on. It clattered into the one next to it. The noisy clang mortified the science teacher and awoke a lot of bored juvenile brains.

The result: a wave of restrained guffaws among the audience of five hundred boys. The headmaster was reading a lesson at a wooden lectern in front of the rows of teachers. He turned briefly to see the subject of their amusement. He registered Wendy's tardy arrival then continued with his address.

Ten minutes later when assembly had finished the head approached the teacher. He waited until they were on their own.

'Is everything okay, Wendy?' He saw that her hand was bandaged. 'Not like you to be late on parade. I noticed yesterday you didn't seem your normal self.'

The headmaster had passed Wendy in the corridor on Monday. He went to say hello but the teacher, seemingly in a daze, completely ignored him and walked straight past.

'Yes. I mean no. I'm sorry, I had a few issues at home this morning. I apologise for being late,' she said, as she dabbed her top lip with the back of her good hand.

He pointed to the white bandage. 'Is that serious?'

'Oh. No, *erm*, I just burnt it on the oven door last night. Stupid,' she said.

'Well, don't worry about your class registration, that was taken care of by Mr Shilling when he realised you weren't here. If there's anything I can do to help, whatever it is, please don't hesitate to come to my office,' said the headmaster.

Whatever it is? She looked into his eyes. *You wouldn't want to help me if you knew,* she thought. She smiled politely. 'Thank you,' she said.

Her day did not get any better. Just after lunch, she had to take the class that should have contained Danny Antonelli. He would have been sitting at the front row desk his eyes locked onto her. She was dreading this lesson as soon as she left for work that morning. How could she talk to his classmates as if nothing had happened? It got worse.

As soon as the class started one of the boys put his hand up to speak.

'Yes, Andrew,' Wendy said.

'I wonder if you had heard anything about Danny, Miss?'

Wendy went to speak but nearly choked. There was something the size of a golf ball stuck in her throat. She felt herself flush. The boy waited, looking puzzled. He turned his head to the boy sitting next to him wondering if he had said something wrong.

The teacher took a deep breath.

'No, I haven't,' she said, curtly. Her short reply was a mask to cover the guilt that was running through her veins. Realising that her rude reaction sounded like she didn't care about Danny, she added, 'The police are doing everything they can to find him. Now get on with the test I have put on your desks.'

As soon as she had mentioned, 'The police are doing everything to find him,' a voice screamed inside her head. She realised that she had to get his body out of the shed. She had to dispose of him but doing so elsewhere would be filled with difficulties and potential dangers. The human package would be too heavy and awkward to get it in the boot of her car without anyone seeing or hearing her. There was only one place she could dispose of this gruesome parcel.

She had to bury him in her garden.

Tonight.

00000

On the journey home, Sam was feeling a little better about the Roth/Cliffordgate situation. James had come up trumps for him. Thank God. Goodness knows what he said to make the headmaster change his mind. He hoped that this outrageous allegation would get sorted before it became common knowledge. Freya seemed to be over her dental problems for the time being. It was time to tell Lucy.

While Sam was recounting the story to his wife, she sat there open-mouthed.

'What! Why would that teacher do that to you? How can some people be so evil? And the boy? Surely no one is going to believe this ridiculous accusation,' said Lucy.

This was the most animated Sam had ever seen his wife. Her voice, normally calm and measured was twice as loud and had climbed up an octave.

'I'm so… *urgh,*' She threw her head up. Her small fists tightening in her lap. 'What are you going to do about it?'

'Well, as I said, James having already helped me, seems to have a plan to force a knife between Roth and

Clifford. He hasn't told me what yet. Thing is, I can't do much myself apart from deny the whole thing. Which is what I've done.'

Sam knew that he could do no more to allay Lucy's worry. He hoped that James could produce another bit of Shilling magic to make this go away for good.

Lucy's anger then overflowed into tears. 'It's so unfair Sam,' she sobbed. Sam held her close in his arms, looked up and said a short, quiet prayer.

00000

Jo Major's boss, Detective Superintendent Jack Jolley was listening to her account of the missing child investigation. Seeing that they had both only been at Wandsworth Nick for a short time Jack was aware of making an impression. More so, he didn't want any glaring mistakes made under his watch. For this reason, he wanted to be kept up to date with all the station's serious cases. A missing child was certainly high on that list.

As in their previous station in Ashford, Jo didn't need much of an excuse to visit Jack's office. Unlike the basic surroundings in her work zone, her boss's room was carpeted in deep royal blue with matching curtains. Pictures of mirrored lakes bordered by mountains and ranks of Noble fir hung from the cream walls. They overlooked a solid oak desk on which sat a silver-framed photograph of his wife and two children. A filter coffee machine sat on a mahogany cupboard in the corner.

It wasn't just the temporary step-up in comfort that Jo looked forward to. It was the quasi-father-daughter relationship that existed between them. The fact that he had continued to guide and encourage her career after her father had died so many years before, gave her a degree of comfort. In a hard-nosed and fundamentally male-driven occupation, Jo was glad of the occasional arm around the shoulder.

Jack was studying Jo's report as she sat the other side of his substantial desk. Her chair, smaller than that of her boss, plus her five-feet-seven inches meant her head and shoulders were all that were visible to Jack. She watched him as he pushed back his pure white hair with his fingers and settle into his chair. He had retained his good looks for a man in his late fifties. His steel blue eyes occasionally expanded as he took in some of the facts before him.

'What did you get from the parents?' Jack said, looking up from the report.

'The parents of the missing boy? Well, I didn't sense there was anything untoward in their body language or their answers to my questions. They live in a very nice house beautifully kept. The father, Enzo, owns a bistro and works all hours in the place, apparently. Karen, his mother just looks after the home and her son as far as I know. I didn't go into what she did outside of that. DC Chand has talked to a few of their neighbours. But nothing helpful came out of it. No overheard rows, no aggro. No one has a bad word to say about them, Guv,' said Jo.

Jack went to speak but Jo interrupted him.

'Oh, there is one thing that could be of importance. I've put it at the end of the report so as to highlight it,' she said, pointing to the last page still sitting on his desk. 'His mum, over the last number of weeks, said he didn't always come home straight from school. Not until five or six o'clock in the evening. And on some of those occasions, she said she thought she could smell alcohol on his breath,' said Jo.

Jack dipped his head and stared at his detective over the top of his glasses. 'I think that could be of *great* importance, especially leading up to his disappearance,' said Jack, nodding. 'That's good work, Jo. Good work.'

Ever since she had been under his guidance, she had been trying to impress him with her work ethic and professionalism. Her face turned a deep crimson. She was suddenly embarrassed by this man's compliment. It was the alcohol that had rung alarm bells as soon as Mrs Antonelli had told her. And her boss had thought the same.

'I'll be following up on that. Maybe some of his mates can help us there?' said Jo.

'How about his phone?' asked Jack,' going back to the report.

'Got the number yesterday from his parents. The team just in the last hour got back to me on that. Unfortunately, they told me that the phone has been turned off. The last activity on it was a received text. Through cell site analysis, we've got the location of the text. But as the phone is not live, we can't get pinpoint accuracy. But it's within a two-hundred metre radius in a residential area just over half-a-mile from the school. But that doesn't mean it's still there. The boy could have received that text while he was en-route to somewhere else.'

Jack nodded. He sat back into his black leather chair. 'CCTV hasn't given us much.'

'No, Guv. He's seen leaving his school at just after three-thirty on his own, then disappears down some back alleys and we lose him. We're still trying to see if there are any more CCTV cameras in the area that we don't know about. You know, on private houses.'

'Okay. Have a sniff around the area where the last text was sent to his phone. Get uniform to knock on doors tomorrow. You've got a photo of the boy?'

'Yes, Guv.' Jo had already decided on that plan of action but there was no way she was not going to accompany DC Kyra Chand on the door-to-door exercise. This investigation had become top priority in her mind. If there was a clue out there, she wanted to be the one to find it. She wanted to show Jack her finger was firmly stuck on the pulse.

Chapter 26

Jeremy Roth laid his knife and fork neatly together on his plate. He dug into his pocket, pulled out a used cotton handkerchief and wiped his mouth. A glance at his watch told him it was six-fifteen p.m. He rose from the pine kitchen table and walked over to the rubbish bin set beneath the heavily stained Butler sink. He hit the foot pedal and scraped the remainder of his dinner into the near-full receptacle. The oily smell of mackerel still lingered in the room. His Siamese cat, Angel, had been treated to a fish of her own. The silver-grey feline finished licking her ceramic bowl turned and sat. The cat's piercing, cyan blue eyes focused on his master. Roth, for once, was not doting on his precious pet. His attention was on another subject. Sam Whitmore.

So far, his plan had not provided the desired outcome. It was Tuesday evening and he was expecting the young English teacher to be suspended by now. He had heard nothing of the sort. His absence would have enabled him, at least temporarily, to take back the running of the football team.

When he first saw the police officer enter the school Monday morning, he thought it was to do with the Clifford accusation. He was excited. When it filtered through that her visit concerned a missing boy, Antonelli, his only emotion was one of frustration. The disappearance of Antonelli would have no effect on him. He wasn't part of his football team. Whether he was found or not he would still re-instate Tommy Clifford as his star striker.

He entered the sitting room. Angel followed. He scooped up a pack of cigarettes and cheap plastic lighter from a sixties teak sideboard that matched the rest of the dated furniture in the room. He sunk down into his shabby, winged armchair. Angel jumped effortlessly up onto his lap and settled. Roth lit his cigarette and began stroking the cat. 'We could have done without the issue of the missing boy, Angel,' he said to the purring animal. 'That was bad luck. Bad timing. Our clever idea has been diminished somewhat. But it's only been put on hold. I'm sure it will work, though. Abusing a child? He's got to go. We've just got to be a little more patient, my precious.'

00000

Thirty-one minutes past eleven p.m., her mobile informed her. She scrolled to the weather forecast for her region. Rain. Cold, heavy rain.

The one thing she prayed for earlier was a dry, cloud-covered still night. It had been a sunny clear-sky day. But the heavens had opened their reserves early evening and had not stopped throwing down its displeasure upon Wendy's plan.

Throughout her life, she had never been convinced that there was a God. A heaven. A reckoning. Tonight, her nihilistic beliefs were faltering badly. She interpreted the sudden change in the weather conditions as yet another punishment. It was a dire warning.

Despite the ominous signs, she persuaded herself that it had to be done. An obdurate sense of survival had forced her nervous doubts to take on this task from the moment she had arrived home from school. There was no turning back. A spot at the rear left-hand-side of the shed afforded the best degree of privacy, she had decided.

Six feet from the wooden shed wall was a large ash tree that stood against the neighbour's fence. The gap there would be the burial site. Next to the tree also on the neighbour's boundary was a seven-by-six-foot camelia shrub. Its position was not perfect, but it was the only location where her neighbours on both sides could not see what she was doing. That was unless they came down to the end of the garden. There, they could peer through the gap between the shrub and the tree.

She threw a cagoule over jeans and two jumpers, slipped on her trainers and headed for the shed. It was now or never.

Chapter 27

With the hood of her cagoule pulled up Wendy reached the shed door, opened it, hit the light switch and stepped inside. 'Oh my God!' she said, covering her nose and mouth with her hand.

The rank odour was even stronger this time knocking her head backwards. Having opened the duvet cover earlier to find his phone, the rotting flesh had been given an airing and clung to the shed walls. It was as though the insides had been sprayed thick with the smell of death. She took a breath, pinched her nostrils together, walked forwards and retrieved a shovel propped up in the corner.

She exited the shed, breathed out, coughed and inhaled the rain-washed freshness of the night. She left the shed light on deliberately. The small window in the left side wall of the outbuilding should afford her enough light to work with. She hoped it would not be too bright to attract prying eyes. If her luck was in, those eyes should all be shut tight in a deep undisturbed sleep.

Wendy trod the short distance through the expanding puddles to where the grave was to be. If there was one advantage to the downpour, she thought, it was that it would make the soil softer and therefore easier to dig. She put her spade to the ground, lifted her foot and pushed her heel downwards. She was pleased with how easily the blade cut through the earth. This may be easier than she thought.

After forty-minutes of digging, she had to stop for a break. The legs of her jeans from the knee downwards were soaked. Her trainers too. But now they were almost twice the size, covered in wet sticky mud. Her back, arms and shoulders were aching. Despite wearing garden gloves the injured hand from this morning was now beginning to throb.

She lay the spade down and stretched her torso backwards, using her arms above her head to extend the stretch. She looked up to the heavens to let the rain beat down on her face. Maybe she was hoping it would cleanse her soul.

She peered down to see the extent of her progress. The dim reflected light from the shed window was not strong enough to see anything clearly. Wendy pulled out a pocket torch from her cagoule. She shone it over the makeshift grave.

She had managed to clear earth across the whole template of the grave. She approximated the dimensions needed to bury the body to be six feet long by two feet wide, two and a half feet deep. She knew it was very shallow but the effort needed to make it any deeper would, she thought, be beyond her physical ability. The beam of her torch lit up the amount of wet earth she had excavated so far. She had piled it up at the base of the ash tree. But it also told her the entire hole was only six inches deep.

'Oh my God! I'm nowhere near yet,' she whispered.

She'd had no experience of digging holes or using the spade other than to plant small shrubs in her garden. It was a skill she badly needed right now. She was already breathing heavily as she inhaled the damp night air.

The constant and repetitive removal of full shovel-loads of heavy earth called upon a set of muscles that she had never used. Initially, she thought the rain would help her task. It did. What she didn't factor in was that the earth, now wet mud, was twice as heavy to lift.

Her first instinct, as she was waiting to get a second wind, was to shelter from the unrelenting downpour. Stay outside or wait in the shed with a stinking corpse? She chose standing beneath the large ash getting colder and wetter.

The teacher spent the next few minutes trying to galvanise reserves of strength she was not sure she possessed. She picked up the spade from the rich, newly-laid grass and commenced the digging. Despite wearing the hood, each time she bent forwards her long, drenched locks slapped across her face like strands of twine. Though weary, she found a rhythm this time and a more economical way of using the spade.

She was allowing the implement to do more of the work utilising the leverage of the long handle. The pile of cloying mud was now expanding much quicker as the hole got significantly deeper. It had to be over a foot deep now, she guessed. Her waning strength was bolstered by her advancing progress.

That was until she hit a large root of the ash tree. Much to her surprise and pain, the blade stopped dead against the tough stem. The sudden impact wrenched and jolted her wrist on the slippery handle. An electric shock shot up the length of her arm. The tool fell from her grip landing in the mud.

'Ow! she cried, as silently as she could manage. She glanced around at the neighbouring houses. They were all still in darkness. She didn't want to cry out – didn't want to make any sound at all. She took a step back shaking and rubbing her wrist. The task, so far, had lasted nearly an hour. She was in pain from her hand and wrist and her lower back was aching. She needed another break. This time it was going to be in the warmth of her house.

Removing mud-caked, soaking wet trainers, that now looked like workman's boots, she plodded into the kitchen. She made a cup of tea and retrieved the biscuit tin. However much she tried she could not release the lid. She wrapped her hands around the teacup, attempting to thaw out her frozen battered fingers as she sipped the hot beverage.

With the warmth coursing through her fingertips, she finally managed to prise the lid off. The hot tea was doing its job inside and out. Along with the following sugar rush she received from the biscuits she began to feel a little more human again.

But the grave was only half finished. Her body was beginning to relax. Worse, it was closing down, she thought. Either way she had to get up, keep moving and finish the job. She calculated that the depth of two feet six inches would be enough to cover the body and a good bit more. It would be a shallow grave but it was all she could manage.

She allowed herself only a ten-minute break to recover. The first thing she did when she reached the shed was to retrieve the pair of loppers to cut out the tree root. She prayed that it would be the only one she was going to come across. Despite the pain in her hand, she managed to remove the stubborn root after a few attempts.

She now got back to the dig. Another hour-and-a-half of physical torture saw the depth finally completed. She had pushed herself further than she thought possible. She straightened up, took off her glove and pulled back the grubby sleeve of her cagoule. Her watch read one-fifty-five. She traipsed back to the house for another rest and more refreshments. It didn't start to get light until around seven a.m. She still had plenty of time to bury the body.

Chapter 28

The muddy trainers stayed on. She was too tired and sore to bend down and take them off this time. The muck clean-up would have to wait till tomorrow This time it was a strong coffee and two chocolate bars that came to her rescue. She slumped back in the kitchen chair. Never before had she felt so utterly burnt out. So empty. So achingly sore.

She sat staring at the calendar on the wall above the work surface. November's picture was of a young father and mother swinging their child between them, wearing carefree smiles. They were strolling in sun-sparkled woods on a carpet of golden autumn leaves.

She loved that picture. She hated that picture.

It was everything she did not have. When her father had suddenly walked out on her mother, three days before her thirteenth birthday, she was devastated. In her mind, the father that she adored had deserted *her*. Her mother, bitter and vindictive had turned to drink. Two months later her eighteen-year-old sister moved in with her boyfriend.

Wendy's secure family life, all at once, had ground to a halt. She never saw it coming. On her seventeenth birthday she finally escaped her wine-soaked mother – sharing a flat with another girl. Her sister, now happily married with three kids, existed in a different world from her. They had nothing in common and rarely contacted each other. She had not spoken to her mother since she moved out twenty years ago. She could be dead. She didn't care.

Wendy leant forwards folded her arms on the table and laid one side of her head on them. She tried to see her life from a neutral's perspective. Her brain had now moved outside of her head, trying to analyse her complex personality. She realised that her life's pilot was not sadness. It was anger that grew from resentment.

At school, she was an excellent student, often top of her class. But she struggled to make friends. Her academic success and insularity had not been popular with her classmates. She had no interest in sport, so camaraderie was alien to her. Classical music and reading were her two loves. Chic lit authors her heroes.

University was not much different. Most of the other girls in uni had active sex lives. In her eyes, it was always other people who were strange – who were wrong. Sadly, the boys she fancied did not fancy her. Her first and only real boyfriend arrived shortly after her twenty-second birthday. She ended up marrying him three years later.

Just then the shrill ring of the doorbell sounded, jolting her out of her session of self-assessment. She instantly went into panic mode.

'Oh! My God. She looked at her watch again. Two fifteen. Someone must have seen me. But what did they see? 'Shit! What do I do now?' she said.

The bell rang again.

'I have to answer it. They may call the police! Maybe it is the police?'

She went to the door and opened it slowly. Waiting in the darkness was her scruffy next-door neighbour again. He stood in an oversized, orange towelling dressing gown this time.

'Is everything okay? I couldn't sleep so I popped downstairs for a glass of water and saw a torchlight in your garden. I thought it might be a burglar. Then when I saw a light in your house was on, I thought I'd better check it out,' he said.

As she surveyed the individual the supressed anger in her began to rise. *Why can't people just mind their own bloody business?* she thought. She stepped two paces forward. The stress and frustration of her plight exploded in his face.

'Fuck off. Why don't you just fuck off and mind your own fucking business,' she said in his face.

The neighbour's jaw dropped open. He took a step backwards. His astonishment quickly turned to indignation.

'I'm not taking those disgusting words from you. You're a disgrace to decency. I don't know what's going on in here but I'm going to call the police.' He turned away and walked back up the brick path.

Her demeanour changed immediately. 'Please don't call the police. Please, please. I'm sorry,' she begged.' She waved her arm in an effort to call him back.

Suddenly there was a loud crash.

Her arm had stretched out knocking the half-full cup of cold coffee off the table, smashing on the tiled kitchen floor. She blinked her eyes open, her head still resting on one arm on the table.

'Another nightmare. Oh, please, no. This is never going to end,' she said.

Still drowsy, she looked at her watch. Her eyes opened wide. It read eight minutes past six. She'd been asleep for four hours.

'Oh, shit! It starts to get light in less than one hour. I haven't even buried him yet.' She sprung up from the table that was now covered in streaks of dried mud. She ignored the broken pieces of her ceramic coffee cup.

An electrically charged dose of adrenalin allowed her to ignore the aches and strains her across her entire body. As she hurried down the garden she looked towards the shed. Jesus!' She stopped dead as if she had walked into a glass door. Wendy's entire body remained static in the middle of the lawn. She screwed her eyes tight to focus through the freezing rain.

'What the hell…' she said.

In the gloom, she could see two black unforgiving eyes standing over the freshly dug grave.

The eyes caught sight of her, stared for a few seconds then disappeared through a hole in the rear fence.

'A fox,' she mouthed.

She exhaled loudly, her breath visible in the chilly air. She was scared of foxes. One had entered her house through the open patio doors several years ago. She had discovered it mid-afternoon pinching biscuits from a plate she had left on a stool in the sitting room. The initial confrontation was scary enough, but it frightened the life out of her when it didn't run off immediately.

It looked to her as if those cold eyes were weighing up its chances against her. When she clapped her hands to scare it off it simply turned, walked back into the garden and disappeared.

Shaken, Wendy continued on to the shed. She wondered what other ominous messages were going to arrive before the night was through. She pulled the door open and stepped straight in. Bending down, she took hold of the feet end of the wrapped corpse and lifted. She slowly dragged the heavy bundle out and around to the side of the shed. Calling upon reserves of her fading strength she positioned the parcel next to the hole.

The smell once again was sickening. She had planned to wear a perfumed scarf tied around her nose and mouth this time but she hadn't expected to fall asleep. In her haste, the scarf had been forgotten. Now, kneeling down in the wet mud, she put her hands against the duvet-covered corpse and with a huge push rolled Danny's body into the grave.

Another look at her watch. Six twenty. She hoped that none of her neighbours rose early to go to work. Already she could see a thin band of light beginning to emerge at the far eastern edge of the sky.

This part of the job was a lot easier but it still took another thirty minutes to shovel the pile of cloying mud back into the hole. But the displacement of the body now meant that there was a large surfeit of soil. The top of the grave was rounded, sitting proud of its surroundings. Wendy could see that it was obvious to the naked eye that something had been buried beneath the mound.

She fetched a rake from the shed that still stunk of death and spent the next ten minutes trying to level the earth around the burial site. Her plan was to plant shrubs over the site, as soon as, creating another flowerbed. Shrubs and flowers that would eventually be feeding on the remains of Danny Antonelli.

Satisfied that the grave was less evident she replaced the rake. As she closed the shed door an upstairs light sprang on in the scruffy neighbour's house. She put her head down and rushed back up the garden and back through the patio doors.

Standing under a hot shower she felt a weight had been lifted off her shoulders. An arrogant sense of survival was now starting to replace the guilt. She had proved she was strong. Strong enough to bury her young lover. Strong enough to carry on in her career. Her reputation would be intact. A small voice in her head whispered, *Freedom is mine.*

Chapter 29

Jo arrived early at the station on Wednesday morning. It was going to be a busy day. She was looking forward to questioning the residents around the area of Danny's last text message. In her experience of knocking on doors there were three main responses from residents. The cagey ones, the gossipers, and the mice.

The defensive lot didn't care about other peoples' troubles. Often, they would be hiding some small misdemeanour or would have had a run-in with the *old bill* in the past. They would want to get rid of you as soon as possible. They did not do police.

The gossipers could not wait to tell you all the low-down of the local community; the names, the addresses, the habits of the neighbours they did not like. They would then want to offer advice on how the police would do a better job if they had bobbies on the beat, riding bicycles up and down the towns and villages. The mice were timid, scared even, acting like they'd never seen a police officer before. But it was often the things that people didn't say that spoke the loudest. The casual asides could prove to be little nuggets of gold.

When Jo arrived at the office, she took off her coat, hung it on the wooden stand in the corner and went to make herself a coffee in the small kitchen. She was deep in thought.

'Guv.' The sudden voice behind her made her jump.

Jo turned to see DC Kyra Chand. 'Jesus! Kyra. Don't creep up on me like that.' She put her hand to her beating heart. 'At least whistle to let me know you're approaching.'

'Sorry, Guv. Not sure I can whistle? Anyway, thought you'd want to know this as soon as you got in,' said Kyra, holding a notepad in her hand.

'Go on,' said Jo, dumping two spoonfuls of coffee into her mug that bore the word *Filth* in dark blue letters on the side. When she saw the mug in a shop window last year it made her smile. She had to have it.

'We had a phone call last night. It was left on the answerphone. I don't know if the caller was a man or a woman.'

Jo lowered her brows, her eyes in a squint.

Kyra tried to explain. 'It was a sort of a, too low a pitch to be a woman but too high to be a man. And a bit squeaky. The person wanted the information they gave us to go to you. So, I have written down the call almost word for word in my notebook.'

'Do you think you'd like to impart that information to me anytime soon,' said Jo.

'Oh sorry.' She opened the front cover. 'They said that a teacher, *erm...*' She scanned her notes. 'a Mister Sam Whitmore, at the Web school, had sexually assaulted a boy in his class a couple of days ago. But the headmaster had not suspended the teacher and was keeping it quiet.

179

They think that may have something to do with the other boy's disappearance and they suggest we interview him on that matter.'

'Do they now? And who is this informant? Don't tell me. They didn't want to leave their name.'

'How did you know?' asked Kyra.

'How long have you been a DC?' Jo said. Before she could answer Jo held up her hand 'Doesn't matter. Well done for copying the call and bringing this to me so quickly,' she said to the young detective.

Kyra's face lit up. She didn't get too many compliments from the DS. Now she was flying. 'What do you think, Guv. Should we interview him?'

Jo picked up her coffee, grabbed two chocolate digestive biscuits from an opened packet and leant forwards towards the DC.

'That's exactly what we're gonna do… but not until I've sat down and had my ruddy coffee.'

Whilst at her desk she was thinking about Sam Whitmore. She had already interviewed him. He was the handsome football coach. What else was he?

00000

Jo was not happy with this latest piece of information, but it did not come as a huge surprise. During their first interview, she had witnessed that the headmaster seemed nervous. She had expected him to be surprised or worried that a boy from his school had disappeared. But he wasn't comfortable with her presence. Now she knew the reason why.

This time she decided to turn up at the school at nine a.m. on the dot, without letting him know she was coming. She parked her car in the school car park and entered with DC Chand through the rear door. The knock on the headmaster's door received a 'come in.'

The headmaster's face reflected his surprised reaction. Jo was pleased that he was caught unaware to see her so soon and without an appointment.

'Detective. My secretary didn't tell me you phoned to say you were coming,' said the headmaster.

'I didn't. And *you* didn't tell me that one of your teachers recently, as recently as Friday in fact, the very day that Danny Antonelli went missing, has been accused of sexual impropriety with a boy in this school. I think that would've been worth mentioning in the light of Danny's disappearance. Wouldn't you?'

Peter Greaves' mouth dropped. He was speechless for a few moments. How the hell did she find out about Sam? He had to respond with a credible reason.

'I didn't tell you for two reasons. Firstly, I don't think there's any chance that Sam is guilty of this charge. And secondly, because of my absolute faith in my teacher, I thought that telling you would simply confuse the issue with the missing boy.'

'I think that should have been a decision for me to make. Not you. I need to talk to Mr Whitmore. And I want to see him in a separate room,' said Jo.

'Of course. I'll get my secretary to fetch him.'

Sam sat in the empty classroom opposite the two detectives. He had just finished telling Jo the full story of the Tommy Clifford accusation. It appeared to him that the detective was fairly happy with his side of the story. The next line of questioning took him by surprise.

'What time did you leave school on Friday afternoon?' Jo asked.

'Erm, around five thirty. I drove straight home. Arrived just after six. My wife Lucy can confirm that.'

Did you see Danny Antonelli at all before you left school or any time that afternoon?'

'No. I didn't take his class on Friday.'

'You're his football coach as well. Why did you suddenly put him in the team?'

Sam didn't like the way this was going. Now I'm a suspect for Danny's disappearance, he thought.

'I've already said that the boy, Clifford, was not playing as a team member but merely for himself. Danny looked useful in training and I thought his size would be an asset. As it proved.'

After a few more questions Jo closed her notebook. 'Okay. That's all for now. As far as the other thing is concerned with Tommy Clifford, that is a matter for your headmaster. Whether he wants to take the matter further or not and involve the police is up to him.'

Sam's shoulders relaxed a touch on hearing the officer's last statement.

Jo was satisfied for now with the teacher's answers, but she didn't like coincidences. For both incidents to occur within the same week at the same school was bizarre. A correlation between the two events may not exist. But she was not ready to strike Mr Sam Whitmore off her list of suspects just yet.

Next on her list was door knocking.

Chapter 30

Shortly after the detective left his office, Peter knew he had to act fast. He hit the button on his wireless intercom to his secretary asking her to summon James Shilling. Twenty minutes went by before James arrived.

Peter stood up from his desk 'I have to tell you this before you hear it elsewhere,' he said.

James stood opposite him. He placed his hands on his hips. 'You're giving me a rise and putting me down to three-days-a-week.'

'That detective was just in here again and wanted to know why I didn't tell her about Tommy Clifford's accusation. Saying it was important information, especially in light of Danny's disappearance. I just wanted you to know that it wasn't me who spilled the beans. Anyway, she was not happy.'

'Oh, bugger it! How has she found out about Sam?' said James.

'Exactly. Anyway, she interviewed Sam straight after she left here. Sam then dropped in here immediately afterwards. He told me she said the Clifford thing remains under my jurisdiction until I say otherwise. So, the police are not going to take that aspect any further. But he thinks he may still be in the frame somehow for Danny going AWOL.'

James moved forwards and sat down at his boss's desk. Peter followed his lead.

'That *is* good news. So we can keep the Clifford thing under wraps for now. I'm sure it won't take the police very long to realise he had nothing to do with Danny's disappearance.'

He cupped his chin with both thumbs and started tapping his lips with his forefingers. He looked up at Peter and threw his arms open wide, palms upward, as if he was carrying an imaginary roll of carpet.

'It's Roth. It has to be. There's no other way our detective could've found out about the Sam/Clifford debacle. It's bloody Roth again. He must have phoned the police station. He's told them. I bet it was anonymous. He's a gutless piece of…' James threw his head up. 'That poisonous excuse for a teacher is trying anything to get Sam out of this school.'

'Unless it was another teacher here at Blackies? I know there are one or two that have got a lot of sympathy for Roth, having lost control of the football team. I wouldn't put it past him to have told his few supporters.'

'That's a fair point, Peter. Do-gooders! The joke is they rarely do any good, these people. They are just waiting to set themselves up against informed majority opinions – they just get in the way; muddy the water,' said James.

'Well, whoever it was, Sam has certainly got my full support now. Roth or one of his cronies is beneath contempt for doing such a thing,' said Peter.

On the drive to school that morning Wendy's mood had changed. Her arrogant feelings of being safe, now that Danny had been buried, were beginning to disintegrate. She was worried about how the investigation was going. It was that damn mobile. If the police had been able to locate Danny's phone, then their attention would be drawn to her location. Her stomach tightened as once more she felt sick.

When she reached her destination, she turned off the ignition and sat in the car park. Maybe there was a way of deflecting any possible unwanted attention towards her by directing those suspicious eyes onto someone else.

The lack of not being socially active and too pally with her colleagues had enabled her to see from a distance their differing personalities – their strengths and weaknesses. It was something she had always done – it served as both a defence mechanism and a way of giving herself a feeling of superiority over them.

She had heard of Tommy's accusation against Sam from another teacher. Roth had told the teacher that Tommy had approached him first to tell him about the molestation and that he had told Tommy to report it direct to the headmaster. Roth must have known that those whispers would filter through to the other staff. And it was common knowledge that he resented Sam for stealing his position of football coach.

Wendy was pretty confident that Sam was harmless. She also knew that James was a friend of Sam and had spoken of his support and determination to help the young teacher. Since James had split from his wife, she thought he was becoming a bit of an amateur sleuth, righting wrongs wherever he could. She also knew that he didn't like Roth.

A plan was forming in her head.

As soon as the bell for mid-morning break went, Wendy headed for the staffroom. She saw James making himself a coffee and went to join him.

'Hello James,' she said, spooning coffee into a cup.

James' eyebrows raised at Wendy's approach. This was a first. She wasn't the most sociable teacher in the school. 'Hi Wendy?'

'I want you to know that you have my support as far as this ridiculous thing with Sam goes. I don't think for a moment that he would do a thing like that,' she said.

'Thanks. He's going to need all the help he can get.'

'I find it quite ironic that the boy went to Roth to complain and that he told the boy to go to the headmaster.'

James turned to Wendy, opened his mouth to say something and thought better of it.

'The thing is, I've always suspected Roth was the one who has been inappropriate around some of the boys. There's been rumours, you know there has.'

'I think...'

Wendy interrupted. 'I wouldn't be surprised if he had a reputation... if something like that had gone on at his previous school?' she said, as she ambled off with her coffee.

James watched Wendy pull out a chair and sit down at the table. He didn't know that Roth had put out the story of Clifford approaching him first. *'The brass cheek of the man. His scheming, evil mind knows no boundaries,'* thought James, with a shake of his head. *'So, that's how the other teachers know of the accusation.'*

He'd had the same suspicions about Roth. But now Wendy had put an idea in his head. His heartbeat broke into a jog. He put his drink down on the melamine counter, left the staffroom and marched off to the headmaster's office.

He knocked on the door and didn't wait for an answer. 'I've got an idea,' he said, to a startled Peter. 'We need to turn the detective's spotlight away from Sam and onto Roth,' said James.

'How will that help? There's no proof that he and Clifford have set this up. And he's not going to be involved in the boy's disappearance, surely,' said the head.

'Maybe not but put that collusion with the boy alongside what I think they may find if they investigate him and it may just put an end to Sam's problems.'

Peter looked confused.

'Have you still got Roth's CV on file? Oh, and his references from his previous employer?' said James.

'It should be on record. My secretary would be able to find it for me.'

'Good. I need to do some digging. And, if you've got the staff to cover for me, I need you to give me the rest of the day off. On full pay, of course,' he said, with his customary Shilling wink.

Peter waited for him to continue, his eyes wide open. James just tapped his nose.

In the school car park, Jo climbed into her car. Kyra waited patiently outside. Jo had to lean across and open the passenger door by hand from within. The key fob opened all the other doors apart from that one. She meant to report it last week when it stopped working.

Kyra swung the door open and slid in.

'Must get that seen to,' Jo said.

'This is a nice car. Apart from the door, obviously,' said Kyra.

'Blimey! You're easily impressed. Mind you, you haven't got your own wheels yet, have you.'

Jo unfolded a map of the location. She began to study the area inside the circle, drawn earlier at the station. It represented the approximate two-hundred-metre radius of Danny's last phone text.

She put the map between them. 'A two-hundred metre radius doesn't sound much but as you can see, Kyra, it constitutes a load of door knockers. In fact, it's about two-hundred-and-forty houses distributed among six long streets,' said Jo.

'Wow!' said Kyra

'We can't possibly knock on every one, we'd be there all day. We'll pick and choose a certain amount per street. Okay?'

'Yes Guv.'

Both carrying a picture of Danny they began asking the same questions over and over again at every house –

when they were lucky enough to find anyone in, that is. The process didn't take long to become monotonous for the two police officers. Especially when none of the residents had provided them with anything worth writing down on their notepads.

Jo knew from past experience that this was one of the most boring and energy-sapping jobs that had to be done on cases such as these. Unless, of course, the valuable piece of information they were seeking was found on one of those doorsteps.

In just over two laborious hours they had managed to ring or knock on just over one hundred and twenty doors. They had nothing. It was now eleven-twenty and a cold wind had begun to bully its way through the tunnel-like Battersea streets. They were getting weary.

Jo looked at her map. 'One more to go. Rupert Street.'

'We'll get the *bear* minimum there,' said Kyra, eyes wide.

'That's all I need. The Chand book of bad jokes,' said Jo.

After they found Rupert Street and knocked on less than twenty doors Jo had had enough. She called a halt to the proceedings.

'Not a sodding carrot. I'm cold, tired and in desperate need of a nice cup of tea,' said Jo shivering, as they reached the car.

After they entered and fastened their seatbelts, Kyra turned to Jo. She looked puzzled.

'Why is it only with tea, that people say, "fancy a *nice* cup of tea". No one ever says, "fancy a *nice* cup of coffee", do they? They just say, "fancy a coffee". Why is that?' said Kyra, with a mixture of mirth and mystery on her face.

Jo turned towards her and studied the young detective. She went to speak, threw her eyes to the roof, shook her head, started the car and drove off.

Chapter 31

James sat in an empty classroom. He looked around him at the all too familiar landscape. The noticeboards filled with school activities and information leaflets that few ever took any real *notice* of: the geometrically spaced rows of desks. Desks, that when he began his teaching career, were made of oak. Their worn worktops, decades old, were scarred and etched into by many a bored and budding artist. But there was a sense of historic grandeur in them – sourced and carved by skilled carpenters from stout English oak trees.

Now they were made of chipboard with laminate tops bolted to skeletal metal legs. The magisterial slate blackboards and multi-coloured chalks now white boards with dry-erase markers. These so-called improvements or money saving exercises had changed the ambience and the smell of a classroom – the smell of a school in general. It was as though a vital part of the history of this revered eighteenth-century place of learning had been expunged. Plasticised.

He marvelled that he had spent thirty years in rooms such as these. Too long.

James picked up the two stapled sheets of A4 paper. There was only one thing that he wanted from Jeremy Roth's CV. His previous employment record. Apart from the fact that he was a bachelor – hardly a surprise – he found nothing untoward. But then he hadn't expected to. Neither had he discovered anything of interest in the job reference that Roth had submitted from the last school at which he taught. In his experience and from what he had heard, there was an unhealthy number of job references that were never checked out. Just taken on face value. A dangerous form of acceptance – of laziness.

But the information he was looking for was there on the printed page. The name of his two previous schools. He may only need one.

Roth had worked at Drake's Grammar in Putney six years ago. He hoped the school still had the same headmaster. Google told him that Joseph Buchanan had been the headmaster for the past nine years.

'Bingo,' he said.

He got the number and went straight on the phone. He saw that the headmaster's secretary was a Mrs Eileen Eddy. When she answered he was pleasantly surprised that he wasn't put through to a recorded message.

But he was not surprised with her response to his request to talk to her boss. 'I'm afraid Mr Buchanan is extremely busy. If you could leave your name and num…'

'Mrs Eddy, this could shed a light on the recent disappearance of the schoolboy, of whom you are surely aware. Which means it could be a matter of life or death. What time does he have his lunch break?' said James, with a stern voice he hardly recognised.

'Er, twelve thirty, if he's not too…'

'Book me in for an appointment at twelve-twenty-seven. I will take only three minutes of Mr Buchanan's busy time. Thank you for your understanding,' said James as he cut off the call.

He placed the phone in his jacket pocket.

'Secretaries. Honestly. Filtering, deflecting virtually everyone who wants to speak to their bosses. Drives me bloody mad. High-powered gatekeeper syndrome. Reflected importance. That's what it is' he ranted, as he stood to put his jacket on.

He then replayed in his head what he had just said to the secretary. He had used the urgency of Danny's disappearance to crowbar himself an interview. He listened again to his own words. They didn't sound so inconceivable. Maybe Roth did have something to do with the boy going missing?

00000

James was on a mission. If anyone or anything got in his way today, they were going to get the full Shilling treatment.

'There is no such thing now as rush hour. It's bloody rush day,' he said, looking at the nose-to-tail cars and lorries that were strangling the country's skinny roads. The traffic-laden car journey from Battersea through Wandsworth to Putney, a quarter-of-an-hours journey, took twenty-five minutes.

At twelve-twenty, he arrived at Drake's Grammar. At twelve twenty-five, he knocked on the secretary's door and entered.

'Mrs Eddy, I presume?' he asked the lady who sat upright at her desk. She was in her fifties, wore a pink cardigan over a mauve floral dress and possessed a look that could chill a bowl of hot soup in seconds. He smiled but still didn't detect any sign of welcome in the imperious face before him.

She looked over her glasses at James. 'You must be Mr Shilling,' she said, as though she was telling off a naughty boy.

'That's me. From head to toe.' James said, attempting another smile.

'The headmaster is waiting for you,' she said, deadpan. She got up and, strangely, didn't appear to get any taller. 'This way,' she said, as she escorted him to his office door.

Mr Buchanan was generously overweight and smartly dressed. He wore a deep blue corduroy jacket, maroon waistcoat and yellow bowtie.

Bloody hell! It's Alfred Hitchcock, James thought to himself, as he shook the headmaster's hand.

'Mr Buchanan. Pleased to meet you,' he began.

'Please, call me John. My secretary tells me you were very keen to see me. You teach at Sir Montague Web Grammar, I understand. Terrible news about your missing pupil. How can I be of help, Mr Shilling?' said the head.

'James, please. I'd like to ask you about one of your previous teachers. Jeremy Roth, who taught history at this school six years ago.'

'Mmm! Jeremy. A rather secretive individual. He ran the under 15's football team. Not too successfully if my memory serves me right. He certainly wasn't a good mixer with the other members of staff, I remember. I wasn't particularly sorry to see him leave, I have to say'

'I'd like to know if there was any misdemeanour or rumour connected to him during his time here?'

'He wasn't a bad teacher, I have to say that. But there was one thing that hung in the ether. An unsubstantiated rumour, I may add, of inappropriate behaviour with one of his boys in the team. It wasn't the boy involved that complained, actually. It was his friend.' He paused and looked away from James as if he was trying to remember details.

James leant forward. 'Please, go on,' he said.

John Buchanan returned his gaze. 'Yes… he said the boy involved told him that Mr Roth would pat then stroke his back on the pretence of praising his performance in the team. When no one was looking, occasionally the hand would go down to his bottom and his inner thigh, brushing his private parts. I immediately got the supposed victim to come into my office with my secretary, Mrs Eddy, in attendance. When I asked him about this, he said nothing had happened. Therefore, we could not take it any further.'

'What do *you* think happened?' said James.

'Personally? The boy in question was quite a timid soul. I think he was too scared. Too daunted to tell me what happened. It's a very serious and worrying thing for a fourteen-year-old boy to accuse a respected teacher of something like that. His parents, especially his father was a bit, *erm,* how can I put this… a rough and ready type. If he had come up here knowing that his son had been abused, God knows what he would have done to Jeremy Roth. I think the boy knew that.'

'That is very interesting. Well, I promised your secretary that I would not take up much of your time so that is me done. Thank you, John. You have been very helpful,' said James.

'May I ask the reason for your interest in Mr Roth?'

'I can't really disclose my reasons at the moment. Suffice to say history may have a habit of repeating itself.'

The headmaster's eyes narrowed as he nodded his head. James shook his hand again and departed.

Chapter 32

As soon as Jo arrived back at the station she was off again. She would have to finish writing her notes on the morning's investigations when she returned. Now she was going to visit the one man in her life that she could only talk face to face for two hours at a time. A brief kiss and embrace was also allowed. The convict, Nick Summers had left a message on her mobile saying he had some information that may help the investigation into the missing boy.

She left Wandsworth station at midday, telling Kyra she was following a lead in the case. It would take her a two-hour drive to get there. She could be back to the station before five if the traffic wasn't too bad.

Whilst in the car she went over all she had learnt this morning. The headmaster, when interviewed, had not revealed that a boy in Danny's class complained of sexual harassment by his teacher. That, on the very same day that Danny went missing had focused her attention on both Sam and the head.

It definitely confirmed her suspicion that there were closely guarded secrets within that school's ivy-covered walls. But having interviewed the ex-pro footballer on the incident she had to admit there appeared to be no obvious link to the missing boy.

At a busy T-junction, she slouched back into her seat, raised her arms high above her head and squeezed out a groan as she performed a long stretch throughout the length of her back. She began thinking of her DC who would be busying herself back at the station writing her notes.

She liked Kyra Chand. She was still a bit green and came out with a few strange and annoying things at times. It was most likely a sign of nerves or a possible attempt at humour which, of course, can be a sign of nerves. But she was honest, a good worker and willing to learn. The three best attributes in this game.

Kyra had told her that she had traditionalist Indian parents who had given her a strict upbringing. So, it couldn't have been easy for a girl with her background to decide to join the police force. There was still a degree of sexism and racism present in the job. She wondered if that would ever change.

Kyra had risen to her present position via the two-year Police Now National Detective Programme. Jo thought a girl from her background must have been subjected to at least a taste of both those prejudices along the way. As far as she could see, it appeared not to have affected her confidence or enthusiasm for the job.

She made a mental note to let Kyra know, at an appropriate moment, that she was impressed with her progress and respected her attitude towards her career. It was important to give that feedback to someone in her position. Jack Jolley had given her similar encouragement when she was climbing the business ladder. There would be a time when she needed her support. There always was in this job.

00000

As Jo approached the carrot-coloured brick walls of Standford Hill Open Prison, she was thankful that he had been transferred here from Wormley Prison. She was thinking of the articles she had read over the past few years. Wormley had a worrying reputation. Prisoner unrest and violence towards inmates and officers were rife within the walls of this detention facility.

In 2014, there was a spate of seven suicides. December of that year saw three men found dead in their cells in as many weeks. The Independent Monitoring Board stated the reason for these incidents was prisoner overcrowding and understaffing of officers. Three men sharing a two-man cell, less time being allowed out of their small rooms. A recipe for disaster.

If he had not been moved, Jo would have feared for Nick's survival. In this gentler environment, Nick seemed to be coping with the demands that his incarceration threw at him on a daily basis. There were still incidents of unrest but if he was being mistreated by his fellow inmates he was not allowing her to see it.

Jo studied him as he walked assuredly to where she was sitting. He moved well and appeared healthy and relaxed. She stood for her brief embrace and kiss. They both sat down at the cheaply made table which kept them eighty centimetres apart. After their same tongue-in-cheek greeting and some preliminary small talk, it was Nick that brought up the subject of the missing boy.

'So, how is the investigation going?' he said.

'Well, we've discovered that there was a teacher/child abuse accusation at the school on the same day as our boy went missing. I've interviewed the teacher and I don't think he's the type to do that sort of thing. Which probably why the headmaster kept that information from me. He was protecting him. I certainly don't believe that it's linked to the missing boy. I think it will turn out to be just a strange coincidence.

'How did you get to know about the abuse thing,' asked Nick.

'We were informed of it from an anonymous caller. I reckon it was from another teacher,' said Jo.

'Sounds like someone has got it in for that particular colleague. Has to be another teacher, surely. Who else would know about it? Unless the boy has told some of his mates and one of their parents has got something against the teacher. Anything else?' he said.

'We've found out through his mobile phone where the boy's last received text was. The phone, sadly, was turned off, so we've only got a two-hundred-metre radius to work on. And it's close to the school.'

'Okay,' said Nick. I've been digging for you and had a word with the guy in here whose mate still lives in Battersea near your school. No obvious candidates as far as child molesters or abductors that he knows of, I'm afraid. This may be of no help, but he told me that there's a woman who lives in a road around that location, been there for ages, who is on the local residents committee. She's in charge of the day-to-day running of the community; complaints or proposals from residents, neighbourhood watch. Things like that.'

Jo put her head to one side. 'And?'

'Well, in June this year, she organised street parties to celebrate the Queen's ninetieth birthday. Part of her job then was to knock on all the locals' doors to ask for a £5 donation towards the cost of the parties. So basically, she knows virtually everyone in that location. I don't know if it's in your two-hundred-metre radius, but it is roughly the same area I would guess.'

Jo raised her eyes above Nick's head, stared at nothing, then returned to his face. She smiled. 'My, you *have* been busy. I'm impressed.'

'Well, there's not much else to do in this place to get excited about. And when I asked the fella in here to get some information from his pal, he was just as keen as me to play the part of detective. Especially when it involved a missing child.'

Jo smiled at Nick's enthusiasm. 'Where exactly does this lady live?'

'I knew you were going to ask me that, so I wrote it down. Hang on.' Nick delved into the back pocket of his jeans and pulled out a slip of paper. He unfolded it. 'Clarence Street. He doesn't know the exact house number but he remembers roughly where her house was in the road. He estimates it to be between number nine and number seventeen. It's not as many houses as it appears,

202

he said, because one side of the street is odds and the other evens. It's a Mrs Ogilvy.'

Jo dipped into her handbag pulled out a pen and small pad and wrote down her details. 'Good work, Sherlock.' She wasn't expecting anything useful from this broad piece of information but didn't want to burst Nick's bubble. Especially when it gave him something positive to do – different from his boring daily routine. 'I'll look into it,' Jo said.

On the drive home, Jo's brain was tumble-drying the information that Nick had found out from his tough prison mate. There was a severe lack of leads to follow up on the investigation so far, and the more she thought about this committeewoman the more she realised that any inside knowledge of the area and its residents could be useful.

Her mind was made up. As soon as she got back to the station, her and Dc Kyra Chand were off to have a chat with Mrs Olgilvy.

Chapter 33

When Jo drove into Clarence Street, she realised that she and Kyra had knocked on a good deal of the doors here already. They parked up and moved over to the odd number side of the street.

'You take number nine. I'm on eleven and so on. Okay?' Jo said to her DC.

Jo struck lucky immediately to find someone in and was told that Mrs Ogilvy lived at number fifteen. They moved up to the house and knocked on the door. A robust woman of medium height answered. Jo thought she was around the mid-sixties mark.

After she introduced herself and Kyra, they were invited into the woman's sitting room that was small, cosy and predominately sky blue. The two officers were perched on a sofa with the homeowner opposite in an armchair 'Would you like a cup of tea,' asked Mrs Ogilvy.

Kyra's eyes lit up. 'That's very kind of you but no thanks' said Jo. Kyra looked at her boss then nodded her head in agreement. After a bit of small talk, Jo went straight in. 'A boy has gone missing from the local school, Sir Montague Web Grammar. We know he was around this area on the day he disappeared. I'm told you are on the local residents committee.'

'Oh, dear, that's awful news,' she said. 'Yes, I am the committee chairperson.'

'Excellent. I thought I might dip into your knowledge of the residents around here. It might be helpful to know, for instance, if any of them may have upset you, any strange behaviour, residents that possibly stand out for a certain reason?'

The lady thought for a few seconds. 'Not really. Nothing particular I can think of.'

'I understand you organised street parties in your area to celebrate the Queen's ninetieth birthday?'

Mrs Ogilvy's face lit up. 'Oh yes, that was a great success. We did the same for her eightieth.'

'And that you approached your residents for a voluntary donation of five pounds. Did they all donate or were there any unusual responses from anyone?

'Yes, it was to help fund the celebrations where we provided free food and drinks and bunting. We even had some fireworks this time. I was very pleased with the response for donations. Of the ones that answered the door, I think there were only six or seven that didn't want to donate and most of them were very old and probably couldn't afford it. Four were all in one street, actually. Rupert Street.'

'Anything about any of them that sticks in your mind?'

'In fact, one of them in Rupert Street is not old at all. She's a teacher. I think she teaches at the Web. I was a little disappointed that she did not donate but I was not really surprised.'

Jo, who was thinking this was going to be a complete waste of time, suddenly perked up 'Why not surprised?' she said.

'Well, most of the residents around here are quite pally. Apart from her, that is. She mainly keeps herself to herself. I don't like to talk about people behind their backs but a few of the locals she has spoken to say she's a bit... *er,* strange,' she said, shifting in her armchair.

Jo's attention tightened. 'What do you mean strange?'

'Apparently, she talks quite a bit about her husband who goes abroad on business trips. Thing is, no one has ever seen him, as far as I know. The rumour is that she's either never *had* a husband or he's gone off with another woman.'

'Do you know the name of this teacher?' asked Kyra before her boss had the chance.

'If I did, I'm afraid I can't remember her name. Our secretary will know,'

'That's okay we will be able to find that out,' said Jo.

After a few more pleasantries, the detectives thanked the lady and left.

On the drive home, Jo's brain was processing the information that the committee member had told her. Kyra spoke first.

'Why would a woman lie about having a husband? Surely, it would be too easy to disprove. But to pretend your husband is still around after he had run off with another woman. That would make more sense, surely?'

'I can think of two main reasons for the last bit you mentioned. Firstly, after her immediate feelings of distress, the rejection could have left a deep sense of humiliation. What woman wants to admit that her partner has shacked up with someone else? Secondly, despite her pride taking an absolute battering, she may still be hoping that he will eventually return to her. Then no one would have to know,' said Jo.'

The car went quiet. Rupert Street. The name rang a bell with Jo. She thought it may have been one of the streets at which her and Kyra had done door-to-door.

'Of course!' Jo said out loud in the car. 'Rupert Street the one that you cracked the silly joke about. Rupert the Bear.'

They had only knocked on about fourteen doors in that street. They had been cold, bored and tired by the time they reached that last one.

As they neared their place of work, Jo had one thought on her mind. First thing tomorrow morning, she was going to ring the headmaster to ask him a question. Which teacher lives in Rupert Street?

00000

James reached his car, which was parked in Drake's car park, feeling upbeat. He climbed in and delved into his pocket for his wallet and pulled out a business card. Jo had distributed them around some of the schoolteachers in the hope that one of them may have thought of something important to tell her. He rang the number.

'Hello, Wandsworth police station.'

'Hi, can I speak to Detective Sergeant Jo Major please?' said James.

'She is not here at the moment. Can I ask what this is about please?'

'This is James Shilling, teacher at Sir Montagu Web Grammar School. I have something that might interest her concerning the disappearance of Danny Antonelli.'

'She is due to be back in the office around four thirty, five o'clock.'

'Okay. Please tell her that I will be at the station at five. It's imperative that I talk to her tonight.'

00000

They sat on bendy plastic chairs either side of a tan, veneered table, the top not much bigger than a paving slab. Jo was the first to speak in the cramped interview room.

'May I call you James?' she said.

'I've been called a lot worse. James is good.'

So, you wouldn't give any information over the phone. What have you got that might interest me?'

'You are aware, I think, of the sexual accusation against Sam Whitmore?'

'Yes. I was informed of that. A little late, I may add.'

'And I'm guessing it was through an anonymous call?'

Jo did not answer. With raised eyebrows, she invited James to continue.

'Well, I know who that was and why.'

'Go on,' said Jo.

'Our history master, Jeremy Roth. He was the football coach for the under-sixteens until Sam Whitmore, an ex-professional player, arrived a few months ago. He took over the team. Roth was incandescent with rage and let everybody know it. Sam then dropped Tommy Clifford from the team which upset the boy. Clifford has a reputation in our school for being difficult and vindictive. He was also Roth's favourite player.'

'I know some of this already and I've told your headmaster that this is a case for him and the school until he tells us otherwise. Anyway, what has this got to do with the missing boy?' said Jo, looking at the clock above James' head. She was hoping to go home soon. It had been a long and exhausting day.

'I'm coming to that. Roth now hates Sam. He won't even speak to him. Roth realising he has an ally persuades the boy to accuse Sam of touching him inappropriately to get him kicked out the school.'

'How do you know that?' said Jo, with a stern face.

'Because I know Sam. He wouldn't do that. He's a popular teacher and an honest man. There's only two people in that school who hate Sam Whitmore. Roth and Clifford. The rest love him and trust him.'

'If what you say is true, how does that tie in with Danny Antonelli's disappearance?'

'I've had my doubts about Roth for some time now as far as being inappropriate with young boys himself. Words got around that when the boys are taking a shower after the game, he will think of any excuse to pop his head around the wall pretending to hurry them up or ask if the showers are hot enough. Things like that.'

Jo folded her arms. 'That could just be coincidence. Hearsay.'

'Rumours will always find a way of echoing down school corridors; entering classrooms; feeding staffroom gossip. Some disappear as soon as they appear. The ones that don't go away are nearly always true.'

Jo nodded. 'Okay?

'I visited Roth's headmaster at his previous school just this lunchtime. He told me that there was an accusation against Roth, similar to Sam's. It was brought up by the boy's best friend. But the boy in question was too scared to admit it because his father, a nasty piece of work, would have knocked the teacher's block off.'

Jo sat up in her chair. James had got her attention.

'And you think he may have something to do with the boy's disappearance?' she said.

'I don't know, is the honest answer. What you may not know is that Danny was the one who took Clifford's place in the team after Roth lost the coaching job. There's definitely a connection there. I think you may just find there's more than meets the eye with our history teacher.'

Jo breathed in and held it… 'So, what are you suggesting I do?' she said, as she exhaled.

'If I were you, I'd go round to his house tonight. Catch him off guard. Ask to interview him inside his home on some trumped-up reason.' James looked upwards, then back at the detective. 'I dunno, say you're interviewing some more of Web's teachers – just routine stuff. What's the downside?' said James, his face lighting up.

'Even if I agree to do that it would have to be tomorrow – when I can get his address from the headmaster,'

'I know where he lives. It's five minutes from here. He's been there all his life, I think. Lived with his parents until they died some years back. I had to go round there last term to pick up some exam papers when he was off sick. Well, he sprained an ankle, supposedly. I say supposedly 'cos he was back at work two days later without a limp.

'Anyway, he kept me waiting at the door while he fetched the papers. I don't know if he was hiding anything at the time, but he didn't want me inside his house,' said James, hoping that might help persuade her.

Chapter 34

Forty minutes later, Jo was walking along the road towards Jeremy Roth's house. It was seven p.m., a clear moonlit night with a cold breeze. The light from a streetlamp several houses away was not bright enough for Jo to make out all the door numbers. The strong beam from her mobile did the trick. She pushed open the low gate and proceed up the crumbling brick path towards the late Victorian semi.

Jo noticed the beds either side were overgrown with weeds and untended shrubs. *He certainly isn't a gardener,* she thought. She stopped at the front door, the bottle-green paint flaking off around the margins. She searched for a bell to press. The torchlight found one on the right side of the door frame, almost obscured by encroaching ivy that covered the walls.

Her gloved finger pressed the button and waited for a sound. Nothing. It probably hadn't worked for years, she thought. After a moment, she lifted the heavy iron knocker and banged it down twice.

'Blimey! If he doesn't hear that, he must be deaf. Or dead,' she whispered.

A curtain moved in the front window to the right. Jo saw it. Moments later, she heard a bolt being slid across the inside of the door. It opened six inches. She was expecting it to creak – as in old horror movies. It didn't.

'Jeremy Roth?' Jo asked, through the gap.

'Yes. Who is it?' came the voice.

Detective Sergeant Jo Major. I wonder if I can have a few words with you, please? Inside if possible. It's freezing out here.'

The door swung open. Roth stood there in baggy corduroy trousers, flannel shirt, cardigan and slippers. He was holding a Siamese cat.

Roth went to speak and instead swallowed, as if he had a stammer. Finally, his mouth started to work. 'What is this about?'

'It concerns the missing boy, Danny Antonelli. It is just a routine call,' she said.

Roth hesitated, then stood back to let Jo inside the poorly lit hallway.

'You'd better come through to the kitchen,' he said.

The foot-worn, heavily patterned hall carpet and floral wallpaper looked like they had been in situ for decades. The kitchen was no different. It was full of clutter. Mustard coloured Formica worktops were heavily stained, their edges flecked with random cigarette burns. Various jars and bottles covered the top. An opened pack of butter sat next to a half-cut loaf of bread surrounded by crumbs. Jo recoiled at the sight of the burnt-food-encrusted gas ring cooker. The surface clearly had never had the pleasure of soap and water for months, possibly years.

'Can we sit, Mr Roth,' asked Jo.

Roth pointed to a chair. She sat down in the kitchen that was not much warmer than the outside temperature. The smell of stale cigarette smoke was confirmed by the packet of twenty Marlboro laying on the drop leaf table. Roth sat opposite with his cat on his lap and a half-finished cup of tea in front of him. There was no offer of one for her, thank goodness.

'What's the cat's name?' she asked. She didn't like cats. She loved dogs.

'Angel,' replied Roth, holding the cat closer.

Jo smiled. She thought she'd just ask a few general questions. 'How long have you lived here?'

He hesitated. 'Since... from when I was a child.'

'You must have seen many changes in that time?'

Roth's eyebrows lowered. 'What do you mean?'

'Well, it was obviously your parents' house and now it's yours. Neighbours come and go, I suppose. Things like ...'

'I don't have much to do with the neighbours,' he said, shaking his head.

Not another one, thought Jo. She saw him visibly tighten when she mentioned his parents. He appeared very unsettled. She was finding it difficult to believe this man was a teacher. He found it impossible to maintain eye contact and had stuttered over his words more than once.

His face when she first arrived was flushed. Now, it was more the colour of alabaster as she probed around his relationships with his school colleagues. The detective's clever phrasing made it appear as though she was more interested in the other teachers than in him. But his clipped, dismissive, replies told her more about the man fidgeting around the other side of the table.

Halfway through their question-and-answer session Angel, possibly feeling his owner's unease, jumped down from his lap to the floor and wandered back down the corridor. Jo watched as the sleek animal pushed open a door with its nose and disappeared inside a room.

After a few more minutes, she terminated the interview. She was not unhappy to be leaving the disagreeable surroundings. A cold shiver crept over her shoulders as she stood away from the table. This physically unimpressive individual, all of a sudden, gave her a feeling of vulnerability.

'Well, thank you for your time, and sorry for any inconvenience caused,' she said to a pensive looking Roth. She did not offer her hand by way of thanks.

As she walked back down the corridor in front of the teacher, she peered inside the door that the cat had nosed wide open. It was obviously the sitting room, with two armchairs facing a small television. It was surprisingly tidy but what caught her eye were the two low shelves running along two walls of the room.

They were lined with teddy bears.

On the drive home, Jo tried to chronicle everything she had seen and heard that day. It had been an interesting one. First, there were questions surrounding the teacher that the committeewoman had told her about. Apart from being a bit secretive, she seemed to be lying about a phantom husband. She also lived in the area where the last text was sent to Danny's phone. Not sure about that one, she thought.

Then there was Roth. She didn't much like Roth. He had a supercilious nature that had engendered a feeling in her of anger and inferiority in equal measure. Both the house and the teacher had left her with an uncomfortable vibe.

'A room full of teddy bears! What's all that about? That's not normal for anyone, let alone a single bloke,' she said out loud in the car.

She thought for a moment. Then she laughed.

'Bugger me. I've got two leads. Rupert Street and teddy bears – you couldn't make it up,' she said, shaking her head.

She stopped at a red light and sat back in the driving seat. 'A teacher kidnapping a boy. No. I don't believe it,' she said, squinting through the windscreen as if she could see the answer through the glass. 'But I'm sure that creepy house is hiding some secrets.' The light went green. 'Rupert Street will have to wait,' she said moving off.

Tomorrow, Roth was the priority.

Chapter 35

Thursday Morning

Enzo Antonelli was in his sitting room talking with his cousin Luca. Luca Antonelli's background was very different from that of his cousin. Both their fathers had come to England around the same time. But the change of country for Luca's father was for a different reason. It was not the promise of new career opportunities for this arm of the family. It was to expand their organised crime syndicate.

Over the years, the Mafia had been moving into less obvious areas of crime. These constantly adapting groups were shifting towards less risky and less violent market niches. They were still lucrative but detection of organised crime in these areas was more difficult.

The largest organised illicit markets were now fraud, drug and migrant trafficking, counterfeiting and setting up illegitimate businesses to facilitate money laundering. They were responsible for eighty-per-cent of cocaine coming into Europe. The days of waking up with a horse's head on your pillow had probably gone. But there was always the silent promise of mental and physical intimidation and occasionally the disappearance of a dangerous obstacle that got in the way. And anyone within the family, active or not, was fiercely protected.

Luca sat in virtual silence as he listened to Enzo's heart-breaking story of the disappearance of his only son, Danny. He could see the effect it was having on his cousin. He looked like a little lost boy. Just then, Karen entered the room.

'Hello, Luca. I didn't hear you come in. Would you like a coffee?' she said.

Luca got up from the sofa. His first reaction was to embrace his cousin-in-law. It was the wrong thing to do. As soon as he hugged her in his arms, she broke down in tears.

'I don't know what to say to you Karen, that will ease your worries at this moment. Apart from one thing. I want to assure you that the family will do everything to help you find Danny. We have excellent and wide-ranging connections all across Britain. If there is any whisper, anywhere, from anyone, we will hear it and act on it,' said Luca.

Enzo looked up at them and broke down himself. Luca moved away from Karen. He looked deep into Enzo's tear-filled bloodshot eyes.

'I know the police are trying to help but this is just one investigation of many they have to deal with. To get Danny back is our priority. We look after our own. The message will go out across the country. You have my word,' said Luca.

The cousins stood together outside the front door of the immaculately furnished but emotionally empty Battersea house. Luca kissed Enzo on both cheeks, shook his hand and left with a whispered promise.

Chapter 36

The bedside digital clock read six forty-five. Fifteen minutes before Jo had to get up to get ready for work. She had been awake since six. Lying in her single bed, her mind had been switching back and forth between two subjects. Nick Summers and Danny Antonelli.

She couldn't pretend to imagine what Nick had gone through – was still going through. Her relationship with him, and how it evolved was not a normal one. Jo had never married, never found an honest, attractive man to make that wish come true. The person with those attributes was now serving a prison sentence, partly due to her.

As the weeks went by, she noticed how much he looked forward to seeing her. At first, she thought it was simply a need to have a regular visitor. One that knew what he had experienced at first hand. But as the months went by that need had grown into affection, exactly what she was hoping. The handshakes eventually went to holding hands. The polite cheek kisses progressed to meaningful ones on the lips.

Her worry was, would it still be there after his release? At the moment, she was the only young woman in his life. But that life was one of constraint. Like holiday romances, the communal surroundings were often the main reason for the temporary accord. Would Nick still feel the same when he was able to enjoy the taste of freedom once more?

Then there was Danny. The last text he received on his phone was in the area where she and DC Chand had carried out extensive door-to-door enquiries. Well, almost. The region where Jeremy Roth lived was just outside that zone, although the technology was not that accurate. But the other teacher, the one with or without a husband – she lived inside the zone.

Mrs Antonelli revealed that she could smell alcohol on her son's breath a few times when he came home late from school. Was he drinking with his friends? Or someone older who was plying him with drink? Roth perhaps? Roth was a complicated character. If what James Shilling told her was true, that he conspired with a pupil to accuse a teacher of sexual molestation… then he was a bitter and twisted man. He was dangerous.

Jo threw back the duvet cover with a sudden burst of energy.

'I need to pay you and your Angel another visit, Mr mysterious Roth,' she said, as she bounced out of bed.

00000

Less than five miles away on that same Thursday morning, Wendy was having trouble sleeping for a different reason. She had carried out an act that, as far as the authorities were concerned, was unforgivable. Punishable by death in some countries. That part of her was remorseful. But she told herself another story. One that would enable her to survive.

She had been threatened in a way that would have initially ruined her career and eventually, her entire life if she had not acted swiftly. To allow her young lover to expose their affair to the school and beyond was unthinkable. After the media had pulled her life apart, her existence would be one of vilification. Her face on the front cover of daily newspapers would brand her a pariah in society.

She had suffered enough in her life. That was not going to happen.

She hauled herself out of bed and went to the bedroom window which overlooked the rear garden. The area of freshly disturbed earth was clearly visible from her aspect. She noticed her two trees over the past weeks had shed a carpet of leaves that lay now beneath each one.

The yellows and golds of the Tulip Poplar on the right of the shed and the blood reds from the Ash on the left were seasonal gifts. In the past, they had provided a soothing spectacle to a predominantly colourless autumn garden. This year they will be used to cover the conspicuous bare piece of ground that contained a boy's grave. She would rake the leaves over the site after work today.

Chapter 37

The staffroom gossip at the Web was predictable– divided between The Antonelli disappearance and Sam's predicament. Amongst Danny's tutors, the atmosphere had been one of incredulity and concern.

James was talking to Sam. They sat close.

'Did you see the piece on last night's TV about Danny and his parents?

Sam shook his head.

'It was another call for witnesses. His mother and father were making a plea in front of the cameras. They were appealing for anyone who may know someone or something that will help the investigation. It was a pitiful sight watching the helpless couple begging to get their beloved son back.'

'I don't know how Lucy and I would cope with losing a child in those circumstances. It makes me go cold just to think about it,' said Sam.

'The programme also did a brief piece on his Italian background.' James went on to tell him the details covered by the programme.

'He's Italian only on his father's side, then. I've got some friends whose parents are Italian. They're a close community in this country,' said Sam.

'Well, here's the interesting thing. His grandfather came from the town of Plati, which was a stronghold of the Ndrangheta,' said James. He waited for a reaction.

Sam's expression did not change from one of mild interest.

'The Ndrangheta was the Mafia of that region. The most powerful organised crime group in Italy. Have you heard of the oil tycoon John Paul Getty?'

'Yeh, there was a recent programme on the box about his life,' said Sam.

'Apparently, the Ndrangheta were responsible for the kidnapping of Getty's grandson. But this is where it gets really interesting. I had a meeting with Google to see who the principal families were involved in that crime network. Guess which family was one of them?'

'No. Not the Antonelli family?' said Sam, open-mouthed.

'Give that man a coconut. Spot on,' said James.

'So, what are you deducing from that connection?'

'Well first of all, I think it's a bloody interesting fact – not often do we get a relative of a Mafia family at the Web. Secondly, maybe there's a possible link to Danny's disappearance – perhaps he's been kidnapped to settle an old score with another Mafia style mob? Who knows?'

Sam stared at James. 'You serious?'

'I asked myself why the television people went into his descendant's history. Does their research team think there's a link? Even if Danny's father is not involved in the criminal element of the family, he's still family. As you rightly said, the Italians are a close community.'

Sam remained speechless. James sat back in his chair.

'I'm not sure why, but I suddenly fancy a nice glass of Barolo and a spaghetti bolognaise tonight,' said James.

The men looked at each other for a few seconds – then snorted with laughter.

00000

DSI Jack Jolley's move from Ashford in Kent had not gone as smoothly as he would have liked. The new-build house he moved into with his wife had cracks up the walls and ill-fitting windows. Like any new-born, it had its inevitable teething problems.

In addition, his wife had left behind all her local friends. Spending most of the day rattling around in the house, she was the one who had to address the home's concerns.

He was aware that she was struggling at the moment...

Jack rose from his desk and walked over to the coffee pot. Concerns for his wife's happiness were on his mind when there was a knock on his door.

'Come in,' said Jack.

Jo opened the door. 'Can I have a word, Guv?'

'Coffee?'

'Ooh, yes please,' she said.

When they were sat at his desk Jo, holding her notes on her lap, began telling her boss of her recent findings.

'A woman that runs the local resident's committee told me that there is a female teacher at Sir Montague Web

Grammar School who lives on Rupert Street which is in the area where Danny's last text was received. Apparently, she's a bit of a loner. When she does bother to talk to any of her neighbours she goes on about her husband. Thing is, no one has ever seen or heard of him. All a bit strange,' said Jo.

She had not told Jack about her prison visits to Nick Summers. She was not sure that he would approve of the association. Especially as he knew she had been instrumental in putting him behind bars. She hoped he would not ask who her contact was.

'Which teacher is it?'

'I've got to find that information from the headmaster. Personally, I don't think a female teacher is going to kidnap a boy in her school. I will follow it up but something that I think is more pressing has arisen.

'Another teacher at the school, James Shilling, told me has had doubts about the history master who used to run the football team. He has a reputation, or so it's rumoured, of spying on the boys taking a shower after the game.'

'Okay. Have you got a name for *this* teacher?' asked Jack.

'His name is Jeremy Roth. Yesterday, Mr Shilling visited Roth's old school where he used to work to get more info on him.'

'Another amateur sleuth. Everyone, it seems, wants to be a bloody detective. They can be a help... or a bloody nuisance,' said Jack.

'I think this guy is pretty trustworthy. Anyway, the headmaster at this school told him there was an unsubstantiated sexual complaint about Roth and a boy in his class. So, I paid this Mr Roth a visit last night.'

'On your own?' said Jack.

'Er, yes. There was no one else around at that time and I wanted to surprise him.'

'I don't want you doing that again, Jo. You don't know what you're walking into. You take someone with you next time. Hear me?'

'Yes. Sorry, Guv. Anyway, he's a strange creature, lives on his own. He seemed very nervous during the time I was there. And I noticed a bottle of red wine on the kitchen worktop. I know half the bloody country drinks wine, but you know. On my way out of his old mess of a house, I looked into the sitting room. I couldn't believe what I was seeing. It was full of teddy bears.'

The DSI frowned. He lifted his cup and took a swig of his coffee.

'Mmm! What do you think?' he asked.

'There's something wrong there. I want to search his premises. See if there's any signs of a boy being held there; get hold of his pc or laptop, whatever he uses. Check out what's on it. Thing is, I know I spooked him just turning up like that at his gaffe. So, if there's a delay for a warrant he could cover his tracks – wipe off any incriminating evidence.'

'I will apply personally for a search warrant. But in a serious case such as this, a delay could affect that search. Which means you can legally enter the premises before the warrant is issued. And I agree with you that Roth is the priority here over the other teacher,' said Jack.

'Thanks, Guv. Me and DC Kyra Chand will carry out the search later today.' She went to finish her coffee then realised that was the end of the conversation. She left Jack's office.

Chapter 38

Jo had taken James' mobile phone number when he had visited the station. She rang it at lunchtime hoping to catch him when he was not in class.

'Hello,' said James, surprised.

'Ah good. I've caught you. It's detective sergeant Jo Major here. I apologise for calling you in your lunch hour, but I need your assistance on the subject we were discussing yesterday.'

'Hang on, I'm in the staffroom. Let me go outside.' He winked at Sam, who always sat next to him, and left the room.

'Right. Yes, I'm more than happy to help. What can I do?'

'I need to know when Roth leaves school to go home tonight. Is that possible?'

'I'll have to find out when his last class is this afternoon. The headmaster's secretary keeps the schedule. She will be able to tell me. There shouldn't be a problem.

'He may have a free lesson and leave early. Normally he doesn't hang around after his last lesson. He's certainly not in the staffroom at the end of the working day. I guess he does most of his paperwork at home.'

'Okay. If you do see him leave, could you give me a bell? I'll give you my personal mobile number.'

Ten minutes later James was back on the phone to Jo.

'No free lessons. There's no staff meeting either. School ends at three-thirty. So, I reckon he will leave shortly after that.' said James.

'That's brilliant. Thanks.'

'Can I ask…'

Jo had anticipated James' next question. 'You'll know soon enough. Thanks again James,' she said, as she ended the call.

James wandered back into the staffroom made himself a fresh cup of tea and took his seat next to Sam.

'What was all that about? Or shouldn't I ask,' said Sam.

He leant into his pal and lowered his voice. 'Things could be moving our way.'

Sam, eyes wide, waited for more.

'All I will say, is that was our detective.'

'You're cooking something up again, aren't you?' said Sam, with a hopeful smile.

James picked up his teacup, went to put it to his mouth, then stopped. He looked at Sam.

'That's the second time she's called me James!' he said.

00000

At four-thirty p.m., DS Major and DC Chand stood outside Jeremy Roth's house. Jo lifted the heavy door-knocker once again. The sun was beginning to disappear behind the spiked tops of a lofty, solid line of firs at the far end of the road. Unlike her first visit, there was still sufficient light to see just how neglected the front garden was. The fascia of the house looked derelict – uninhabited almost. Drab curtains hung behind grimy windows, parts of the frames being little more than bare wood. They had not seen a paint-brush for decades.

Roth must have recognised Jo through the window as the door was opened wide this time. Jo noticed he was wearing the same clothes as yesterday. His hands lay over his protruding stomach, rubbing his fingers over and over as if he was thawing them out.

'Mr Roth, we have reason to believe that you may be detaining someone or possess something in this house that will help our inquiry into the disappearance of Danny Antonelli. We are here to search the premises,' said Jo.

Roth's face turned grey. He stood rooted to the inner doormat unable to move. After a few moments, his blood started running through his veins once more.

'I don't understand. What have I done to deserve this treatment? I'll get my solicitor on this. This is an outrage. I want to see your search warrant,' he said, standing his ground.

'Where possible danger to a child's life is involved, a warrant is not needed, Mr Roth. And it is, of course, your right to call a solicitor. Meanwhile, if you would stand aside and allow us to carry out our search,' said Jo, stepping forward.

Roth took a pace backwards on unstable legs. The two officers squeezed past the teacher and entered the house.

Slipping on latex gloves the two officers commenced the search.

One hour and twenty minutes later, they were finished. They discovered nothing to suggest that anyone had been imprisoned or entertained there. In the main upstairs bedroom, they took a laptop and a personal diary, both of which would go back with them to be scrutinised. Jo was not sure what they would find but the forensic digital examiners should be able to get into the laptop to look at the historic material on the machine.

Jo found Roth sitting in the kitchen, his eyes closed, his lips moving without any sound coming from them. She thought he might be praying. As she approached, he opened his eyes. She held up the two objects in front of his face.

'I am confiscating these two items. They will be examined. If we do not need to keep them for any reason after the examination, you may retrieve them from the police station. Thank you for your compliance in this matter,' said Jo, as they left.

Back in the car, Kyra was the first to speak.

'Well, I don't expect to see that place in Homes and Gardens anytime soon,' she said.

They looked at each other in silence. Then erupted in laughter. They had no idea what they were going to find when they entered the creepy surroundings of the teacher's home. The giggling was a welcome release valve for them both.

'Did you see him when we left? He looked as if he had shrunk six inches. He looked ill. He has dark secrets,

231

that man. Secrets that he does not want us to find out. I've seen that look before,' said Jo, with an exaggerated shiver.

'So, not a good idea to invite him to the Christmas party?' said Kyra, straight-faced.

The girls laughed again. 'Blimey, you're on form today. What did *you* have for breakfast?' Jo said.

When they got back to the station, whilst still in her car, she had a quick look inside Roth's diary. This was the only chance she had before handing over the two confiscated items to the exhibits officer. They would then go off to the forensic lab. Most of what she saw were weekly or monthly entries. Basic reminders.

Things like take Angel to the vet – Tesco delivery – Doctor's appointment, and so on.

She flicked through to more recent entries. There were additional ones here. Most of these had initials instead of names. *PG is a snivelling bastard. An arse licker. He had no right to do that to me.* The following day – *Must find a way to make PG look inept.* Two days later – *Get rid of SW pretentious fucker. Get C to help me.*

Looking through her notes on the investigation, Jo was pretty sure that PG was Peter Greaves the headmaster, SW was Sam Whitmore and C, presumably, was the boy Clifford. James' theory that Roth had coerced Clifford to accuse Sam of sexual interference looked pretty accurate.

Chapter 39

Wendy awoke on Friday morning with one purpose in mind. She needed to visit the garden centre to buy three or four shrubs. On returning from work yesterday afternoon, she noticed that the burial site was visible again. The wind had blown away the cover of leaves. At the same time, she witnessed her scruffy neighbour, who had been working nearby, gathering up those very leaves that had ended up in his garden.

That nuisance of a man seemed to be in his garden more often of late, she thought. Although she questioned whether it may just be her nerves that were causing her to scrutinise the outside area much more often.

Her dream of a beautiful garden turfed and full of colourful flowers, a haven of relaxation, now represented pure fear. Would she ever be able to sit on her patio in the summer sunshine with a glass of wine without thinking of Danny's rotting carcass lying thirty feet away? Her brain reacted with a resounding *no*. When she deemed it safe, she would have to move house.

Her neighbour was bound to have noticed the sizeable empty area of freshly dug earth, she thought. Was he just a nosey sod or did he suspect her of something? Her calculating mind realised that there would be no logical reason for that bare patch to suddenly appear unless it was to prepare the ground for a new flower bed. At least, that is what she hoped.

November was not the best time to buy plants. The choice was very limited. The spring and summer varieties had all disappeared from the shelves. But as long as it looked as though the plot was there for horticultural purposes as opposed to what it looked like now – a burial site – it would not matter. Any plants should fit the bill.

She had rung the school last night and left a message on the secretary's answerphone. Her excuse was that she had the beginnings of a migraine and probably would not make it to work on Friday. Anyway, she needed a day off. She had not called in sick for over a year.

Her existence, a constant state of tension, was draining her of energy. She had not heard anything back from James since dropping the hint about Roth's previous record at his last school. She was sure he would follow up on it but she needed confirmation.

On the drive to the garden centre, she started to think of Edward, her husband. Her ongoing pretence that they were still together was a pathetic effort to appear normal to her neighbours. As long as she perpetuated the lie there would still be an element of truth in her own mind. To admit to anyone that he had left her for her best friend was not going to happen.

'That bastard is not going to get the pleasure of seeing me fall apart,' she whispered to herself in the car.

Edward's job as a furniture buyer and seller for a large company took him all over Europe. That was also a convenient excuse for him to disappear for days at a time.

Those days, it turned out, were spent in the bed of her divorced friend. During one of his supposed trips, sensing something was wrong with their marriage, she had phoned his company to be told that he was not abroad but working in London.

When she confronted him on his return home, the unbearable reality punched her right between the eyes. He admitted everything. Their affair had been going on for over a year. He moved out the following week and moved in with his lover. After just one phone call, she had lost her closest pal and her husband. Her mind went back to when she was a fifteen-year-old girl. It had happened again. The nightmare had come back to haunt her.

She only saw the red light at the last moment. She slammed on the brakes, skidding to a halt two yards past the stop line. She missed a passing car by a matter of feet. The other car's horn assaulting her fragile mind as it continued across the junction. Her knuckles white, were still gripping the top of the steering wheel as she bent forwards and dropped her head onto her fists.

The word 'fuck' came out in a scream. Her powder keg brain, a clutter of anger and confusion, had caused her to lose concentration. She was lucky this time.

At the garden centre, she bought five small shrubs and put them in the boot of her car. Her inclination was to find the largest ones for the most cover. But the big plants had large root balls in large pots meaning she would have to dig deeper and bigger holes to plant them.

Danny's grave was only a shallow one. With smaller shrubs, there would be less chance of hitting the corpse with her trowel when planting them. Her nostrils flared at the thought of digging down into the fifteen-year-old body of one of her pupils.

When she arrived home, she placed the shrubs over and around the grave. She knelt on a kneepad and started planting. After the second one had been successfully put in the earth, she heard a rustling noise behind her. She turned to see her scruffy neighbour standing by a pile of leaves. He was leaning on the boundary fence watching her.

'Hi, do you need a hand?' he asked.

She closed her eyes and turned away. 'For pities sakes,' she mouthed. She turned her head back to him.

'No thanks, I'm fine,' she said with a pained smile.

'Those plants are not going to get much light around that side of the shed. I hope they like the shade?' he said.

She ached to say, *Would you please fuck off and leave me to get on with my job?* She took a breath. Instead, she compromised. She turned to look at him with a face that conveyed those very sentiments then swung away from him once more.

Seconds after she had continued planting, she heard the sound of his back door close. She looked around to check that he had vacated his garden. It had worked. But she could still feel his presence hovering over her.

'I bet he's still watching me from his kitchen window,' she said.

She could not believe it. During the five years that she had lived there, she had seen this neighbour no more that half-a-dozen times and spoken to him even less. Now she couldn't get rid of him.

He was still watching.

Chapter 40

Jo was at her desk writing up a report when Jack Jolley entered the room holding a piece of A4 paper. Jo looked up at the six-foot man now looming above her.

'Hello Guv,' she said, putting her pen down in front of her. She went to get up but Jack put his open hand towards her as if he was telling a dog to sit. But this was a warm gesture. Kyra, sitting at the desk behind her, stopped writing.

'The forensic team have had a lot on their plate lately, but I asked them to prioritise my request. I've asked you both to come in on this Saturday morning because this was emailed to me late last night,' he said, holding up the sheet of paper.

Jo had been busying herself with other less pressing enquiries since Thursday, all the time waiting for the results of the confiscated items from Roth's house. An unexpected feeling of tension washed over her. It surprised her.

'Fingerprints on the diary match those found on the laptop. So, it's safe to say they are both Roth's. The latter end of the diary contained some cryptic messages but I think you will know what they mean, Jo. That's not what we are interested in at this moment,' said Jack.

Jo nodded. She had told Jack about Clifford's accusation and Roth's possible involvement. They both had accepted that presently it was being handled in-house.

'The guys got into his laptop without too much trouble. On it, they found videos of boys getting undressed and showering in what looks like a sports changing room. You've already told me that he was the previous football team coach. So, I assume these videos are of schoolboys at his place of work.'

Jack paused, then looked straight at Jo.

'They've also found a raft of child porn pictures and videos that have been downloaded over a period of some years.'

'Yes!' shouted Jo, standing up.

'The forensic team had been given a picture of Danny Antonelli. But as far as they could determine he doesn't appear in any of the school changing-room videos.'

Jo's excitement all at once became flaccid. Then it dawned on her.

'Bugger! Danny isn't in the videos because he was not in Roth's team. He only got in when Sam took over,' said Jo.

'Okay, that makes sense. But that doesn't necessarily mean that he had nothing to do with his disappearance, does it?' said Jack.

'Could I watch the videos of the Webs' schoolboys, Guv. I want to see if Tommy Clifford appears in any of them. I've interviewed him so I know what he looks like.'

'Why's that?' asked Jack.

'Cos if he is, then I think that would help the truth to come out concerning the accusation of the teacher. I'm not exactly sure why, but I think if the boy knows that Roth was videoing him in the showers then he's going to be disgusted with him – and less likely to validate the story they've concocted.'

'How does that help the Antonelli situation?' said Jack.

'Well, it doesn't directly. But it will show us the type of person we're dealing with if he is proved to be lying. If he doesn't care about trying to ruin a fellow teacher's life with what is a disgusting allegation, who knows what he is capable of?'

'All right. But don't lose sight of what we are trying to do here. Which is to find the missing boy and the person or persons responsible for his disappearance. We have a responsibility to Mr and Mrs Antonelli to discover why their only son did not arrive home last Friday and hasn't been seen since.'

'Yes, Guv,' said Jo.

'If Roth has nothing to do with Danny's disappearance at least we've taken a paedophile out of that school and off the streets. But if it's not Roth then who is it? You need to continue to concentrate your efforts on the missing boy but perhaps in other areas. I will get uniform to go and arrest Jeremy Roth. I presume we will find him at his house today?' asked Jack.

'I would hope so. I've got James Shilling, the geography teacher and deputy head keeping me in touch with Roth's school attendances, but we've not been watching his home.'

'No. Why would we when we didn't know what we were dealing with? Okay, good work, Jo. Keep it up,' said Jack.'

As he went to walk away, he turned back to Jo and Kyra.

'Now go home you two and get some rest. That's where I am going,' he said.

Jo watched him leave, got up from her desk and wandered over to make herself a coffee. Jack's words, *if it's not Roth then who is it,* were a whisper in her ear. She began to ask herself questions. From the moment, she met Roth she had a feeling that all was not right with him. She could understand why James had his suspicions about the teacher. She was happy that they had found some damning evidence against him yet disappointed there was nothing more.

When Jack left the room, Kyra was the first to speak.

'If Roth had a fixation about Danny and lured him to his house somehow…'

'No! It doesn't make sense. There was no evidence in Roth's house that a boy had been kept or harmed there. More significantly, if he was obsessed with Danny or he was one of his favourites, surely we would have found a photo or video of him somewhere. He could have easily taken one of him during school hours.'

As she waited for the kettle to boil Jo's thoughts were fixed upon the pros and cons of the small piece of technology that was now part of everyday life.

'Mobile phones. They all come with still and video cameras. Someone appears to be texting when, who knows, you could be appearing in their bloody video.

Kyra nodded.

Jo took her coffee back to her desk, dug in her handbag and pulled out a Snickers bar and unwrapped it. 'So, what else have we got,' she mumbled to herself, as she bit into the chocolate. She sank back into her chair, closed her eyes and ran through the last few day's events.

Nick's lead, via Mrs Ogilvy, had given her the strange teacher with a fantasy husband. If she had lost her husband or he had done a moonlight, she could be angry or frustrated. Both.

But would she lure one of her schoolboys back to her home – back to her bed. If so, where the hell is he now?

Jack's whisper was growing louder.

Teddy Bear Roth, for the time being, had drifted out of contention. Could the other teacher provide the answer? She would have to wait till Monday, when school reconvened, to ask the headmaster the question. She opened her eyes.

'Which one of his teachers lives in Rupert Street?'

00000

When Jo arrived home, she could not stop thinking about what had happened with Roth. When it got to early evening, after a couple of glasses of wine, she decided to phone James. The conversation went as follows.

'Hi, James, it's Jo, your nuisance-value detective here.'

James also had a glass of wine on the go and was halfway through a joint.

'Oh, hi Jo. Have you phoned to tell me you're coming to arrest me? I'll deny everything?'

'No such luck. Look, I'm sorry to bother you at the weekend but seeing how much work you've put in on this case, I thought you might want to hear my news on your favourite teacher, Mr Roth,' said Jo, taking a quick swig of her Sauvignon Blanc.

James laid his roll-up in in the glass ashtray and swapped the phone to his other hand and sat up straight. 'I'm all ears,' he said.

'Really? Well, no one's perfect,' she replied. She heard laughter down the phone. 'No, seriously. We searched Roth's home on Thursday, as you may have guessed. We found nothing of interest in the house, but we took his diary and laptop. In the most recent part of his diary, there are entries with just initials for names. They seem to point to his hatred of the headmaster and Sam and the plotting between him and Clifford.'

'That's great news. But is it enough to make him admit to his collusion with the boy?'

'Probably not, but I think that what we found on his laptop will be enough to persuade the boy to change his story. For obvious reasons I can't give you any more details at this time.

'I've got a bloody good idea what you've discovered on his laptop. I've had my suspicions for ages about our

Mr Roth. I'd already heard that a few boys were unhappy that he was always in the changing rooms on his phone when they got undressed.'

'Look. Keep your theories to yourself for now. I'm not at liberty to confirm or deny any of your speculations. What I can tell you is we arrested Roth this morning at his home and charged him. And, unless I am mistaken, I doubt if Tommy Clifford is going to want to play dangerous games with his teacher anymore.'

'I know Tommy Clifford inside out. That boy would not want to be party to anything like that. It's not him. If he is on his laptop, it will come as a great shock to him. Then he'll be furious with Roth.'

'As I've said, I've rung you tonight because of all the help you have given me in this investigation. You can keep guessing but if I hear any of those guesses have escaped into the public domain, I'll be on you like a ton of bricks. But for some reason I trust you. I'll give you a bell on Monday if I can tell you anymore. Have a good night. Cheers.'

'You can trust me, absolutely. Cheers, Jo.'

James put his mobile down, picked up his wine and said one word… 'Yes!'

Chapter 41

Monday Morning

Kyra Chand had started work at Wandsworth Nick just two weeks ago. On her arrival, she wanted to know what type of person DS Jo Major was. When she asked her colleagues about her immediate boss, she had received mixed views. A few said that she was ambitious and didn't suffer fools; one said she was up Detective Superintendent Jack Jolleys' arse; but most said that when you got to know her she was a likeable and loyal team member.

After two weeks of working under Jo, she could see that they all had a point. The DS had been quite tough with her throughout the first week. She jumped on any mistake or slack attitude, but she hadn't expected anything less.

One of the reasons that she wanted to be a detective was that, even as a child, she had always been naturally inquisitive. She had enjoyed watching and analysing people in her class at school. So, it was not difficult to notice the relationship between Jack Jolley and Jo Major. It was perhaps a little warmer than the rest of the officers under his guidance. She saw nothing wrong with that, so long as it didn't bleed into favouritism.

What was also noticeable, as the days went by, was her relationship with Jo was already improving. She sensed that her boss was starting to trust her. Gradually, she felt her own personality was beginning to emerge, like making the occasional light-hearted comment, for instance. A silly joke here and there. It was part of her personality from her school days onwards. She believed a sense of humour was important in life. It had got her through some tough times.

In this job, it was essential.

00000

At ten-fifteen, Jo strode into the office as if she had just discovered an oilfield in her back garden. She had spent the morning at the forensic laboratory in London. Back in the office, Kyra had been awaiting her arrival, constantly looking at the clock on the wall. Jo had texted her to say she had gone to study Roth's videos of schoolboys in various sports changing rooms. As soon as she sat down at her desk, she winked at Kyra then picked up the phone. Destination – James Shilling.

James was standing in front of the whiteboard delivering a geography lesson on map contours lines to his year nine pupils. He had the class's full attention partly because the boys were expecting one of his geographical jokes any time soon. He didn't let them down.

'To be able to read maps is very important. Even the other day I got an email from Google Earth telling me they can read maps backwards. But I thought to myself… that's just spam.'

As most of the boys were laughing while the others were trying to work out the joke, he felt the subtle vibration of his mobile that was sitting in his jacket pocket. He took out his phone. Jo Major's name appeared in the window.

'I've just got to take this. Get on with drawing and labelling those contour lines,' he said as he left the classroom.

'Hi James. It's Jo. I know you are probably teaching at this moment but I wanted a quick word.'

'What have you got?' said James.

'Roth's laptop has given us everything we need. I'm coming up to the school at lunchtime. I need to ask the headmaster or his secretary a question. Also, I want to speak to Clifford. I think he might be able to tell us more. Could you locate the boy and ask him to wait outside the head's office at twelve thirty?' asked Jo.

'Yep, no problem. Look, sorry, Jo, I've got to shoot. I've got thirty boys trying to get their heads and pencils around contour lines. But thanks for telling me. I'll sort Clifford for you.'

James pressed the end button and returned to his class. In the lunchtime break, he needed to do one thing. Find Master Clifford.

00000

James had downed a coffee and prawn sandwich in the staffroom whilst talking with Sam about the weekend's London derby between Chelsea and Spurs. He purposely did not tell him about the phone conversation with Jo. He hoped he could surprise him with some better news. He looked at his watch. Twelve-twenty.

Having swapped views on the finer points of the game, James excused himself and made his way out to the playground. He had ventured outside only wearing a thin jacket over a shirt and tie. He glanced up at the bright sky.

Cumulus, he said to himself. *Fluffy balls of cotton wool.* This cloud type was his favourite. The temperature was not. He soon began to shiver in the cold November air, rubbing his hands together whilst trying to pick out the spikey head of Tommy Clifford.

There were three boys standing in the far corner, partly hidden by the smoky-brown trunk of a sycamore tree. They appeared to be having an important meeting, in other words, plotting mischief, thought the teacher. And the head poking out from the rear of the tree was, James screwed up his eyes, yes it was Clifford.

As he approached the huddle through a sea of blue blazers, all three looked up at him. Two heads then checked out the concrete floor and four feet began to shuffle. One boy stood firm and met the teachers' eyes.

'Tommy, could you wait outside the head's office please? You have done nothing wrong, but I think you will want to know what the detective, the one you saw before, has to say to you,' said James.

'What, now?' asked Tommy.

'Yes, please,' said James.

Jo and the headmaster were now standing in his office. After she had finished telling him that they had arrested his history master and the reasons why, the head's face dropped.

'My God! More shame attached to our school. When will it end,' he said. Feeling slightly giddy, he stepped back and slumped down into his chair.

'We still don't know if he has anything to do with Danny's disappearance. We are still looking into that,' said Jo.

The headmaster shook his head in disbelief. He gathered himself together. 'You said on the phone that you wanted to know some details about one of our teachers here. It's obviously not Mr Roth. Who is it?' he said, his voice unsteady.

'I don't know, is the answer. But I know their address to be Rupert Street, Battersea.'

The headmaster pressed the intercom button on his desk and gave the address to his secretary. The reply came back in less than a minute.

'The only teacher to live in Rupert Street is Wendy Jacks. 24 Rupert Street,' the secretary replied through the small loudspeaker.

Jo already had her notebook open to write the name down. She was surprised she already knew of the teacher. She had interviewed her when she first came to the school. She flipped over pages to her notes. *Wendy Jacks. Head of Science. Taught Danny. Seemed very nervous.* Her pulse gave a small jump. She and the headmaster looked at each other.

'Can I ask what this is about,' asked the head.

'I don't know yet. It may be nothing. But I want you and your secretary to keep my enquiry about Ms Jacks to yourselves. For obvious reasons, I need to speak to

Tommy Clifford now. If your Mr Shilling has done his job, he should be waiting outside the door. I would like to speak to him and would ask you to be with me when I do. It's a very delicate subject as, I'm sure, you appreciate.'

'Of course,' said the head.

'If Tommy admits that it was Roth that persuaded him to accuse Sam, I would ask you not to punish the boy. I think, having talked to Sam, that he wouldn't want that either.'

No. Quite. I will put all this down to Roth. I just want this over and done. I'll just be glad that at least one nightmare at this school can be put to bed.'

'Thank you. Could you ask Master Clifford to come in please,' asked Jo.

Despite James telling Tommy that he had done nothing wrong, he didn't really believe him. He did wrong on a regular basis and was used to people berating him for it. In a strange way, he enjoyed doing wrong. It made him feel braver than his contemporaries. Accordingly, when he entered the office Jo noticed him fold his arms high up across his chest.

A defiant look spread across his face when she asked him to sit down. But his expression changed dramatically when Jo finished telling him what they had found on Jeremy Roth's laptop and in his diary. He was not sure he believed the story at first.

'He's been arrested and charged with these terrible offences, Tommy. I would not lie to you about something as serious as this. More importantly, as far as you are concerned, he's betrayed you and your friends. And this is a man you trusted,' she said, raising her voice slightly.

The boy's face froze. He was lost for words whilst his brain tried to compute what he had just heard. The corners of his mouth turned downwards.

He unfolded his arms. 'That's disgusting. He's a pervert.

'He will be tried as a paedophile and almost certainly be convicted of that charge. I'm assuming that you would not want to have anything to do with him now?'

'No bloody way, dirty bas…' he stopped mid swear word, looked at the police officer then down at the carpet by his feet.

'Look, I know Mr Roth persuaded you to accuse Mr Whitmore of sexually abusing you. And I know the reasons that you agreed to go along with it.'

Tommy's eyes darted up and straight into Jo's face, as if he had just seen a ghost.

'I need you to admit this to me, Tommy. There will be no blame directed at you from me or your headmaster.'

Tommy's eyes move across to the headmaster who nodded in affirmation.

Jo continued, 'Because of what we know about him now, you will face no consequences. He has groomed and taken advantage of you, to try and get a good teacher sacked. I know Mr Whitmore dropped you from the team, but he doesn't deserve to have his life and career utterly ruined by this false accusation. He is a decent man.'

Tommy looked anywhere but at the detective. Telling the truth did not come easily to him. He thought about his reply.

'And I won't get in trouble and get thrown out of school,' he asked.

'No. I promise.' said Jo.

'Yes then,' he mumbled. 'Mr Roth persuaded me to say that Mr Whitmore had touched me up.'

'Thank you, Tommy. That could not have been easy,' said Jo.

The headmaster congratulated Tommy on his honesty and reiterated that he was not in trouble and that the matter would be forgotten.

'Before we finish here, is there anything else that you could tell us about Mr Roth? For instance, was he particularly friendly with Danny Antonelli,' asked Jo.

The boy shook his head. 'No. Not that I ever saw. Roth thought I was a better player than him. But that was all.'

Now she had got him on her side, she felt he was beginning to relax. She pushed again. 'Is there anything else that comes to mind that you may have heard from or about Danny. Anything he may have said that was a bit unusual.'

'Not really.' He looked away from both of them. 'Oh, there was something a bit weird,' said Tommy, his face beginning to flush.

Jo looked at the headmaster then back at the boy. It was the first time either of them had seen him look self-conscious.

'You can tell us anything in confidence here. Whatever it is will stay inside these four walls. You have my word as a police officer.'

It was almost the wrong thing to say. He and his mates didn't trust the police. But this conversation was different. He was starting to feel more at ease and confident in front of her.

Tommy took a breath. 'There was a conversation in the playground, probably a couple of weeks back. One kid was boasting about having sex with his girlfriend who had just turned sixteen. We didn't believe him. Then everyone turned round to Danny when he said, "You've never had proper sex until you've had an older woman." Some other boy said, "Bollocks! When did *you* have sex with an older woman." But he suddenly shut up,' said Tommy.

Jo's demeanour changed in an instant. A klaxon sounded in her brain. The one lead she had not followed up on. The one possibility that she thought was unimaginable.

That Danny Antonelli was having an affair with the teacher who lived at 24 Rupert Street.

Wendy Jacks.

00000

When it filtered through to the other teachers that Roth had been arrested, Wendy was privately elated. Maybe now, she could relax a little bit more. Her plan had worked. That creep, Roth, was under the spotlight. He deserved it. There was no reason now, she thought, for the investigation to be pointed her way. She was pleased with herself. She breathed easy.

Chapter 42

When Jo arrived back at the police station, she sat down with Kyra and kept her up to date with all she had learnt that day. Throughout Jo's debrief Kyra sat gripped. She longed to butt in but held her tongue till her boss had finished.

'So, you think that this female teacher is somehow responsible for Danny's disappearance?' said Kyra.

'I don't know. But there's a lot of small things stacking up and leaning in her direction. If she's having an affair with the boy and something has gone wrong like, I dunno, maybe he's stolen money from her and done a runner. Perhaps he was not as happy at home as we thought?' said Jo.

'So, a respected teacher, mid-thirties, is having an affair with a fifteen-year-old schoolboy? That would be madness. She could lose everything if she was found out.'

'She wouldn't be the first, Kyra. This type of thing happens more than you know. I'm not saying it's common place. Danny is virtually sixteen. Boys of his age are eager to break into manhood. I should know, my younger brother demonstrated exactly that. He was a bloody nightmare – thinking he knew everything about life at the age of sixteen. To some young men, an older woman is very desirable. It represents that step up from adolescence. A welcome to the adult world.

'The same applies to some middle-aged women, who are single or unhappy with their partner. To know you're desirable to a young man must be a boost to a flagging ego. A chance to feel young again. This teacher, by all accounts, has a missing husband and lives on her own. Add that to the fact she is surrounded by growing lumps of testosterone dressed in school uniforms. See what I mean?' said Jo, to her wide-eyed DC.

Kyra raised her eyebrows and nodded her head.

'This afternoon, when this Wendy Jacks gets home from school, we need to pay her a visit,' said Jo.

'Why don't we go to the school after lunch to interview her? Early bird catches the worm.' said Kyra.

'I want to see where and how this teacher lives. How she reacts to two police officers suddenly turning up at her home – the possible love nest for her and Danny. I'm hoping to see this worm wriggle.'

00000

Monday Lunch

Sam Whitmore was waiting for James to return to the staffroom again. He had come back once, got a phone call and disappeared again. He sat reading the sports pages of the Daily Express that someone had left on the table but he was only taking in half of what he was reading. James had dangled a carrot in front of his nose this morning, with that wink. Could he allow himself to think it was good news?

At this moment, he was still the accused – the trusted teacher who turned out to be a sexual predator of young boys. As he listened to his inner thoughts, the idea of that label referring to him made him feel unclean, even though he was innocent. If it had not been for the support of James, he would have felt totally alone, terrified of gaining a reputation that would ruin his and his family's future.

As he turned the page of his paper, he heard the soft creak of tired hinges. He swung around to see James enter the room. His face looked like his numbers had come up on the lottery but he'd forgotten to buy a ticket. Sam shivered.

Jo had phoned James to tell him of Clifford's admission. She added, 'This thing with Roth was obviously a police matter but as Tommy's accusation has been kept in-house and not officially been reported to the police, the headmaster and I thought you'd like to tell Sam the good news yourself,' she said.

Instead of joining Sam, James walked straight over to the food station to get a coffee. Eventually, he sat down next to Sam.

'Well?' said Sam.

'Well, what?' said James, straight-faced.

'What's happened with Tommy Clifford?'

'Oh, that! Yes, everything's fine. He's admitted to it all,' said James, nonchalantly.

The men looked at each other. James broke out in an enormous grin showing all his teeth.

'You bastard,' he whispered through tight lips as he motioned to strangle the geography master. Sam then sat back and placed his hands on the table. 'So, it's all okay then?' he said, relaxing for the first time in days.

James leant in and said, 'It's going to get bad for Roth and he deserves all the shit he's going to receive from his prison pals when they lock him up.'

'Thank God this is all over.' He looked at James. 'Apart from being a bloody tease you've done a brilliant job for me. You've saved my career, my reputation... I can't think of a way to thank you enough,'

James half-turned his head towards his pal, went to pick up his coffee then stopped. 'Don't worry. I'll think of one,' he said, rubbing his hands together.

Chapter 43

At five-o'clock Jo and Kyra set off from the police station on the way to interview Wendy Jacks. The journey, even on busy roads, would take under ten minutes. The positive atmosphere in the car was palpable.

When Jo turned into Rupert Street, she noted that the houses were the same as all the other adjoining streets. They were a mixture of three and four-bedroom semi-detached dwellings all built in the early nineteen hundreds.

'We didn't knock on hardly any doors in this street, did we,' said Kyra.

'No. But even if we did, we didn't have the knowledge then about the teacher who lives down this road. More to the point, she wouldn't have been in at that time of day anyway. However, let's look forward. I've got all the odd numbers my side and they're going downwards. So, it's up to you to spot number twenty-four.'

In the half-light, it wasn't easy to see the door numbers. Jo proceeded forwards slowly in her unmarked pool car. Towards the end of the street, they pulled up outside Wendy Jack's house. It appeared in good order and the small front garden was well-looked after. A car was in the drive. Hopefully, she was in.

Wendy had arrived home twenty minutes before them. She had put a bag full of books to be marked on the kitchen table, changed into joggers and sweatshirt and poured herself a large glass of rioja.

It was her favourite wine and constant companion – a deep red mask blurring the lines between deceit and reality. Denial in a glass. But it worked; most of the time. She was getting through a bottle a night, sometimes more. It was the days that were the problem; threatening to unravel her make-believe world. Looking at those boys in her class, knowing that Danny's head was missing – knowing that lovely face would now be unrecognisable lying in her garden beneath thirty inches of earth.

She had almost finished the glass of wine when her doorbell rang.

'If it's that blasted nuisance next door again...' she said, as she walked to the door.

She stiffened at the unexpected sight that met her eyes. At once, she recognised the detective who had interviewed her at the school. Now there were two of them.

'Hello Mrs Jacks. This is DC Kyra Chand. I'm Detective Sergeant Jo Major. We met before at your school,' said Jo.

'Yes, of course. What is...' in that split second her brain clicked into Road Runner speed. She had to keep calm, get on the front foot. 'Have you any news about the missing boy?'

'This is just a routine call. We are trying to cover every possible angle. May we come in,' asked Jo.

'Please. Come through to the sitting room,' said Wendy, opening the door wide.

As the officers filed past the kitchen door Kyra was the one who noticed the bottle of wine and partly filled glass on the table. When they were all seated, Jo spoke.

'Actually, I tell a lie. It's a routine call in so far as your house just happens to be within the estimated location where Danny received his last text.'

Jo watched the teacher closely. She flinched, as if a low electrical charge had passed through her body. The detective knew the question had hit a nerve.

'Oh, I see,' was Wendy's only reply.

'You have a nice house. Been here long?' said Jo.

The teacher knew they were not here to ask her polite, fluffy questions. So, why were they here? What did they know?

'About four or five years,' said Wendy.

The general chit-chat continued for a few minutes. But the longer it went on, she could feel herself getting more tense. She was waiting for the detective to dig deeper. It didn't take long.

'Do you live here on your own?' said Jo.

'No. I am married. But my husband's job takes him abroad quite a lot,'

'Oh really. What does he do?'

What's that got to do with you, she thought. 'He works for a company that buys and sells bespoke furniture,' her voice was starting to sound shaky again as it did during the school interview.

'Oh, really. I could do with some of that myself. But it's probably out of my price range. The Met don't pay that well, I'm afraid,' Jo said, with a brief chuckle. Kyra gave a polite smile. 'Since we last talked, I wondered if you may have thought of anything else concerning Danny. His friends, his relationship with other teachers?'

His relationship with other teachers? Where was she going with this? Wendy pretended to think. She merely shook her head in response, pursing her lips as if she was kissing an unwanted auntie goodbye. The less she spoke the better.

'How about his nature, his mental state? Had you noticed any change over the weeks and months?'

'No. As I said before, he appeared much the same as all the other boys in his class. Quite normal really.'

Kyra suddenly got up from her armchair.

'Would you mind if I used your lavatory? It's all the tea I drink at the station. I'm sorry to ask.'

Despite there being nothing obvious to hide, that she could think of, Wendy did not want a police officer wandering around the house. She had no option.

'Yes, of course. It's up the stairs, first door on the left.

When Kyra reached the top of the stairs, she entered the bathroom. She had a look on the shelves and in the small wall cabinet. Then she flushed the loo, washed her hands and walked back out onto the upstairs landing. Before she came down, she poked her head in the three bedrooms.

Hearing that the conversation downstairs was in full flow, she went further into what she guessed was the main bedroom. It was the largest one and contained a double bed. Kyra had a quick scan of the room. As she opened the wardrobe door to look inside, she was aware of the sudden silence down below swiftly followed by approaching footsteps.

She promptly headed for the bedroom door. Just seconds after she squeezed outside she met the teacher at the top of the stairs. Wendy narrowed her eyes.

'Everything okay?' she asked the police officer.

'Yes, I am now, thanks,' said Kyra, her heart tapping on her ribs.

Wendy did not want to appear as if she had something to hide. She had to have a reason to check up on her. She thought quickly once again.

'After I heard the toilet flush, I was a bit worried about you because the door sticks sometimes. Don't want to be accused of locking our local police in my bathroom, do I.'

Kyra giggled politely. As Wendy followed her down the stairs, she thought to herself, *being accused of locking the police in the toilet is the last of my problems.*

When they arrived back in the sitting room, Wendy saw that the other officer was not in her chair. She turned to see her standing at the patio doors, looking out onto the garden. She was relieved that it was now too dark to see any details.

When Jo heard them behind her, she turned.

'You found her then?' said Jo.

Wendy smiled.

'Well, we will leave you to enjoy the rest of the evening. Apologies again for the disruption of your downtime.'

The teacher closed the door behind them as they left the house. Kyra went to walk to the car. Jo turned the other way.

'Hey,' Jo called to Kyra. Not yet. You knock on the neighbour's door that side and I'll do this. Just ask them if they had seen or heard anything. Okay?'

'Oh. Yes, will do.'

On Jo's side, the door was answered by a middle-aged man in baggy tracksuit bottoms and an off-white vest. He was finishing a mouthful of food.

'Hello, I am Detective Sergeant Jo Major. We are carrying out some house-to-house inquiries concerning a missing boy from Sir Montague Web School. You may have read about it or seen it on the TV?'

'Yes, I read it in the paper. A terrible thing for the parents,' he said, wiping his mouth with the back of his hand.

'She pulled Danny's photo from her jacket pocket. 'I wondered if you may have seen this boy in the local area last Friday or any time since?'

The neighbour took the picture. He studied it then screwed up his face.

'I'm not sure,' he said, slowly.

Jo was at once encouraged by this man's response. This could be the first possible sighting of Danny since the beginning of the case.

'Take your time looking at his face. This could be important,' said Jo.

He stared at the photo. 'How tall is this lad?'

'Five-ten, five-eleven.'

'Yeh, it could be,' he said, handing back the picture.

The suspense was killing Jo. 'Could be…?' her eyes wide.

'There was a boy, did some work in the garden. The lad was laying turfs, creating a new lawn. He was around here quite a few times actually.'

'He laid some turfs in your garden?'

'No. Not my garden. Hers next door,' he said, pointing to Wendy Jack's house.

Jo's skin tingled. 'How old would you say this lad looked and what time of day did you see him?'

'*Er,* sixteen, seventeen. Time of day?… *erm,* mid-afternoon. Three-thirty, four-thirty, maybe.'

Jo wrote down some details, thanked him, and headed for the car. Kyra was already waiting there.

On the journey back to the station, they swapped stories. Kyra kicked off.

'It was a lovely old lady my side. But she couldn't help us at all. She could hardly hear what I was asking her. But back in the teacher's house, when I popped upstairs, it wasn't to have a wee it …'

'Yeh, I realised that. Smart move for a rookie.' Jo interrupted.

'Thanks. I looked everywhere in the bathroom. No sign of a man. No razor or aftershave and only one toothbrush in a glass. I stuck my head in the bedrooms.

Nothing out of the ordinary. In the main bedroom, there were no men's clothes in the wardrobe. Her husband, if she's got one, does not live there. More importantly, there were no other rooms to check out so Danny is not being held prisoner upstairs.

'Good stuff Kyra. When Wendy went upstairs to find you, I had a quick look around downstairs. There's only a kitchen and a sort of boot room. Same thing – he's not in this house. There's a tiny shed at the bottom of the garden that I could just about see in the twilight. She would hardly keep a prisoner in there.'

'Ah! I almost forgot, I saw a bottle of red wine on the kitchen table and an unfinished glass,' said Kyra.

'Yeh and me. So, it's only five o'clock and she's already on the sauce. Danny's mother told me she had smelled alcohol on her son's breath more than once when he came home late from school. Did you see how nervous she was when I asked her whether she knew of any other teacher's relationships with Danny? A bit too close to home, methinks.'

'What about *your* neighbour?' said Kyra.

'I've been holding this back. I've just had the best lead yet. My man next door, by the state of him, looks like he's got nothing better to do than spy on his neighbours. And thank God for that because he thinks he recognised Danny. He told me there has been a boy that matches Danny's description who has been doing some gardening work for our teacher. Laying a new lawn. And he was a regular visitor. I wonder how she paid him?'

Kyra's face was like a child's unwrapping a Christmas present, as Jo continued.

'Tell me if I'm missing something, she said, as she drove through the Battersea traffic: 'We've got her house that's inside the area of Danny's last received text: Wendy, his teacher, strange woman who lies about an absent husband and is probably a heavy drinker: We've got Danny telling his mates about having sex with an older woman: him coming home late from school smelling of alcohol: And back to Wendy, who we now know as a liar, and has been very twitchy in both interviews.

'And the deathblow – a witness who tells us a boy of his description has been frequenting her house. And at a time that fits in with immediate after-school hours.'

Jo lifted one hand from the steering wheel and made a fist and pulled it down as if she was pulling the communication cord on a tube train.

'Get in,' she cried, to her impressed DC. 'We, Miss Chand, have got ourselves a prime suspect.

Chapter 44

Wendy did not know how she had managed to appear even semi-normal during the police officers' visit. Inside she was a wreck. When she closed the front door behind them, she turned and suddenly felt faint. Then her legs gave way. The bulk of her weight hit the nearby wall. In doing so, she knocked over a tall standard lamp. Dizzy, she slid slowly down the lilac wallpaper to the floor. She held her stomach and swallowed hard as bile rose up from her gut into her throat.

She sat in that position for minutes waiting for the knots in her stomach to unravel, the blood to return to her panic-stricken brain. She sat thinking. *Why have those detectives turned up at my door? My door! They've discovered the area of Danny's last text. Shit! They had to know more. They were testing me with their intrusive questions.*

She began mumbling to herself. 'That other bloody nosey detective – sneaking around upstairs. I definitely heard my bedroom door close just before I got up there. If she looked in the wardrobe, she would've seen I live on my own. Why did I lie about my fucking useless husband?' She scrambled back up to her feet.

She picked up the overturned lamp then headed straight for the wine. Just ten minutes after the detectives had left, the bottle was empty, and she was convinced. They were coming back. She opened another bottle and refilled her glass. She put it to her maroon lips. The teacher whispered into the darkness of the wine.

'And this time they won't be asking how many bloody years I've been living here.'

00000

When Jo arrived home, she was thrilled by what they had discovered. It had been a productive day. She was sure that Wendy Jacks was or had been having an affair with Danny Antonelli. There were too many coincidences. What she could not work out was where the hell was he? Was he safe?

When she and Kyra had returned to the station, Jack had already gone home. She would have to wait until tomorrow morning to put the facts before him. If he was agreeable, she would ask for another search warrant. She wanted to go through that house from the roof to ground floor. There had to be something in there that linked her to the boy.

She couldn't wait to see the teacher's reaction when told that she knows about the boy working in her garden. That piece of information, when delivered, would pin her down. She'd have nowhere to go, Jo thought, getting increasingly excited at the prospect.

She made herself a gin and tonic, threw her shoes off and sat in the solitary armchair she possessed. The five weeks in the apartment had flown by. Most of the old furniture she had in Ashford had been left behind or thrown out. Apart from her mother's favourite armchair. The memories and cosiness it provided made it a must keep.

Since her arrival, she had not found time to go shopping to furnish her new home. She was looking forward to decorating what was a blank canvas. Her desire was to share it with someone. That someone had arranged to ring her at six-thirty. It was almost that now.

Her mobile lay on the only other item of sitting room furniture she had brought with her. A fifteen-inch-square teak coffee table. On the stroke of half-past-six, the phone began to shimmy across the shiny surface. She always kept the phone on vibrate only, as it stayed with her throughout the working day.

'Hi, Jo. This is your resident jailbird reporting in,' said Nick Summers.

'Hello Nick, how's your day been?' His upbeat tone never failed to surprise her. For a bloke who shouldn't really be in prison he was coping really well, she thought.

'Fabulous. But I still haven't received that cake with the file in the middle. What's going on?' he said.

She smiled. 'Nick, you know that this phone call is probably being listened to, or at least recorded, don't you?'

'Well, what are they going to do? Put me in prison? Anyway, you told me you don't bake cakes. So, I should be safe. What I want to know is what is happening with this missing boy?'

'You will be pleased to hear that your information about the committee organiser has led me to my prime suspect. Can't tell you much more at the moment. But hope to have some sort of result pretty soon.'

'If it helps you to find the kid that would be fantastic. Keep me in touch. Oh, and if it does prove to solve the case maybe you could ask to get the rest of my sentence quashed.'

'Don't hold your breath on that one,' Jo said.

Nick was only allowed to make a call on the prison phone for a period of fifteen minutes. They spent much of that time laughing. After they said their goodbyes, Jo spent the rest of the evening in a positive frame of mind. How bloody ironic, she thought, that when she had at last found a man that she wanted to spend the rest of her life with, she ended up putting him behind bars.

Chapter 45

Tuesday Morning

Despite Jo having to scrape a layer of ice off the windows of her car this morning, she still managed to arrive at the station by seven a.m. The office was not a great deal warmer than the outside temperature at that time of day. Her blue puffer jacket and matching lambswool scarf was staying on for now.

She was aware that the room always had a different smell when she was one of the first in. The absence of warm body scents gave way to the chemical odours of the chipboard and melamine desks, the computers, plastic folders, the thin tweed carpet tiles, seasoned over the years with tea and coffee spills and heavy traffic. The air seemed thinner in an empty room somehow.

She had enjoyed a comfortable and dream-sprinkled sleep last night. She was surprised how relaxed she felt when she woke up. The reason for her early arrival was to prepare and finish the report that would contain all that she had learned yesterday. The neighbour witnessing the boy's visits to the teacher's house being the shiny pearl.

She needed to present her case in the most concise and professional way. Danny coming home late from school and his mother smelling alcohol on his breath was the most important bit of info that stood out in her last report to Jack.

This next report was the one. This was going to turn on the lights, pull back the curtains and start the show. She wanted to dazzle Jack with what she thought had been, her best performance to date.

Shortly after, Kyra walked into the office carrying two cappuccino coffees bought from the local café. She plonked one in front of Jo and sat down at her desk opposite. Jo's eyes opened wide. This was a first.

'To what do I owe this pleasure? If it's bribery... I don't give a flying. It's very welcome. Thanks,' Jo said, taking off the lid.

'Absolutely, it's bribery,' said Kyra, straight faced. 'Actually, it's to celebrate our first major breakthrough on this case. Do you get it? MAJOR breakthrough! Jo Maj...'

'Yes, yes I get it. Thought there'd be a KC pun somewhere mixed up in this offering. I'd be disappointed if there wasn't,' said Jo, rolling her eyes around their sockets.

Just then, Jo heard the automatic snap of the outer door to their office as it shut. She watched Jack Jolley, immaculately dressed in a silver-grey suit, white shirt and knitted pink silk tie stride along the corridor to his office. Minutes after she had finished her coffee, she scooped up her report and headed for the meeting she hoped would finally get this case moving forward.

'Come in,' Jo heard, in reply to her knock on his door.

'Morning, Guv. Sorry to disturb you just after you've arrived but I need to run this report past you. We're going to need another search warrant or preferably your approval to search another house.'

'What have you got?'

'It's Danny's teacher, Wendy Jacks. I've got good reason to believe she was having an affair with Danny.'

Jack's heavy grey brows lifted his forehead up into a series of furrows as he took in Jo's controversial supposition.

She then went through all the evidence they had accumulated over the past eight days. Jack scribbled on a notepad as she took him through each separate piece of information. When she had finished, she watched him underline a few items on his pad.

Jack leant forwards and marked off each point. 'This doesn't need the issue of a search warrant.' He looked at his watch. It read twenty minutes past seven. 'School teachers don't normally get into work much before eight-fifteen, at least they didn't when I was at school. From her house it's a five minute, at most, drive to the Web. Take a team, get in the property before she leaves for work. Put her under pressure and see what you can find. This info is not telling us where the lad is but it's a great start.'

The DSI's last statement: 'Do it!'

Chapter 46

At seven-thirty-five, Jo and Kyra drove into Rupert Street. It had been a rush. Another police car containing two uniformed officers was due to join them in the next ten minutes.

'I'm really nervous. My heart's taking a trip around everything I've got above my waist at the moment,' said Kyra, patting her chest.

'Is this your first serious case?' asked Jo.

Kyra nodded.

'Understandable. But you need to get it in perspective. The only person that should feel nervous is our teacher when we knock on her door again.'

When they parked opposite Wendy's house Jo was the first to notice it.

'Fuck it!' she breathed loudly. The parking space on her drive was empty.

Kyra looked at Jo and then at the vacant driveway. 'Maybe she's parked it further down the road?'

'Mmm. Why would she? She can't have left to go to school this early. I don't like this. Let's go and knock,' said Jo.

She looked out of the car window and up at the crowded sky. The early dawn gloom was exaggerated by dense black clouds that hung low over them like a voluminous cloak. Jo pulled a torch from the glove box. They both got out of the car and approached Wendy's house. As they walked up the path, Jo noticed the neighbour peeking out from a gap in the curtains. They knocked loud and many times on her door. The interior of the house was in darkness. When they received no answer, Jo tried the side gate to the garden but the inside bolt had been drawn across.

'Right as soon uniform get here with the big red key we are going in without her,' said Jo, as they made their way back to the car.

Five minutes later the other officers arrived. Jo got out of the car to meet them. After a brief conversation, one of the men pulled out a battering ram from the boot of the car. They all approached Wendy's front door. After knocking on it again, Jo spoke.

'Let's do the side gate first. Less damage. There may be an unlocked door or window at the back,' she said.

The officer with the battering ram smashed through the bolt on the thin wooden gate with ease. After checking there was no easy access, they moved around to the front again and did the same with the front door. It yielded on the second attempt to the unnerving crack of splintering wood.

The team, after turning on all the lights in the house, then set about searching the premises. After thirty minutes, nothing incriminating had been found by any of the officers. What was noticed was the lack of clothes in the wardrobe and bedroom drawers.

Jo turned to Kyra. 'There's only a few things left in the bathroom – no toothbrush – and most of her clothes have been taken. She knew we were on to her. Our teacher has done a moonlight.'

'There's your confession. If we had got it wrong and she hadn't done anything illegal she would still be here,' said Kyra.

Jo realised Kyra was stating the blooming obvious, gave her a quick look but didn't pick her up on it. 'There's got to be something in this house that links her to our boy. I'm going to try upstairs again,' said Jo.

Kyra followed her up the stairs.

'You take the small bedrooms. I'll take the main one again,' said Jo.

After searching the wardrobe and cupboard drawers once more, she slumped down onto the unmade bed. Jo looked at the ruffled sheets. Possible DNA. The forensic team will be able to tell her that. She took a deep breath and slowly scanned the room. No photos of her and her phantom husband. Her eyes moved around to the two gloomy pictures. She looked at the rosary beads first and then at the Virgin Mary holding the baby Jesus.

'Religious? Huh! Don't make me laugh,' she said, leaning back on her arms. 'Where are you, Danny? What's she done with you?'

Jo had already looked under the bed the first time she searched the room. Because she could not think of what to do next, and in desperation, she leant forward, adjusting her position slightly, and ducked her head under the bed again. Perhaps she had missed a chain that had come off his neck or a paper tissue that could have Danny's DNA on it.

There was nothing.

As she began to straighten up, her legs brushed across the bottom sheet causing it to reveal a small piece of the mattress. On the lower part was a tiny red smear. Jo sprang off the bed, pulled the sheet right back and heaved the mattress up. There it was. A large deep magenta stain the size of a beach ball. The mattress had obviously been turned over.

'Kyra,' Jo shouted.

Kyra ran into the bedroom not knowing what she was going to find. She saw Jo holding up the heavy mattress.

'What the hell happened here? Whatever it was I'll bet a year's wages that the forensic guys will find it's Danny's blood,' said Jo.

Kyra stood transfixed. She blinked hard. 'Oh, my God! That does not look good for Danny, does it?'

'This is now a crime scene. Get one of the officers to seal off this bedroom.

Just then, one of the uniformed officers, who had responded to Jo's shout, appeared at the bedroom door. 'I heard that. I'll get it done. Also, I came up to tell you that there's a bloke downstairs, says he is the next-door neighbour. He wants to speak to you.'

Jo looked at Kyra. 'This better be good,' she said.

Jo recognised the neighbour. He was standing on Wendy's front path.

'I couldn't help noticing you all here. Is this got to do with that missing boy from the local school,' he asked.

This is a police matter, It's Mr…?'

'Relish. Leonard Relish. I just wondered if I could help in any way?'

'You have already been helpful Mr Relish. Unless there is…'

'It's the phone, you see. The mobile phone.'

He had got Jo's attention. 'What about the phone?'

'Well, I could hear this ringing coming from inside her shed. I was weeding in my garden and heard it a couple of times. I thought she might be in there. But it went on for a few days. When I told the lady who lives there, she said she must have dropped it in the shed last time she was in there. And she thanked me for it.'

Jo and Kyra looked at each other again. 'Thank you. That's good information Mr… *erm,*'

'Relish. When you arrived back here, I knew there must be something going on in that house. So, I've been thinking. She had never planted any shrubs before. They were already here when she moved in. Not a good time to plant coming up to winter, either.'

Jo was getting impatient. This man was rambling now and she wanted to go and check out this shed. She had to get rid of him. 'As I said, thanks for your help but we must get on.'

'I told her that was the wrong place, the other side of the shed, to create a new flower bed. Not enough sun, you see.'

Jo went cold. She turned away, headed through the side gate, turned on her torch and followed the beam straight down to the garden shed. Kyra almost had to run to keep up with her. Jo opened the door and stepped in. It was not a strong smell, but she recognised it immediately. She saw that the shed had an inner light. She switched it on and killed her torch.

The shed had only what most garden sheds contained but she knew what a rotting corpse smelled like. It would take a while for the odour to disappear in a small, enclosed space such as this. A body had been kept in here. She was sure of it.

'Kyra leant in through the door. 'That smell. Is it what I think it is?'

Jo nodded. The wooden floor of the shed was dirty with dried mud and dust but to one side there was a long smear, maybe two feet wide, that was cleaner than the rest.

Jo pointed to the dirt-free area. 'It looks as though something heavy has been dragged along the floor and out of the door.'

'Yeh. Looks like,' said Kyra.

Jo walked out of the shed turned right and right again. Then stopped dead. She pressed the button on her torch and lowered it to the floor. There it was. The new flower bed. The beam lit up the large area of earth that had been recently turned over. In the middle, a rectangular area was slightly raised. The plot contained various newly planted shrubs.

She knew instantly what she was looking at. Her worst fear had been realised. There was no doubt in her mind that beneath these carefully placed young plants lay the fifteen-year-old body of a schoolboy. She felt sick.

'Get uniform to seal off a large area around here, including the shed. I'll get on to the Duty Officer. He'll take care of supervising the securing of the scene,' said Jo.

An hour later, the rear of the garden was lit up by police searchlights and screened off from concerned onlookers. An hour after that, the covered body of Danny Antonelli was carried out of the garden, towards a waiting ambulance. Jo and Kyra, who were standing on the pavement outside, watched in silence as the body was carried past them.

Jo turned to Kyra. I just need to check on something. I know what the answer is going to be but I don't want to look stupid,' she said, as she pulled out her mobile. She punched in a number.

'Hi James. Has Wendy been at school this morning?'

'No. I've had to take her registration again. Is there…?'

'That's all I wanted confirmed. Thanks James,' she said and ended the call.

Kyra looked at her DS with a frown.

'Of course she hasn't. But if for some weird reason she had gone there, even for a short time, maybe to pick something up from her locker, for instance, and I had not checked…? Now I've covered my arse and can include it in my report. A lesson to be learned there, DC Chand.'

Kyra nodded.

Two members of the press that had already turned up were taking pictures of everything and everyone. One of them approached the two detectives. Jo recognised him.

He worked for one of the red tops. 'Hello Jo. Anything you can tell me?' he asked.

'No more than you've seen I'm afraid, Tom. A deceased body has been taken out of the premises. We have an ongoing investigation,' said Jo.

The reporter knew he was not going to get any more from the detective. He moved off to speak to the half-a-dozen or so locals that had now gathered around. She knew the neighbour would tell him it's connected to the missing schoolboy. She couldn't do anything about that.

'I'd love to know who calls the journos. They often turn up before we even get to the bloody location. At least one of our lot is getting a tickle for keeping them in the loop. Maybe it should be me,' said Jo. 'Before you go and report me, I was joking, Kyra,' she added.

Kyra smiled. Then her face changed. 'I know you said that affairs between teachers and pupils were more common than most people think, but to kill him. Why? How can that happen? How does a female teacher murder an innocent fifteen-year-old boy?' said Kyra.

'Your guess is as good as mine. But something went suddenly and seriously wrong with their relationship. Maybe he was threatening to tell his parents of their affair. If it got out she'd do time inside, lose her job. She couldn't teach again, that's for sure.

'So, where the hell is she?' asked Kyra.

'I can't believe she thinks we won't be able to find her, eventually. More importantly for now, I've got to ring the boss to tell him what we've found here. He will get an FLO to attend his poor parents,' said Jo.

'God. What a job the liaison officers have to do. He was their only child. The parents are going to be in bits' said Kyra.

'Thank goodness I haven't got any children. If I were his mother I'd want to find that teacher myself. I'd probably kill her with my bare hands and bugger the consequences,' said Jo.

Chapter 47

When the family liaison officer knocked on the Antonelli's door it was just before eleven a.m. Her offer of ongoing support whilst searching for their son had been much appreciated. Every time she turned up at their door they were hoping for good news and dreading bad. When all three entered the sitting room, the FLO asked them to sit down. It was then that they noticed an expression on her face they had not seen before. She appeared self-conscious. Respectful.

Danny's parents shrunk down on the sofa. Neither dared say a word. Their eyes were locked onto the officer. They could sense her brain choosing the right words before she addressed them. They wished that moment of silence would last forever. Because until she spoke Danny was still alive.

Instinctively, Karen and Enzo held hands as the officer took a breath.

'I have to inform you that a body, who we believe to be your son, has been found earlier this afternoon.'

'No!' Karen emitted a long, agonizing scream. 'No,' she repeated, this time in a high whine. She collapsed into her husband's arms. Enzo sat there stunned, his face ashen, as he held his sobbing wife.

'Where was he found,' asked Enzo.

'He was discovered on the premises of one of his schoolteachers,' said the officer. Enzo's reaction was one of astonishment. He could not make any sense of her words.

'What are you saying? That a man, who is also his schoolteacher, is responsible for my son's death?' said Enzo, whose demeanour had changed from shock to anger.

The officer handed Mrs Antonelli a tissue she had ready in her pocket. 'It's not a man, Mr Antonelli. It is a female teacher.'

They both looked at the officer. 'A female teacher and her husband?' said Enzo.

'No. She lives on her own.'

'On her own? Who is this woman; what's her name?'

'It's his science teacher. Wendy Jacks,'

'Mrs Jacks? We've been to the school before at parents' meetings. We know who his science teacher is. This can't be true,' said Karen.

'As unbelievable as it sounds, I'm afraid it is,' said the officer.

'So, you have arrested this woman for murder?' said Enzo. On the word murder, Karen broke down once more.

'No, I'm afraid. Not yet. The detective interviewed her yesterday. The information gathered, led us to believe she was having an affair with Danny. Then we added our suspicions to her next-door neighbour's vital information. He witnessed a boy resembling Danny visiting her house on a regular basis. This was around the time, school had just finished for the day. The officers came back to search the house first thing this morning.'

Both parents could not comprehend the shocking story that was laid before them. It was inconceivable to them that their young boy could behave like this behind their backs.

'Danny was found in her house?' asked Karen.

This was the question the officer was dreading. She lowered her voice. 'He was found in a shallow grave in the teacher's garden.'

'Oh Danny. My lovely Danny,' Karen whimpered. Enzo looked helpless. His son was dead and his wife was falling apart in front of his eyes. So was his world.

'Why haven't you arrested her?' Enzo finally managed to say, struggling to hold back his tears.

'When we returned to search her house, she was no longer there. She obviously knew we were coming back so she did the cowardly thing and disappeared. We have got our people looking for her and we will do everything in our power to bring this woman to justice. We *will* find her,' said the officer, setting her jaw.

00000

After Jo had informed Jack of their dreadful find, it left him with mixed emotions. He was proud of his DS for discovering the body of the boy and the culprit for his death. His poor parents will at last know what has happened to him. Terrible news for the two of them but they can now at least mourn him. But they would have wanted the culprit in police custody.

She probably packed her bags just after the first police interview at her home and left that night, he thought. Now he was going to have to put in motion a nationwide search for the murdering teacher, Wendy Jacks.

Chapter 48

Later that morning, Enzo was on the phone to his cousin Luca. He struggled to hold himself together as he informed him of his son's murder. It was when he reached the part where he told Luca that his boy's body had been callously buried in a shallow grave that his resolve shattered. With his wife in another room, he cried like he had never cried before.

Luca, listening to his cousin's anguish, was fighting back the tears himself. After his initial feelings of sorrow for the close member of his family, he soon became enraged.

'Enzo. This fucking woman. She has taken your beautiful boy, from you. Your only child. If the police find her you will, I am sure, have a degree of justice. You will see her go to prison, certainly. The other prisoners will know she has killed a young boy.

'Maybe she will get a hard time inside. But prisons in this country are too comfortable. Televisions, computers, games, pastimes. Fucking gymnasiums. If she pleads manslaughter, she gets maybe ten years. If she behaves herself, she gets out in five years. Is that justice?' asked Luca.

Enzo wiped tears from his face. 'No. But nothing will bring my boy back.'

'No, it won't Enzo. But you know our family. We believe in an eye for an eye. You are an Antonelli. We are a proud family. Would you want this woman to be free in five years and do this to another father's young son?'

'No, of course not. I don't… I don't know what I feel at the moment, Luca. I just want to go and see him, but the police won't let me. They have to carry out an autopsy first. But they said I wouldn't want to see him anyway. They are certain that it is Danny's body but they will take a DNA sample from me to make sure.'

'Last time we spoke I made you a promise. If the police don't find her, we will. The family and friends of the family will be informed. You know they cover a big area in this country,' said Luca.

'I was told that there will be an appeal to find her in the national papers tomorrow or the following day. I guess her picture will be part of those appeals.'

'Okay. If you or Karen want or need anything, you only have to ask. We will always be here for you both. My heart is bleeding for you and Karen. I love you Enzo. We will talk soon.' Shortly after the call, Luca downloaded a photo of Wendy Jacks from the school website to distribute amongst the organisation.

 The next thing Luca did was to break the sad news to his immediate family. He then spent the rest of a difficult day ringing his close contacts.

Enzo put the phone down next to him on his expensive Italian sofa. There was always an element of fatherly protection whenever he spoke with his older cousin. He was grateful for that as his own father had died suddenly last year of a stroke. Collapsing backwards on the furniture his heartache now turned to hatred as five of Enzo's words lodged in his brain. *'An eye for an eye.'*

His mind went back to soon after he and his father opened their Italian bistro. The leader of a local gang and his three friends, who began frequenting the restaurant, had eventually been barred for repeated drunken behaviour. When, two days later, one of the gang threw a brick through the bistro's window Umberto contacted Luca. Within a week, the gang's leader was admitted to hospital with extensive facial bruising, broken ribs and the end of two fingers missing. He never told the police who did it. Those kind of stories spread more swiftly than forest fires. Umberto had not had any trouble since.

Enzo blinked the memory away and looked around the room at all the beautiful furnishings on which they had spent so much time and money. The décor was exquisite. It meant nothing to him now. The room and the rest of the house, in his eyes, was an empty shell.

He stood and went looking for his wife. She was not on the ground level. He climbed the stairs to find her. She was sitting on the bed in Danny's bedroom holding one of his jumpers to her face, breathing in her boy.

Enzo sunk down next to her. As he put his arm around his wife, he wondered how their lives could ever be normal and happy again. Karen was now too old to have another child. Their son was all they could have hoped for. Danny was everything he was not. Well educated, handsome and confident. His boy was not going to work in a café like his father. He was not going to serve at other peoples' tables.

He was going to be a successful businessman, a doctor, a city banker dining in swanky restaurants where he, himself would be waited upon.

That dream now was dead. And so was his beautiful boy.

Chapter 49

Jo was in Jack's office. She was staring at the deep blue curtains either side of the white-haired head of her boss. There was no coffee on offer this time. Jack was reading her latest report.

'There's a lot of good work in here, Jo. Getting the boy, Clifford, to talk about Danny's sexual boast. The news of the somewhat strange behaviour and reputation of a teacher that lived in our identified area. God knows where you found out about that. And the neighbour's statement. All excellent detective work.

'Good teamwork is paramount in this job. I don't expect you to get everything right all the time, but you and DC Chand have done an admirable job so far, on what was an uncomfortable and potentially inflammatory case. Well, two cases actually. But it's only half-done.

Now we need to get out there and find this dreadful teacher. Look into her background. Friends? Where's that absent husband of hers? Bank accounts? Family?'

'Will do, Guv.' When Jo got back to her desk, she took her bosses' words with her. There was a murderer to hunt down. But there was an important phone call, she had to make first.

00000

Jo called James Shilling's mobile. It went to answerphone. 'Hi James. It's Jo Major. Call me back when you get a moment.'

She took a breath and stood up from her desk. 'I need a coffee,' she said. It was the third one of the morning. It was only eleven-thirty. 'Blimey! I'm living on the stuff,' said Jo, as she approached the small food station. By the time, she had made herself one and got back to her desk her phone rang.

'Hi, Jo. It's James. I was in the middle of teaching my kids the savage power of tsunamis, but I've held them up, they can wait until I've spoken to you. I'm dying to know what's going on. Is Wendy Jacks a suspect?' said James, his voice a high whisper.

'That was my reason for calling. We went to search Wendy Jack's house last night. We found evidence that Danny had been a regular visitor to her house.'

'What? You mean they were having an affair? Danny and Wendy?'

'It looks that way. But I've got worse news to tell you.' There was silence at the other end of the line. 'We found a considerable amount of blood in her bedroom, which we believe had come from Danny. Then, following a neighbour's witness account we found a body buried in her garden. We are also confident that it is Danny's body.'

James went cold. 'No! For pity's sakes, no!' For a moment, he was completely lost for words. The shock had rendered him dumb. His usual buoyant energy dissolved in an instant. *This cannot be real*, he thought. *Things like this don't happen at Sir Montague Web School.* Finally, he found words, 'What the hell did our teacher have to say for herself when you found his body?'

'She didn't. She wasn't there. Nor were her clothes, passport or personal items.'

'She's legged it. Jesus! So, you think she's murdered the boy somehow?'

'We don't know yet how he died. But it's not looking good for her, is it?' I don't suppose you know where she could have gone? Does she own another property or caravan somewhere?' asked Jo.

'If she does, she wouldn't have told me. No, I can't help you there, I'm afraid.'

'Okay, James. Well, there's nothing that I've told you that won't be in the papers and on the box in the coming days. So, if you want to inform the headmaster and whoever you think should know, you can. I will be coming up to the school early afternoon. I'll be asking the staff if they have any relevant information concerning Ms Jacks. If you hear anything that may be useful to our search please let me know. Okay?'

Yes, of course. All right. Bye,' said James. His arms dropped down by his sides. His mobile held loosely in his hand almost slipped from his grasp. The news that had just come out of that phone had shaken him to the core.

He had already had personal experience of how dark and treacherous people could be. Yet, the thought of him working in the same close environment as the murderer of a child. 'Wow!' he said. That handsome lad that he saw and taught every week – he won't ever see again. A lung-draining sadness came over him as he wandered back to his class.

As he stood behind his desk, he looked at the fresh-faced boys in front of him. He struggled to imagine how someone could kill a young and innocent child with their whole life in front of them.

He finished his lesson in a puddle of confusion. When his brain had given up computing the why's and how's of what Jo had told him, he went straight to the headmaster's office. The story was related to the shell-shocked head who said he would call a brief meeting at lunchtime to inform the rest of the staff.

At the dinner break, the full complement of teachers gathered inside the staffroom. The men and women stood rooted to the spot as they were informed of Danny's death. They had only recently been told of Jeremy Roth's arrest and the reasons why. Their shock and disbelief were heightened tenfold when the headmaster revealed that the prime suspect was Wendy Jacks. There were audible gasps around the room.

One elderly female teacher, who had been on friendly terms with Wendy, almost fainted on hearing the news. She had to be helped into a chair by two nearby teachers where she broke down in tears.

After the meeting, the headmaster approached James. 'Could I see you in my office tomorrow morning, James?'

'Yes, of course,' he replied. It was a serious request. *What next?* thought James.

On her visit back to the Web, later that afternoon, Jo discovered nothing new about Wendy Jacks. She could see all the staff were deeply upset by the news and was pretty certain that none of them were holding back any relevant information. Before she left James approached her. They went to the empty gymnasium.

'Jo, on top of all this horror that has come to light, I need to ask you a favour.'

'Fire away. I need something to take my mind off all this, even for a minute or two.'

'Tommy Clifford. I've found out that his mother's live-in boyfriend is a lazy good-for-nothing. He knocks her and the kids about and has got it in for Tommy, especially. Which tells me a lot about why the boy is what he is. She's too scared of this bloke to report his behaviour. I wondered if you could send an officer around to her house and, I don't know, warn him somehow, get him kicked out maybe?'

'That certainly will affect Tommy's behaviour. I've seen it many times before. I'll get uniform to pay her a visit. But if they can't get her to make a statement pertaining to his maltreatment of them all, then there is nothing we can do. But I will do as you ask, certainly.'

At six-o-clock that evening, Jo took a phone call from Stanford Hill prison. Yesterday's events dominated the conversation. The account, when relayed to Nick, hit a raw nerve. He and his wife had had no luck when trying for a child. Something they both dearly wanted.

Locked inside a three by two metre cell every night on his own, gave him too much time to think. But one thing was getting him through his sentence. His determination to build a new life and his desire to be a father someday.

'That is terribly sad news. Blimey! If we can't trust our schoolteachers now to look after our nation's children, who can we trust?' said Nick.

'I know. I love this job – most of the time. After a while, you become hardened to depravity and wickedness. But there are some incidents that you never get used to. Occasionally, you come across behaviour that is just beyond comprehension. Evil. It catches you out and pierces right through your professional armour.'

'I don't know how you can do that job, Jo? The things you must see. The people you have to deal with. Whatever you get paid is not enough,' said Nick.

'Can I quote you on that to my boss?'

Although the evening chat finished on a lighter note, Jo went to bed that evening with an overpopulated mind. Her dreams consisted of whispered voices in gloomy houses: prison cells that mutated into stark bedrooms that suddenly became garden sheds with blood-spattered floorboards.

It was not the first time she had experienced sinister visions. Whenever she was on a disturbing case, her mind would gather up these dark events and weave them into haunting, disconnected dreams. There was only one way to stop those unsettling nightmares. She had to find and arrest Wendy Jacks.

She had to prevent this happening again.

Chapter 50

Wednesday Morning

Jo was back in the boss's office again.

'I went to the school this afternoon but drew a blank as far as any new info goes concerning Wendy Jacks. But I found out where she used to work from the headmaster and gave them a ring. It was Castle Vale High School in Stockport, Greater Manchester. She was only there for two-years.'

'And that was how long ago?' asked Jack.

'*Er,* five years. Yes, she's been at the Web for five years. Anyway, the Castle Vale headmaster had only been there under a year but the deputy-head had worked there a lot longer. He remembered Ms Jacks.

'Much like James' enquiry at Roth's old school, I asked him if there was any unprofessional behaviour with her pupils during her time there. He said there was some talk amongst the teachers that a boy was getting bullied by his contemporaries for being Wendy Jacks' pet. Some of the boys were saying he must be having an affair with her. There was a bit of tittle-tattle in the staffroom, but it was nothing more than rumours. Mind you, he said their suspicions were aroused when, shortly after, she handed in her notice and left soon afterwards.'

'How about the school before that?' asked Jack.

'The deputy head said she could not remember exactly where she worked before, but she thought it was a school in Devon somewhere.

'This woman likes to move around, doesn't she?'

'It looks as though she's got a bit of a fixation with young boys,' said Jo.

'Find out if our teacher owns a property in or around Stockport' Maybe she could be holed up there.'

'Will do, Guv. But I doubt it cos we've already discovered that her house in Battersea was only rented. Which is why, I suppose, she couldn't care about dumping it. By the look of it, I think she rents and moves on as soon as trouble arises.'

'Mmm. Have we got a serial child abuser on our hands? If she hasn't managed to get out of the country, which she could easily have done, then it should only be a matter of time till we catch her. Her face will be all over the papers tomorrow. Someone must have seen her somewhere,' said Jack.

00000

At eight a.m., James walked through the open door into the headmaster's office.

'Ah, please close the door and take a seat. I've been thinking very deeply about what I am going to say and do. And I want you to be the first to know my thoughts.'

James sat there with his most inquisitive face on. He did not have a clue as to what his boss was about to say.

'When my affair with Ami first started it was the most exciting thing that has happened to me over the past ten years. My marriage had become devoid of any intimacy shortly after the birth of my son. Naughtiness usually belongs to children and teenagers. My God James, we should know that. We are surrounded by them here.'

James shifted in his seat. He was beginning to feel awkward listening to this man's personal life.

'But to be doing something naughty at *my* age, plus having the sexual release that I had given up on, especially with a beautiful young woman, gave me a new lease of life. But here's the thing. It was daring and exciting when it was a secret.

'Now you have found out about us it ceases to be naughty. In fact, it now feels sordid and irresponsible. Also, as head, I am supposed to be in charge of good behaviour. Carrying on with a member of my staff is not good behaviour. Is it?'

'Peter, I'm a man of my word. I told you that I would never tell on you if you didn't suspend Sam. And you didn't,' said James.

'I know that, James. But secrets are only fun, only mischievous when no other person knows or guesses what you've been up to. One or two of the other staff may have had suspicions, I suppose, but they never let me know. The reason I'm telling you all this, is when this awful situation comes to a conclusion with Danny's death and Wendy's arrest, I will be looking for a job in another school.

'I will never leave Ruth, I love her. But in a different way. If Ami still wants to continue seeing me, for however long, that will be my personal choice. Right or wrong. But it won't be under the same business roof, which is definitely wrong.'

James took a long deep breath. 'Your relationship with either woman is none of my business. I'd hate to see you hurt, Ruth, she's a good woman. But it's your life. There's a well-used phrase about shitting on your own doorstep. So, for that reason, I think your decision is the right one.'

The conversation ended with a handshake. A somewhat startled James left the room.

At the end of school, he headed straight for the Tradesman's Arms next door. The stunning conversation with the head was still fresh in his mind.

'Usual,' said Sheila.

'Usual? Ha. I used to think that usual was bloody boring. You would not believe how *unusual* my life has been these past weeks. The things I could tell you would make your beer mats curl up at the edges. Read the papers or watch the television tomorrow night. I'll fill you in on the rest when I can,' said James, picking up his freshly poured pint of bitter.

'Sounds like what you've got to tell me deserves one on the house. That one's on me,' said the landlady. 'This story better be good?'

'Oh, believe me, it's good. It's bloody good. It's better than good,' said James, swallowing a third of his pint in one gulp.

Chapter 51

3 Months Later

James and Sam were in the headmaster's office.

'Jo Major, you know, our school detective, texted me last night. She told me that Roth has been convicted of his crimes at long last. For downloading child porn, he would have probably got three years, she said. But taking videos of his pupils in changing rooms and showers was deemed to be more serious. The judge said, as a teacher, he was in a position of parental trust and responsibility, and he betrayed that trust. So, he bumped it up to five years,' said James.

The two teachers, that were now inseparable, both shouted 'yes' and pumped fists.

'When I think of the hell that he put me through when I first started here. He's evil, that man. Thank goodness, that lowlife will never be allowed near children again... Headmaster,' said Sam, one side of his mouth turning upwards in a smile.

James looked over at Sam. 'You can stop that *headmaster* lark. It's James when there's no blue blazers in earshot. Yeah, it wasn't the best start to a new job for you, Sam, was it? Anyway, it's done and dusted. I hope that creep gets a hard time inside; paedophiles are not best loved amongst the inmates.' said James.

'If there was one person in this school who was not going to change when promoted to headmaster it's you. I know it has been a week since your promotion, but this is the first time I've had the opportunity to say, face to face, congratulations on your appointment,' said Sam.

'The reason I'm sitting in this chair is down to the previous incumbent, Peter Greaves. Before he left to take the job at Wimbledon College, he was the one who recommended me to his bosses to get this post. So thanks for your kind words… but you're still not getting a rise,' said James, deadpan.'

Sam laughed. 'Anyway, did our detective say anything about Wendy Jacks?'

'Only that they are still looking for her. I can't believe she hasn't been caught yet. She's either been bloody lucky or she's a clever bugger. Web's Slippery Science Teacher – good title for a book, eh? Let's face it, if Fifty Bloody Shades can be a best seller, who knows?' said James.

00000

The late January weather on the Scottish Isle of Mull was not for the fainthearted.

Tobermory, the capital and most northern part of the island was sitting beneath two inches of snow. In January it rained, on average, twenty-seven of the thirty-one days. The temperature needle rarely climbed above freezing. But it was the ice-tipped wind that cut along the Firth of Lorn that tested the performance of the residents' winter clothing in this harbour town.

303

Alex Dalglish and Hugh Baxter were sitting in the upstairs bar in MacGochan's waterfront pub and restaurant. Both were drinking pints. The sweeping curve of the harbour, even in winter, was a heart-warming sight. The array of colours were more than the eye could take in at first glance.

Brightly painted coastal shop fronts and hotels decked the bay either side of the two drinkers. Their coruscation was an invite to come, browse and enjoy. On the water, the many vibrant dinghies and tall-masted yachts, swaying to and fro, gave perpetual movement and life to this picturesque Scottish port.

The middle-aged locals were both teachers at Tobermory High School, just a five-minute walk away.

'I am going to miss Jimmy Campbell. He was a good teacher. Always made me laugh,' said Alex.

'Aye, he was a good man. Retirement comes to us all though, Alex,' Hugh lifted his glass. 'May he live a long and happy life.'

'Aye,' said Alex, bringing their glasses together in a toast. They both downed a mouthful of beer in honour to their friend.

'I hear our replacement science teacher is a lady. She starts Monday, I think. The headmaster was telling me she hasn't worked for the last five years. Busy caring for her sick mother apparently. Her CV is very impressive I'm led to believe,' said Hugh.

'Scot's lass?'

'No, English. Worked in England all of her career so far. She is going to find it different here with only one hundred and thirty odd senior pupils to teach. Most English schools are at least five hundred plus. Why she wants to take a job in the wilds of the Scottish Inner Hebrides is anyone's guess,' said Hugh, with a weak laugh.

'What's her name?' asked Alex.

'Winona Jackson.'

'Have you seen her yet.' asked Alex.

'Aye. Met her briefly after her interview. Late thirties early forties. Short blonde hair. Glasses. Seems quite nice. Busty lass,' said Hugh.

The men looked at each other and said in tandem, 'Well, she will be a hit with the boys.'

Chapter 52

Jo sat in her car in the small car park, leant forwards and looked out of the window. The air was just above freezing. The only surrounding colour was from the line of verdant Douglas Firs in the ranch-fenced meadow to her right – their sharp peaks stabbing the silver-blue sky. The rest of the neighbouring trees were a jumble of twisted limbs – undressed, unprotected from the miserly English winter.

She had been sitting there for over twenty minutes with the engine running to keep the car interior warm. Jo was on her mobile searching for new furniture in the January sales at knockdown prices. She still hadn't got round to furnishing her new two-bedroom flat yet. She needed to get it done.

Every so often, she would glance up at the entrance to the single-story building directly in front of her. She was getting impatient. Whilst she was looking at a blue corduroy three-piece suite, there was a sudden loud tap on her passenger window. It made her jump. She looked up from her phone to see a man standing close to the car carrying a holdall. She did not want to open the car door, so she pressed a button. The automatic window slid down.

'Any chance of a lift, darlin'. I'm freezing my cods off out here,' said the man, in an exaggerated cockney lilt.

'Only if your name is Nick Summers,' said Jo. She sprung out of the car then stopped. Suddenly she was uncertain of herself – not sure what to do next. Nick was definitely not uncertain. He put down his holdall, stepped forwards and opened his arms. The couple fell into a long, close embrace. Then they kissed.

It was the first private kiss between them. All the others, mostly goodbye pecks on the cheek, had been monitored by prison guards; overlooked by inmates and their visitors. She had been waiting for this moment for eighteen months. She had taken the day off work. Today Nick said goodbye to prison.

The plan was for him to stay at her flat, initially. His house had been closed up for the duration of his sentence. The interior would be cold and musty. She offered him the spare bedroom and he gratefully accepted. It was just until he got himself sorted out, they agreed. In Jo's mind, though, it was more than that. A trial period for both of them.

She knew that most normal relationships would be: meet, start dating, intimacy, possible cohabitation. Theirs was certainly not normal. Apart from the meet, they had all that to discover. Their one was all about face – this would be a test of their compatibility.

Jo knew that another reason Nick was keen to accept Jo's offer was fear. How would he feel going back to the house where his life had been ruined? The place where he found his broken wife's body hanging from the bannisters. His nightmares must have all taken place in that house. Nick told Jo he was probably going to sell the property as soon as it looked lived-in once more. But she sensed there were still a lot of questions and doubts growing inside him.

She was nervous on the drive back to her flat. Their platonic romance, if you could call it that, had only ever been carried out across a table and surrounded by convicts. They had occasionally held hands. Could they live together? Would they sleep together? She was pretty sure that he must be having the same feelings of uncertainty. They drove the first few minutes in virtual silence. It was Nick who spoke first.

'So, your teacher is still on the run, then?'

'Afraid so. We've tried everything we know to track her down. She seems to have disappeared into thin air. We've had all number of potential sightings – half of them from bloody crackpots. None of them turned out to be her.'

'What did the boy die of?'

'After the body was confirmed as that of Danny, the forensic pathologist found death was due to an intracranial hematoma. Basically, bleeding on the brain. This was caused by the crushing of his temporal lobe with a blunt instrument. In other words, he was hit on the head with enormous force. They found wine in his stomach and there were small traces of wine around the injury. So, the probable weapon used was the wine bottle.'

'I would imagine that not having closure on this case has been frustrating for you?'

'Yeh, you could say that. I would have loved to have got that woman behind bars. But I've had to move on. I've got other cases to concentrate on now. We just haven't got the budget and man-hours to carry out a protracted search with no end date. Obviously, the investigation has been left open but I'm really disappointed that she's still out there somewhere.

'Now that she knows the dust has settled and she's not top priority for the police, she may even have got another teaching job in another, I dunno, remote part of the UK or another English-speaking country?' said Nick.

'I know she's got skin like a bloody rhino but I can't see her being that arrogant or stupid enough to put herself at risk by working in another school?' said Jo, eyeing Nick with a frown.

One Week Later

Her first week had gone better than Wendy had expected. The school was a lot smaller than she was used to. She preferred it that way. The staff all seemed more friendly than those in her previous schools. It didn't come naturally to her to have close relationships with her colleagues. Although, this time she had to become part of the fixtures and fittings as quickly as possible. She could not afford to draw attention to herself or alienate anyone.

She remembered James saying that most job applicants C.V.'s are not checked by their employers these days. She prayed that he knew what he was talking about.

The teacher had rented a small, two-bedroom bungalow just outside the centre of Tobermory. The dwelling was situated along an unmade track, passing between rusty, corrugated farm sheds and then down the end of a long gravel path. Two round-top picket fences ran either side down the whole length. These were fixed in front of broken lines of dense gorse bushes. The dwelling was invisible from the main road.

It was just a five-minute drive to the school. She was pleased that it sat on the outskirts of the bustling little harbour town. The out-of-the-way location was ideal to maintain a low profile outside of her work hours. She had coloured and cut her own hair. With a blonde bob and the addition of heavy-rimmed glasses – instead of her daily contact lenses – she felt she had successfully altered her appearance to the casual onlooker.

Tobermory was a pretty little harbour village, with virtually no crime and therefore a very small police presence. Perfect. She was going to enjoy working here.

Chapter 53

Jo was putting the finishing-touches to a report of an armed robbery at a local store run by a father and son. The young thief, who had been the son's friend at school, was caught on CCTV twenty yards from the shop, when a strong wind blew the hoody off his head, exposing his face. When the fingerprints left on the counter matched the accused, game over.

Temporarily free from work she started thinking about Nick. Living in the same flat was a little awkward to begin with. The relationship had been slow to get going with both of them unsure of how to progress their cordial romance. They needed to relax. It was a restaurant meal with wine and more drinks back at the flat that did the trick. They had made love for the first time that night. It changed the dynamics immediately.

But it was his words about Wendy Jacks getting another teaching job that began to rattle her detective's brain. *No, surely not? But then again, she has to work to survive.* The more she thought about the possibility the more it began to grow in her imagination. If Wendy Jacks was brazen enough to do it, the school would have to be in a remote part of the UK, because her picture had been all over the papers and television.

'But to be a teacher in the UK you must have to be member of an association, or something, for security's sake, surely?' she said under her breath. 'And that would be under her true name, which means she could easily get caught. Jo realised she was digging in the dark. She needed to do some research.

After searching on the internet, she found what she was looking for. In state run UK schools, a teacher was required to achieve Qualified Teacher Status. Whereas, independent and private schools did not require QTS. Wendy Jacks would've already achieved QTS but if she went private, she would not need any proof of her real name apart from her CV, which she could easily change.

It was a stab in the dark, but Jo had got the bit between her teeth again. 'Well, Nicholas Summers, let's hope you have once again provided a potential lead in this investigation,' she said to herself, as she Googled a map of Great Britain. The obvious places to start were the furthest away from London – far Western parts of Devon and Cornwall and remote Northern reaches of Scotland. But before she started on this speculative journey, she had to run her idea past the boss, Jack Jolley.

When she had finished telling him her plan, he spoke. 'Do you know how many private schools there are in the UK?'

'No Guv. But if we just keep to the really out-of-the-way places, which I think she would try first, there shouldn't be too many of them,' she said, her fingers crossing beneath his desk.

'It's a bloody long shot, Jo, but if you are sure that there's nothing pending or pressing at the moment on your desk, you've got two days to come up with something,' said Jack.

Her search would begin with non-state-run schools in the smaller towns and villages and mainly on the coastline. Remote seaside towns, certainly from the ones she had visited, tended to exist in a more sedate, separate little world. This, of course, was their attraction when it came to short breaks and holidays. When these schools were located, she was going to ask, via email, if they had employed a new English, female science teacher in the past couple of months.

When she got back to her desk, she called over to Kyra, 'I'm going to need a hand.'

Three hours later they had compiled their list. It ran to fifty-three. When the email addresses had all been entered, Jo put together a letter stating the information required but not giving a reason why.

All they had to do now was wait.

By the following morning Jo was holding her breath as she checked her emails. They had received forty-one replies so far. All negative. By ten o'clock, the number had risen to forty-eight. She was beginning to realise that this was all a waste of time until her screen, a minute later, showed another email had been delivered. 'Be lucky forty-nine.' she said, staring at the screen.

'Kyra,' Jo called, whilst waving her hand in a beckoning motion. Together they read the email: Tobermory High School, Isle of Mull, Outer Hebrides.

Sorry for the delay but we only picked up your email an hour ago due to a power cut. We get more than our share up here in the Inner Hebrides. To answer your question: Yes, we employed a new Science Teacher from England two weeks ago. She started work last week. Her name is Winona Jackson.

Kyra stared at Jo with her mouth open. 'It has to be. It's too much of a coincidence. It's Wendy. Wendy Jacks.'

'Gotcha!' breathed Jo. She then replied to the email playing down the importance of the enquiry and asking her not to report this conversation to the teacher in question. She then thanked her for her time. What she didn't want was to alarm the teacher and risk missing her again.

One minute later, she had informed Jack. 'Crikey! I have to be honest, I wasn't expecting that. Well done, Jo. Have you got the school address and the teacher's home address?'

'Er, we've got the school address. It's on the email. But I was so excited...'

'Get back to your emailer or even better, give the Headmaster's secretary a bell 'cos you're going to need to know where she lives if you get there after school hours, which is going to be the case.'

'Yes, Guv. Sorry, Guv.'

Jack got the map of Scotland up on his computer screen. 'Blimey, that's a trek-and-a-half, all the way up to the northern reaches of Scotland. We'll get you up there on one of our choppers. We do not want to lose her again. Take DC Chand. And you need to inform the commanding officer at Tobermory police station what you are going to do and ask them to provide two officers in a car to drive you from the copter to her premises. And I want them there when you arrest her in case she throws a wobbly.'

Jack hit a few keys on his computer, while Jo stood waiting in front of him. 'Okay, you've got over five-hundred-and-fifty miles to Mull. It will take in the region of three-and-a-half to four hours, that's with a stop. Copters can't fly much more than five-hundred miles without refuelling.' He then made a phone call. When he finished he looked up at Jo. 'We can get you both on a chopper at three o'clock this afternoon, which means you probably won't get to Wendy Jacks' house much before seven-thirty this evening.'

'Okay, Guv. I'll get her address and brief DC Chand.' Jo nodded and left the room. When she phoned Tobermory police station which, due to its small size, was not manned full-time, the phone call was diverted to the larger station in Oban.

When the commanding officer came off the call wide-eyed, he related the contents to two of his colleagues. For London detectives to travel all the way up there to arrest a murder suspect in sleepy Tobermory, of all places, was unusual. In fact, it was unheard of and worthy of sharing.

One junior officer who overheard the conversation picked up his mobile and disappeared into an empty office. He pushed a few buttons on his phone.

'I thought you'd like to know that two detectives from London are travelling up to Tobermory School to arrest a murder suspect. A female teacher. And she is English. I think you have a friend who may be interested in this information.' He waited for a response, then replied, 'By chopper. I doubt if they can get here before early evening.' He then hung up.

Chapter 54

After Danny's funeral, Enzo took to working even longer hours at his bistro. He didn't want time on his hands to think of where his life was going to go after the loss of his son. His way of coping was to blank out all thoughts of children. It was almost as though Danny had never existed. His wife, Karen, also wanted to keep busy, but unlike her husband, she had a need to be in daily contact with young children.

During the long wait before she gave birth to Danny, she worked as a creche assistant. The necessity to care for and handle babies was strong whilst her and Enzo were trying for a family. When a nearby vacancy arose last week, she applied for the job. She already possessed the required qualifications. Her application was successful, securing the full-time job in nearby Fulham.

Enzo had mixed feelings about her taking the job. Due to his long hours working in the bistro, added to Karen's new commitment, it meant they were spending less and less time together. It was beginning to pull them apart.

Enzo was at his desk in the cramped office at the rear of his restaurant. The walls were full of shelves stacked high with folders and piles of paper; he was busy with the company's accounts when his mobile rang. The name of the caller came up on his phone. It was his cousin.

'Hi Luca. How you doing?'

'Not bad Enzo. Listen. I may have some good news for you. As you know, I have made everyone we know and their contacts aware of what has happened to you and Karen. Through our network, we have a 'relative' who lives and works in Oban in Scotland. One of his mates is a young police officer deployed at the local station. He's overheard his commanding officer talk of a phone call today from a London detective. Two of them are travelling up there to a little island called Tobermory just across from the mainland.

They are going to arrest a female murder suspect. A science teacher. And she's English. Our contact knows a woman whose daughter works in the kitchens of the school where this teacher is. Apparently, it is very rare for a teacher from England to want to work up there as it's so remote.'

Enzo sat glued to the phone, his neck muscles contracted exerting pressure across his entire skull. Was it out of anger, excitement? Fear? 'What does she look like this woman?' he asked.

'We're not sure yet. I've emailed a picture of this Wendy Jacks to my man. He and one other are on their way at this very moment, to take it down to the school and give it to the girl who works there. I am waiting for a reply. If it does not turn out to be her, I will let you know. Sorry Enzo I've got to go,' said Luca, cutting short the call.

Enzo was left stunned by the abrupt phone call. Unlike his cousin, he did not have an aggressive bone in his body, but now a part of him wanted Luca to find Wendy Jacks first. He went to pick up his pen and noticed his hand was damp with perspiration. He took a deep breath, got up and opened his office door. He walked into the bistro and pulled a bottle of wine from one of the coolers and a glass from the shelf above. He went back into his office. As he unscrewed the cap both his hands now were shaking.

He had a strict rule. He never drank at work.

00000

The morning had gone well for Wendy. She already felt more at home in this neat little Hebridean school than at any time at the Web. The children were surprisingly well-behaved, and the staff had all accepted an English woman into their Scottish bosoms.

She still had a nagging worry though. It was that C.V. But as far as she could see, no one else was checking up on her.

She was wrong.

One employee was more than eager to check out the new teacher: twenty-eight-year-old Sarah Boyd. She was under strict instructions to make eye-contact with the woman to compare her with the picture she now had in her overalls pocket.

As kitchen assistant, she would only have to wait until lunchtime when she prepared and served dinners to the staff and pupils. She had been working at the school for over three years and knew all the teachers by name and appearance. So, the new recruit was going to stand out like a cuckoo in sparrow's nest.

At twelve-thirty, the staff and pupils poured into the dining hall. By twelve thirty-five, the room was full of hungry stomachs and lively conversation. Sarah was watching the rear view of everyone from the open kitchen hatch as they passed through the swing doors. She had not yet seen her target. She was looking for a woman with shoulder-length, wavy brown hair. The only figure she did not recognise was now sitting in the far corner of the hall. A rather plump woman with short-cropped blonde hair.

When it was time to serve her table, Sarah pulled out the downloaded image given to her and once more studied the woman's face. She approached carrying a large tray of four full dinner plates. As she distributed the hot meals around the table, she paused in front of the blonde. The woman looked up at her. Sarah smiled and returned to the kitchen.

She looked at the picture once more. Her face appeared to be a little fuller than the photo. She thought that was probably down to the shortness and colour of her dyed hair. Her features were a good match, though. But it was the eyes when she looked up at her. The glasses were an addition but the questioning hazel eyes were the give-away. She had made up her mind.

When she reached the kitchen, she walked to the back door where she knew two individuals would be waiting outside. She opened the door, simply nodded in affirmation and returned to her duties.

00000

Wendy had only two classes that afternoon. She arrived home from work at four o'clock in her seven-year-old grey Ford Fiesta, a car that would certainly not attract attention. Being the new addition to the school, she was expecting many questions from the other members of staff. She had already rehearsed a set of answers that would get her through the first few weeks. But her novelty value had already cooled it seemed.

She felt very pleased with herself, all was going to plan. She climbed out of her car and approached the front door. Her attention was drawn to one of the side windows. It was wide open. She knew she had not opened that window. It was far too cold to open any windows at the moment. It rang alarm bells.

She had been told at her school interview that the island was virtually free of serious crime and police presence was sparse. It was one of the reasons that she chose to work there. But someone had broken into her house. She was sure of it.

With her heart pounding up into her throat, she turned the key in the lock. Bit by bit she opened the front door and stepped inside. Would the burglar still be in there? Standing by the open front door, she shouted. If he or she was inside they could escape past her. She certainly wasn't going to attempt to stop them.

After a quick check in the rooms to see there were no intruders, she took a close look at the window. The dated mechanism had a simple drop latch. Easily opened with skilled fingers and the edge of a credit card slipped through the gap.

322

What was mystifying and slightly worrying was the window looked like it had been deliberately left wide open. It was secured on the last hole of the stay. It was as if the intruder was boasting. Blatant.

She took a more thorough look around the house. Nothing obvious, as far as she could see, had been taken. It baffled her. That was until she walked into her bedroom. There it was on her bed. Her passport and driving licence set neatly side by side on the white pillow. It was like a calling card. A cold shudder drove deep inside her bones. She now knew the reason for the break-in. Whoever had entered her property was looking for one thing. Her real identity.

They had found Wendy Jacks.

Chapter 55

The helicopter carrying Jo and Kyra touched down on the finely mown grass of Glenforsa Airfield, Tobermory at five forty-three p.m. It was already dark. A car parked in the gloom outside the Glenforsa Hotel flashed its lights at the disembarking detectives. The arranged signal came from the two officers who were waiting in a police car. They were to take them the twenty-five-minute journey to the school where the headmaster would be waiting for them.

When Jo had phoned through to get Wendy's address the head had insisted on taking them to her house as it was off the main road and difficult to find. He also asked the reason for the phone call. Jo had told him, swearing him to secrecy. Apart from his generous gesture, Jo thought that he must be intrigued and not a little worried that he may have employed a child murderer at his school.

When they arrived at the school, they were greeted by David Hanson, the Headmaster, who was standing hunched, rubbing his fingers together. It wasn't from the cold night air, Jo thought.

'I've not said a word to Win…' he hesitated. 'Ms Jacks, as requested.'

'Thank you, Mr Hanson,' said Jo.

'Right. *Er,* the house is a little off the beaten track. You can follow my car,' he said. In normal circumstances, the headmaster was probably a genial and confident person. But Jo could see by his staccato phrases and servile manner that this man was in shock. This episode was out of his comfort zone by a thousand miles and expanding.

After they turned off the main road, the car's headlights enabled Jo to see them passing by numerous dilapidated farm outbuildings, mud-spattered diggers and tractors. As they drove up the winding track to Wendy's house Jo could see why she had chosen such a location. The first thing they noticed when they got out of the two cars was that there was no vehicle on the premises and the house was in darkness.

Jo's heart sank. 'Bollocks, not again,' she said, under her breath. She couldn't have missed her this time, surely? With torches pointing the way, the detectives walked up the single step to the one-story dwelling. After knocking on the front door and getting no answer, they and the two police officers made their way around the boundary of the building. Stepping over brambles and around overgrown weeds, Jo and Kyra peered through each window for signs of life. They found none.

It was not difficult for one of the local officers to force an entry through the slim front door with a hefty kick. Kyra flicked the light switch. The interior was sparsely decorated. That wasn't a surprise to Jo as Wendy had only been living there for two weeks. The surprise was that they found her belongings were still evident. Clothes hung from a rack in her bedroom, items of jewellery were on the bedside table next to an alarm clock. What they did not find was her passport and driving licence.

'Bloody hell. Our teacher was in a mighty hurry to leave,' said Jo.

The headmaster spoke for the first time since arriving at the empty house. 'I hope you don't think it was me or my secretary that spooked her. We both said nothing of your visit.'

'I believe you, so you have no worries there. But someone or something has made this woman flee from her home with just the clothes she is standing up in, plus her personal documents,' said Jo, shaking her head. 'She'll be off the bloody island by now.'

Jo looked up at the clear night sky. She wanted to scream.

Chapter 56

Four Days Later

Jack walked into the office where Jo was working on a case of mistaken identity on the mugging of an elderly woman. Her boss was carrying a newspaper. He approached Jo and put the paper on her desk. It was opened on an article. The headline read: *'Body of woman washed up on the shore on a remote Scottish island.'* Jo read the headline and lifted her head to her boss with a furrowed brow.

'Page fourteen. Carry on reading… out loud,' said Jack.

The story went on to say that yesterday a woman's body was found floating next to a yacht that was anchored in Tobermory Harbour, on the Isle of Mull in the Inner Hebrides. She has been identified as Mrs Wendy Jacks, the woman wanted for the murder of Battersea schoolboy Danny Antonelli.

Jo's mouth fell open. She glanced up at Jack again then straight back down to continue reading.

It went on to say that the woman had just started work at the local school but under a different name. Her car was found abandoned on a clifftop one mile from the town. The police found her passport and driving licence neatly laid out on the passenger seat.

An autopsy found her stomach contained nearly a bottle of whisky. Her terrible injuries were commensurate with a long fall onto rocks. But the coroner said the death was due to drowning. Summing up, he said that the careful and deliberate display of her documents in her car led him to believe she wanted, whoever found her, to know who she really was. Perhaps she was showing remorse for what she had done, he surmised.

The empty bottle of whisky was found on the back seat of the car. The coroner thought that her idea was to get drunk, sitting in her car, parked on a cliff-edge with one thought in her mind. To end her life. The coroner considered it to be suicide but the evidence was not conclusive and therefore declared it an open verdict.

'Bugger me,' said Jo. 'So, she goes to all the trouble of changing her name, getting another teaching job in one of the remotest Hebridean islands of the UK only to throw herself off the nearest bloody cliff. And just a week after she started work. So maybe no one spooked her. Perhaps she'd just had enough of hiding, had an attack of guilt and decided to top herself?' said Jo.

'Yeh, maybe,' said Kyra, who had sat dumbfounded throughout the story. 'But it's a bit of a coincidence that she tops herself just before we turn up to arrest her. I think she knew we were coming.'

'Or maybe someone else had found out who she really was and she panicked. If that was the case, I don't expect that person to come forward after she has committed suicide,' said Jack.

'That's if she did commit suicide, Guv?' said Jo, her brain still throwing around ideas.

'Well, the case is closed as far as I'm concerned. There is no doubt in my mind that she killed the boy. Unfortunately, we will never know the reason why. At least Danny's parents can move on at long last. It's a shame you could not get the arrest, Jo. Especially after going so bloody far to achieve it. But your clever work in locating her will not go unnoticed.

'Thanks, Guv. That means a lot.'

00000

The following day Jo thought she ought to ring the headmaster of the Web in case he had missed the news of his teacher's demise. Then afterwards, a quick call to James to let him know and thank him for his help in the case.

'Hello. Can I speak to the headmaster,' said Jo.

'Certainly. Can I say who's calling?'

'It's Detective Sergeant Jo Major.'

A moment later. 'Hello, Jo. How are things?' said James.

Jo was silent for a few seconds. 'James?'

'You wanted to speak to the headmaster didn't you? Well, here I am. And I'm very busy, so what do you want?' he said, suddenly sounding like a fifties BBC announcer.

'You cheeky bugger. You've been promoted. Why didn't you tell me? Congratulations, Mr Headmaster.

Actually, you saved me a phone call. You were next on my list to phone.'

God knows how I got this job, Jo. I certainly wouldn't want to go to a school where I was the headmaster,'

'Every school should have a headmaster like you, James. I for one would have loved to have a pot-smoking, pisshead running my school.'

'Who told you I smoked pot?'

No one. I guessed. But now, I know. Listen. The reason I called…'

'I know, Jo. I've read all about it. My feelings? An accident, suicide or whatever, she's gone and not costing the taxpayer thousands to put her in prison for the next thirty years. Good riddance.'

'My thoughts exactly, though I'm not supposed to think like that in my profession. And I'm not sure that Mr and Mrs Antonelli would regard that as the perfect end to this story. I'd guess that they'd want to see their son's murderer suffer in jail for the rest of her life. But, at least, it has some finality.

'Also, I wanted to know how Sam was doing after the nightmare start to his new career. How worrying must that have been to be accused of such an awful thing.'

'I can't imagine. But with Roth out of the picture things have settled down. Sam's fine. It's all good,' said James.

'How about Tommy Clifford, the accuser,'

'That boy, would you believe, is unrecognisable. I've got you to partially thank for that. The officers you sent round persuaded Mrs Clifford to lodge a complaint against her nasty piece of work, boyfriend. I think it was going to go to court to get a restraining order or something on him, but he disappeared before the date. Never been seen since – so my Oracle from the local pub told me.

'Tommy's got his head down with his studies and is back in the football team. And actually playing as part of an eleven-man side for a change. I've got hope for the kid now.'

'I'm embarrassed to admit I didn't keep tabs on what happened after I arranged the visit from our guys. But that's great news. Well, give my regards to Sam. I've got to shoot. Lovely to catch up. Keep your powder dry. Bye.'

Chapter 57

Enzo got a text early that morning. It was from Luca. *Read the Daily Mail. Page 14,* is all it said. The paper, that was delivered every day to the Antonelli household, was sitting on the breakfast table. It was folded and unread. Enzo picked it up. He turned to page fourteen. The headline confused him at first. Though, it didn't take long for the story to make him sit up.

He called Karen over. They sat together in silence and read the article. When they had finished, they stood and embraced each other, both shedding tears of sorrow and relief. Enzo could feel the anger gradually escaping from his body.

He made himself a promise that this news was going to be the start of a new life. He was determined to recapture the close bond that he and Karen had enjoyed before they lost their son. He was sure that Danny would not want his death to split his loving parents apart. He expressed those thoughts to his wife. She was relieved to hear her husband talk and feel that way. Through her tears, she agreed.

They both decided that they would share with each other any negative emotions that they experienced from now on. They had kept their own feelings about the loss of their son a secret from each other. It was destructive. Enzo decided that he would never keep a secret from his wife ever again.

Apart from one.

The End